THE MARLOW PROJECT

by LM Barrett

L M Barrett

Copyright

Cover designed by Digital Mojo Ltd.

Original photos by Vlad Tchompalov on Unsplash

DEDICATION

To the readers who enjoyed my first book. It's all your fault that I've written a second one!

PROLOGUE

The two men stood up and shook hands. A gentleman's agreement. No contract signed. No paper or email trail. It was a done deal and the stranger guaranteed a completed job without further discussion once he'd received the payment.

Henry Marlow watched as the stranger walked out of the pub. Once the door shut, Henry sat back down next to the roaring open fire in the country pub. A pub miles from home, where no one would recognise him. He stared deep into the flames and imagined it was hell and he was in it. He might as well be – he'd just made a deal with the devil. And he was okay with that.

CHAPTER 1

"Dr Marlow, it's a pleasure to meet you and I'm honoured that you've chosen to speak to my newspaper," said Joe Slater as he entered the room and introduced himself.

The two men shook hands. Dr Marlow sat at a desk with his computer in front of him; he was a well-known workaholic.

"That's a rather retro looking piece of machinery," Joe said as he pointed at Dr Marlow's laptop.

"Yes, it's old, I believe. But it still works – a bit like me."

He appeared frailer and older than Joe expected. Unkempt and unshaven, his hair was grey, his skin was pale and he'd lost weight, which accentuated some deep lines on his face. Famous since Joe was a little boy, he was used to hearing about Henry Marlow on the news. Although the doctor was regularly mentioned in the news, Henry himself preferred to maintain a low profile. Interviews and footage were kept to a minimum. Even still, the transformation of the younger more confident doctor that Joe was used to seeing was unsettling. Now he looked tired, with his shoulders slumped, like a man who had taken on the world and failed.

"It's nice to meet you too, Joe. I've always read The Daily Telegram ever since I was a young man with my cup of coffee in the morning."

"Speaking of which, I asked ahead and got you a cappuccino, your favourite."

Joe handed over a cup of takeaway coffee. "Can I say again, I'm honoured to meet one of the most prominent scientists of our time, if not in history."

Joe regretted this sudden gushing towards Dr Marlow, knowing this humble doctor preferred to downplay his achievements.

"I know you're due to write the specifications of 'The Marlow Project' for the benefit of the medical and scientific world but I'm here to record the more personal side of your story. I want to put together a comprehensive record of your work in our newspaper; written in layman terms so the public can understand everything you've achieved and how you got where you are now. I'd also like to hear about some of your patients as the press haven't been permitted to report many details about them up until now. Some of your patients have also volunteered to give their side of the story."

"That's good to hear and thanks for the coffee, Joe. The coffee here tastes terrible. Where do you want to start?" he asked as he closed his computer.

"At the beginning please, I've got all day and can come back tomorrow," said Joe.

A warm smile radiated from Dr Marlow, appearing more consistent with the old Dr Marlow that Joe recognised.

"I wouldn't want to bore you?"

"You won't. Please go ahead," insisted the eager reporter.

"I was born in a pleasant, leafy suburb in Bristol almost fifty years ago. My father worked as a web developer and my mother, a teacher. As an only child, I had a close bond with my parents. I had a comfortable, conventional, middle-class childhood. My father taught me to program a computer from a young age and I became fascinated by coding. Remember, those were the days when jobs were more varied and not everyone used a computer to work. However, my father knew the importance of technology and believed everyone should know the ins and outs of programming. He was right. Nowadays, everyone uses computers to program the AI gradually taking over the jobs that humans do. People used to clean their own homes, drive their own cars, there were people at check-outs in supermarkets. In supermarkets, we'd hand-pick our own goods. There was more human contact in those days. You could walk to the bus stop and someone might speak to you but even in those days, you could see us all becoming increasingly obsessed with technology. I must admit; I was guilty of it too – always on my phone or watching a screen during any free-time. It didn't take too long before the majority of the population were working from home from their computers, ordering every good or service they desired from the comfort of their settee."

Joe smiled politely at this familiar monologue of how technologically obsessed youths were today. His father said the same thing and remarked how different it was in his day.

Henry continued. "At any rate, I found school easy. I was a gifted child and loved science and computing. I also loved animals and wanted to be a vet from an early age. However, my father always encouraged me with computer programming. He wanted to ensure I had a solid future; coding was the way to go. As well as helping me carve out my future, we played football and cycled in the woods. At weekends, we barely spent any time at home; we were always exploring."

CHAPTER 2

2013

"Look at the state of you two. Where have you been all evening?" asked Rachel, Henry's mum.

"Biking in Leigh Woods. It was awesome, Dad fell off his bike twice. You should have come," said Henry as he walked past his mother and opened the fridge.

"What was awesome, Henry? The bike ride or me falling off my bike?" asked Frank, Henry's dad.

Henry just sniggered.

"Oh dear, you've got a few cuts and bruises. I'll have to kiss them better later," Rachel said to her husband.

Frank kissed his wife on the cheek.

"Gross," said Henry. "What's for dinner? I'm starving. Can we get a Friday night takeaway?"

Great idea, agreed his dad. Rachel ordered a takeaway while Frank and Henry cleaned up. They all settled in the living room for a film, eating their takeaway; which quickly became their Friday night routine.

As well as having fun together, the Marlow household was an ambitious one. Henry's potential was evident from an early age. Many questions were asked as soon as he could speak. Why is the sky blue? How does the internet work? What happens when we die? What are black holes? Frank answered all as best as he could but sometimes his toddler stumped him. Why are bananas yellow? What makes me think? How are babies made? This final question was always directed back to Henry's mum. Rachel thanked her husband for this.

Growing older, Henry's questions increased to the point Frank and Rachel were frequently stumped. Soon, it got to the point where Henry knew more than his parents; not that his parents lacked in the intellect department. Both had successful careers and worked hard. Rachel was a teacher and Frank ran his own design company. Frank encouraged his son and pushed him into learning about all aspects of technology.

"This is the future, Henry. Everything is already computer driven and our dependence on it will increase in the future. If you know the in's and out's of how it all works you'll be ahead of your peers."

With her background as a science teacher, Henry's mum encouraged him in her area of expertise. Frank sometimes suggested his son skip a couple of years at school but Rachel insisted there was enough time in Henry's future to study. Childhood was fleeting and would fly past in the blink of an eye. No, instead of studying and worrying about the future, she insisted they spend as much time together as a family. Henry's future was bright and she knew he would amount to great things. Work and fun were currently of the correct proportion, which led to a well-balanced boy. So Henry always remained in the correct year group at school, even though it was evident he exceeded the intellect of his peers.

One day after school, Henry walked home. On the way, he popped into the newsagents to pick up the latest gadget magazine and a chocolate bar. His plan was to lie on the sofa and read his magazine for the rest of the evening before his dad got his hands on it.

There was a police car parked directly outside his house. Henry wondered what it was doing there. It wasn't often he saw police on this street. However, he heard burglary was on the increase in the area. Maybe his house had been burgled? They better not have stolen his new iPad. If only he was allowed to take it to school, but his father wouldn't let him. Nor was he allowed to have it at the dinner table or after nine in the evening. He's not sure why his father agreed to buy it for his birthday in the first place. It always led to the same old lecture.

"Stop ignoring us and talk to us," his father demanded. "Honestly, you kids will forget the art of communication by the time you've grown up. We talked and played out in the street when I was a kid. There was nothing on television and no internet. Such a simpler life."

"Yes, yes, I know old man. In your day you worked

down the mine and were lucky to get some bread and water for your supper," teased Henry.

"Cheeky, I'm not that old," Frank usually replied.

Henry chuckled to himself as he opened the front door. He loved his dad but he was always so predictable. He almost forgot about the police car outside until he walked into his kitchen. Two police officers were sitting with his crying mum.

"Mum, what's the matter? Have we been robbed?"

"Oh, Henry, something awful's happened."

"Where's Dad?" he asked. He should be here if something terrible happened.

"Oh, Henry," was all his mum could say before the uncontrollable crying continued.

The police officer stood up and approached him.

"We have some bad news about your father," she said.

Henry stepped back; he didn't want to hear any bad news about his dad.

"I'm sorry, but your father was in a serious accident."

"No, no!" Henry covered his ears.

He sat in shock, staring at the wall as the police told him his father was involved in a hit-and-run and was on life support at the hospital.

The next couple of weeks were a blur for Henry and his mum. Henry insisted on accompanying her to the hospital, where they both sat by his bedside all day. Waiting and hoping for some improvement or any reactions from Frank. But nothing. His internal injuries were severe and his head injury, life-threatening. Initially, the doctors found a degree of brain activity and kept him artificially alive. Eventually, the doctors concluded irreversible brain damage; the respirator was the only thing keeping him alive. In an agonising decision, Rachel and Henry agreed it was for the best to turn off the machine. Within a few hours, Frank, beloved husband and father had died...

CHAPTER 3

"**A**nd that was the end of my happy childhood. Months passed and our house was devoid of any joy or laughter. It was just the two of us and my mum retreated into her own little shell and performed only the most basic parental duties. She ensured I was well-fed, safe and had clean clothes but she barely interacted with me anymore; simply going through the motions. She asked about my day and what I was up to. I tried to engage her and give details to these questions but she didn't listen. Not only did she give up work, she hardly left the house. No more bike rides, holidays or Friday night takeaways. My mother lost the will to live. My father was her life. Ten years later, she took her own life.

From the moment of my father's death, I couldn't stop thinking about him lying in that hospital bed and nobody could do anything to help. I thought about his brain activity and wondered if there was a way to transfer it, or part of it into a different body? Would that have been enough to save him? My father always said it would be possible one day. He talked of a time we would be able to upload all our thoughts and experiences and save them, so our family and loved ones could access them when we were long gone. As I grew up, thoughts of helping sick pets were gone. I wanted to do something. I wanted to make a difference, so I thought what if it was possible to transfer the code from our brain, not into a machine but into a different body?"

"I'm so sorry one of the world's greatest scientific discoveries was inspired by something so tragic," said Joe. "What happened to the driver?"

"It was some idiot high on drugs. He stole a car and drove it onto the pavement, knocking my father down. He never saw it coming. They arrested the culprit and imprisoned him for involuntary manslaughter but released him after three years for good behaviour. He received such a short sentence in the first place because he used his drug addiction as an excuse. Can you believe it? Only three years for killing my brilliant dad and indirectly killing my mum. I heard he died of a drug overdose about fifteen years later; I can't say I was sorry to hear about that."

"Completely understandable," Joe agreed. "I hope you don't mind but I did some delving into your past. I spoke with some of your fellow students. They all seemed to think you were...what's the word?" Joe hesitated.

"A complete and utter arse perhaps?" suggested Henry.

Joe laughed, slightly embarrassed to bring it up.

"Yes, to put it politely," said Joe. "There was also

a neighbour who said you killed her cat? And you were expelled from school?"

"I was an arse, although I didn't kill any cats. My behaviour went off the rails a bit but I didn't resort to murdering a domesticated animal. I still cringe now about how my younger-self behaved. Until my father died and my mother drifted away, I was a happy well-behaved boy with many friends. After-wards, my teenage years consisted of withdrawal from my friends and spending most of my time on my own, becoming obsessed with how I would have helped my dad. I read endless journals and books on neurology and followed all the notable neuro-scientists. I thought all the other kids my age talked about mindless drivel, such as football and TV shows. I forgot I was like them at one point when I enjoyed playing sport and reading my comics. Once, I happily watched mindless drivel on TV too. But I lost interest. I had nothing in common with the kids my age any more. I got into fights; kids didn't seem to like it when I compared their brain size to that of a pea..."

CHAPTER 4

2014

"Henry, you've been called into my office numerous times for fighting. I can only excuse your behaviour up to a certain point but I'm reaching my limit. Do you have anything to say for yourself?" asked the head, Mrs Gorman.

Henry just shrugged. He didn't care.

"This attitude won't do. I can't accept it. The teachers and your classmates are scared of your temper. They have no idea when you're going to blow up. You're always interrupting the teacher in class as if you know more than they do."

Henry just checked his nails as he informed Mrs Gorman that he did know more than his teachers. In fact, he knew more than she did.

Mrs Gorman placed her pen on the desk and folded her arms across her chest as she stared at Henry for a few moments.

"Well, you're obviously not getting anything useful from this school. It's been a year since your father's death but I see no improvement in your behaviour. You've left me no alternative but to expel you. I'm really sorry, Henry. Perhaps you could enrol in an institution which deals more effectively with gifted children."

"An institution? Do you mean a school? I thought this was supposed to be a school?" asked Henry.

She sighed.

"Don't be so facetious. Good luck, Henry. I'll call your mother to explain why you're home so early today. If she needs to come in and talk to me, please let her know my door is always open."

Henry shook his head, his mother stopped turning up to the meetings with the head a few months ago. She wouldn't come in now.

His mother called him as soon as he walked through the front door.

"Sorry, Mum."

As usual, she was sitting in her armchair, placed by the window. She spent most of her day there, staring out of the window.

"That's okay. It's not your fault. You're obviously bored at that place. Your father was right; we should have made you skip a couple of years at school."

Henry's mother enrolled the help of a personal tutor who could challenge Henry a bit more. Good ones were difficult to find and they went through a number of them. None of them stuck around for too long and Henry didn't want to go back to school so he spent most of his time alone, either designing and playing computer games or researching medical experiments and the workings of the brain.

One day, Henry was sitting in his room with the window open. He heard a car hit its brakes followed by a squeal from a cat. He rushed out to find the cat lying dead in the middle of the road. The car was nowhere to be seen.

It was Mrs Palmer's beloved cat, Remy. She lived across the street. Poor cat, thought Henry. Left for dead in the street, just like his own dad. He found a cardboard box and placed the cat in it before Mrs Palmer saw and he took Remy inside. Back in his bedroom, he double-checked for a pulse but the cat was definitely dead. Unsure what to do with the cat, he left it in the box and continued with his study.

Later that evening the temptation was too much. He was desperate to see what a real-life brain looked like and although it felt slightly wrong, the cat was already dead. His mum was in bed so he went into the kitchen and sliced the head open to dissect the brain. Lost in thought, he didn't hear his mum walk into the kitchen.

"Henry!" she screamed at him.

He quickly covered Remy's body with a tea towel. But his mum had seen enough as his hands dripped blood on the floor. He explained how he found Remy lying on the road and was curious.

"Please don't tell Mrs Palmer," he begged.

"Oh Henry, she loves that cat so much. She has to know; it would be awful not knowing what's happened to him. You must take him to her first thing in the morning and explain. Please make his head look normal before you do so."

Henry agreed and tried to sew the head back together as best he could. The next morning, he took Remy in the box across the road. The poor woman screamed as she saw her mutilated cat lying dead in the box. Unable to say much he ran home and cried.

"Ah, so you didn't actually kill the cat?" asked Joe.

"No, of course not! I was a brat as a child but I wasn't a monster. I felt awful for poor Mrs Palmer and regretted my actions. Instead of remembering Remy as the handsome cat it was, her last image was of the poor thing covered in blood with a badly stitched head. Sewing was definitely not my forte. Anyway, she heard I was expelled from school and marked me as a troublemaker. She didn't believe I found Remy dead in the street. As the local gossip, I think she preferred her version of events.

The rest of my teenage years at home were largely uneventful. My mother was depressed and I guess I must have been as well. I sat my GCSEs and A-levels at an independent study centre and passed them all with straight A stars. Cambridge University accepted me and that's when I started becoming a normal teenager again. It helped to be away from the melancholic atmosphere at home. I integrated myself with my fellow students and put my troubles behind me. It was a new chapter in my life. That's where I met my best friend Charlie Gregson. We're still friends now; he's always been supportive of my project. In fact, my first official operation was one of his patients.

At twenty-one, I got a place at Harvard University where I pursued a neurobiology concentration in mind, body and behaviour and where I learnt to use maths and science to evaluate brain signals. It was fascinating. I lived and breathed it and that's when I first believed my obsession could become reality; the transfer of brain waves from one animal to another. This is what I based my thesis on. From writing it, I knew it was theoretically possible. And that's when my life's work really began. The thesis was widely applauded by experts in the field. Based on that thesis, I received funding from the British Government when I returned to the UK to see if I could turn it into reality."

Joe sensed Dr Marlow relax once he got past his difficult early years. He decided not to interrupt again and let Dr Marlow continue his life story from his twenties.

CHAPTER 5

"**H**enry, you've got to get out of this stuffy lab and come out for the night!" Charlie Gregson yelled over to Henry as he barged through the doors of Henry's lab.

The two had been close friends since meeting at Cambridge University and remained in close contact during Henry's stint at Harvard University. Although Charlie followed a career as a GP, he always showed an interest in Henry's work. He found the project fascinating but knew it might never happen in their lifetime. Unlike Henry, he didn't want to hang around a lab for the rest of his life waiting, hoping and yet seeing the experiment fail time after time. That's why he became a GP; he was a people person and wanted to help now. Henry was more patient and knew one day he'd get a breakthrough. This quiet confidence and persistence from Henry always impressed Charlie.

"I can't leave. If I don't have anything solid or practical to show for my work then my funding might be withdrawn," Henry said as he continued to stare at his screen.

"It's Friday night, the bars are full and the ladies are waiting for us!" Charlie exclaimed as he towered over Henry.

Henry laughed; he knew the ladies were definitely not waiting for two guys like them. Charlie was tall and gangly. People always noticed him when he walked into a room but not in a good way. He was clumsy, he banged into tables and his large sideburns made him look as though he belonged in a different era. He was fun though and people liked him. Henry was quieter and preferred keeping a low profile. He was of average height, medium build and with sensibly cut brown hair. Henry was less noticeable as he dressed conservatively, usually in a shirt and smart suit.

In the past, he joined dating sites, as he worked many hours. He was relatively successful in the first few dates. Women were attracted to him due to his friendly face and warm, hazel eyes which lit up when he smiled. However, after a few dates, it always became apparent Henry never had much in common with these women. Whenever his dates asked what he did for a living, he told them – in great detail – all aspects of his work. Hoping to impress but instead, he could almost see the point at which their eyes glazed over with boredom. Charlie advised him to stop being so dull and to pretend he was an astronaut or something slightly more interesting. After a few unsuccessful dates, he deleted his profile.

Henry decided to shut his computer, stand up and put his jacket on. Charlie was right; he needed to get out more and a couple of beers wouldn't do any harm. They walked to the nearest bar and as usual, it was full of young, twenty-somethings typing away. Occasionally someone looked up just to take a picture of themselves; no doubt to post on their blog. Charlie started pouting and pretended to take a selfie.

"Honestly, when did the world become so damn narcissistic?" he asked. "How are we supposed to get laid when everyone is either too busy taking selfies or has their eyes stuck to a screen?"

"It's been like this ever since I was a teenager. I think we were too busy studying and we missed the great blogging revolution, thank god!" Henry replied. "Let's get out of here."

The two men found a quaint, less trendy bar nearby and ordered two pints.

"This is more like it, although I don't like the look of yours," Charlie gestured to his left towards a group of older ladies.

Henry laughed; the group of women were probably in their sixties.

"At least they're talking to each other and not one of them has their phone out."

Henry proceeded to fill Charlie in on the latest findings of his experiment. He had so far developed the receptor which could mimic the artificial brain waves from one avatar on a computer to be downloaded to another avatar. The second avatar, without any programming, behaved exactly the same as the original one. This was the first stage and the most straightforward part of the experiment. The next stage was to reproduce these results into a live subject and this is where Henry was failing. No matter how many times he tried and altered the code accordingly, the subject matters died. Henry was experimenting on lab rats.

Various experiments, for example, included one rat living in an enriched environment with running wheels and mazes which they learnt to complete and other tests where they learnt they could release food from hatches. They were also designed to hate one certain type of cheese. The partner rat, in contrast, had a less exciting environment. They didn't learn any tasks; they were kept in smaller cages and grew to be less confident. They were also trained to love the cheese their partner rat loathed. Whenever Henry felt the test subjects were ready, Henry downloaded the first rat's brainwaves and injected it into the second rat's brain via the implanted receptor. However, the second rat rarely survived and if it did, it was permanently brain-damaged.

Charlie, fascinated by the subject, discussed with Henry all possible hypotheses of what was failing. Charlie occasionally doubted the viability but knew to keep that to himself. Henry wouldn't take it very well and he never gave up once he had his mind set on something.

As they were talking, they were interrupted by a woman at the bar.

"Excuse me? I couldn't help but overhear, neither of you seem even the slightest bit concerned you're causing unnecessary harm to an animal, even if it's just a rat. You're talking about leaving half of them bored out of their minds throughout their short lives and causing brain damage and death. Then it's simply 'oops,' on to the next one. Don't you feel a bit guilty?"

Henry and Charlie stared at each other, feeling slightly embarrassed. They hadn't expected anyone to listen in and rarely had to justify themselves. They usually left out the part of testing on animals whenever talking to members of the public. Their fellow colleagues knew it was part and parcel of this particular work and never questioned it. Experiments on animals were highly frowned upon and only permitted when it meant the chance of saving lives or securing a huge breakthrough. Henry was trying to do both.

Henry spoke first; "I'm really sorry we appeared blasé and I assure you that I do care about the welfare of all animals, even my lab rats. They're well treated during their lives and they don't experience any pain or undue stress."

The woman argued back; "how can you know for sure that they don't experience pain or stress?"

"Because, their entire lives are monitored, from their heart rates, blood pressure right down to their brain waves. Their outputs are always pretty constant, I promise you," Henry replied.

"What about the poor rats that you keep bored?"

asked the woman at the bar.

"I can't be responsible for the entertainment of all rats," said Henry.

Finally, the woman at the bar smiled at them although not convinced on the subject. Charlie interrupted, offering Henry's services to give her a tour of his laboratory to put her mind at ease. He nudged Henry and said goodnight to them both. Left alone, the woman introduced herself; "I'm Annie by the way."

"Henry, pleased to meet you," he said as they shook hands.

"So, what exactly is it that you're trying to do?" she asked.

Henry smiled and tried not to get carried away with the explanation of his work. There was something about Annie and he didn't want her eyes to glaze over. Henry was happy when Annie's friend cancelled and she remained in the pub with him. The two continued to talk over drinks until closing time. Henry was pleased to learn Annie was a web developer and keen to discuss coding. It reminded him of old times with his father. As they left, Annie made him promise to give her a tour of his lab, to which Henry gladly agreed.

CHAPTER 6

As promised, Henry arranged to show Annie around his workplace the following week. She arrived one evening after the last of his colleagues had left. He was keen for the opportunity to assure her of his decent treatment towards the lab rats. Henry held his breath when security buzzed him to let him know he had a visitor. He felt rather nervous and checked himself in the mirror; he had on his best shirt that day and adjusted his hair with his fingers. He discreetly breathed onto his hand to check for bad breath. 'Calm down,' he told himself. It's just a girl.

Although Henry had girlfriends in the past, he'd never been in a serious relationship. The few girlfriends he'd had prior never lasted beyond three or four months. He always lost interest and immersed himself in his study and forgot about them. Annie was the first girl in a long time he felt excited about. When he saw her standing in reception he couldn't help but smile; she returned a beautiful, warm smile. He hoped she felt the same as he did.

Usually, highly confident when talking about his experiments, he found himself flustered. The only time he ever felt nervous in a professional capacity was when he found himself justifying reasons for additional funding.

The experiment was high tech and required the latest equipment as well as experts to build the receptors to attempt the transfers. He also required the expertise of genetic engineers and fellow neuroscientists. There was no way to give a time frame of how long it would take. Initially, he received a large injection of funding which he hoped would be enough but that was five years ago. Now Henry was forced to apply for additional funding every six months, which required jumping through hoops and preparing major presentations. Patience was being lost and the funding council didn't feel as though they were getting their money's worth. However, Henry always felt he was just on the precipice of the major breakthrough that he was looking for. He just needed a bit of luck perhaps or some inspiration. He wasn't sure what was missing but knew it was something within his grasp.

These nerves were different to the ones he experienced when engaged in presentations; he hated presenting in front of the funding council. Although he knew his stuff, he worried the people judging him didn't and wouldn't quite understand what angle he was coming from. They might freeze his funding because they were less intelligent and didn't completely understand.

His nerves tonight were because he wanted to impress this girl. She looked so pretty – he hadn't quite noticed the first time they met. Petite and lovely, Annie had wavy, mid-length, blonde hair and large, friendly brown eyes with a smattering of freckles across her nose. Her smile accentuated her cute dimples and she was dressed casually in a raincoat over her top and jeans. With a kiss on the cheek, Henry took hold of her hand; it was cold. As he rubbed her hands to warm them up, she laughed at him. Not wanting to let go, he led her to the lab. She didn't pull her hand away and Henry felt re-assured by his forwardness, which was very forward for Henry.

Normally, Henry always waited for the woman to make the first move. In such circumstances of romance, he always felt awkward as though he couldn't read the signals correctly. Usually, when the subject of the consent form came up, Henry knew he was no longer in friend's territory. Since 2028, it was illegal for people to engage in sex without signing a consent form.

This was in the form of an app connected to all of a person's personal electronic devices. All adults above the age of sixteen were required to register with this app. Some argued this interfered with any spontaneity and was intrusive to their private lives. Others argued, in this day of blurred lines and harsh punishment, the device could only be a good thing – it was an alibi. Only that person had access to their own consent form, where they could view the names and consent of past lovers. It was frowned upon for anyone else to view it or for spouses to share the information with each other. However, doctors had access to the information and although doctors were sworn to uphold their Hippocratic Oath, there were some that believed this information may have been shared elsewhere such as the government or agencies of the government. Some of these people rebelled and refused to sign consent forms. If caught, they were usually heavily fined. Persistent offenders might be imprisoned and now that rape was recently added to the list of capital offences it was becoming less and less common for people to ignore the consent form.

Henry liked the consent form; he liked the black and white of romantic situations. He preferred to know where he stood, but with Annie, he felt something he hadn't felt before and he put it down to a chemical reaction that he'd never experienced.

"What are you thinking about?" asked Annie.

"Nothing," said Henry as he led her to his lab to distract her. He daren't tell Annie he was thinking of consent forms and chemical reactions, it was hardly romantic and he didn't want to put Annie off.

Once in his lab, he guided her around explaining the use of each piece of equipment and showed her some of the coding behind his idea. She showed genuine interest and understood some of the finer details that went over other people's heads. This seriously impressed Henry and he couldn't help but smile at her.

"What are you smirking at, Henry Marlow?"

"Are you sure you're not bored? Does this really

interest you?" he asked.

"Of course it does. I find it fascinating, especially the way you found a synthetic way to copy the complexities of the brain and simply turn it into a piece of code. I get it; I'm impressed."

A surge of pride hit Henry as he explained he rarely spoke to people, outside of the lab, who showed such an interest. "People are always interested by the overall idea but they usually switch off when I go into the details."

"You're probably just speaking to morons, Henry. Now lead me to your rat friends so I can make sure they're well cared for."

Annie pulled him away towards the cages.

CHAPTER 7

"So that's how you met your wife Annie? The rat experiments obviously didn't put her off?" asked Joe the reporter.

"No, I successfully reassured her about the conditions of the rats and one thing led to another and we began dating. Soon afterwards, we signed the damn consent form. You still have to do that?" asked Henry.

He'd been out of the loop for a while and had no idea what went on in the world of dating and sex any more; that was long behind him.

"Yep, we still have it. I can't imagine not having it. It's good to have a backup," said Joe.

"It'd been introduced just before I met Annie. People thought it was the end of civilisation as we know it; passion and spur of the moment would become a thing of the past," reminisced Henry.

"I can safely say, I still experience plenty of passion in my life," winked Joe.

Joe could sense Dr Marlow becoming slightly uncomfortable and steered the conversation back to when Dr Marlow met his wife.

"I heard the 'The Marlow Project' was named after your wife and not yourself as many people believe," asked Joe.

"Yes, that's right. I wanted to call it 'The Annie Project' but it didn't sound quite right. Then I considered her maiden name but somehow 'The Legg Project' or anything with the word Legg in was completely unsuitable. She didn't want to take any credit for the project but without her inspiration and continuous support, the project may never have happened. We went through many connotations but unfortunately, our imaginations failed us and we simply came up with 'The Marlow Project'. However, it was apt as we were both called Marlow as we had been married for about a year at the time. Annie inspired me and it was her input that turned the project around..."

"Henry dear, now we're married, you must stop working so many hours. I need sustenance; I need to go out for wine and food once in a while. We need to see the outside world occasionally and get some fresh air," Annie demanded.

"I know, I know! We will," Henry promised.

They had the same discussion every week. Annie was just as much a workaholic as Henry. She didn't demand too much of his time and with Annie working all the time, Henry stayed at the lab most evenings. In bed at night, they often promised each other to make more of an effort. Henry always agreed but told Annie she had to make the first step in shutting down her computer. Annie loved her web-development work as much as Henry loved his work and she also found shutting off just as difficult. She'd just started a job with a new company in the health service. The eventual ambitious goal of the company was to monitor the health of the entire population. There was a huge strain on hospitals due to the increase of cancers, so monitoring would lead to early detection. It could save lives and treatments would be less costly.

During these bedtime hours, they caught up with each other about their day and bounced ideas around about their work. Although she wasn't involved in the medical side of the project, she was creating the website responsible for collating all the information, Henry loved hearing the updates and inputting his ideas. This would be a huge undertaking for Annie and it paid well.

As before, still fascinated by Henry's project, she always encouraged him during his failures. One night, as usual, he talked Annie through the latest on his project. Eager to hear, she was just as desperate for a breakthrough as Henry. Even with variations in his calculations, in the last year progress appeared to be at a standstill. This worried Henry; who was reaching a point of running out of ideas.

"So, you're still replicating pretty much the same code to mimic the brain waves with minor alterations here and there?" asked Annie one night.

"Yes," said Henry.

They'd been through this many times.

"I'm just thinking out loud, but the process always worked from computer to computer but not from organic matter. You're using the same process from computers and trying to apply it to animals. Computers work from code but animals don't."

"What are you getting at?" asked Henry.

"The one thing that has always made me question the experiment is that you are essentially replicating the brain by using your complicated algorithms. So when this does work, the implanted brain wouldn't be an organic brain but just a computer mimicking the workings and functions of the old brain. You'd be essentially creating a cyborg, yes?" asked Annie.

"No!" protested Henry.

He detested the term cyborg. The implanted brain was human, with living thoughts and memories and would continue to generate future thoughts and memories. He was convinced they'd feel love and pain and all the usual human emotions. It had been questioned numerous times before if these emotions would be real or just computer generated emotions.

"Annie, you know I hate that word, cyborg!"

"I know and I'm not trying to upset you but you've been following the same path for a long time. I think you're so blinded and obsessed with what you're doing that you're leaving out something obvious. Yes, we all know you're a brilliant coder but why use code? Why not use the actual dark matter in the brain? The experiment works from computer to computer but not animal to animal because we're not computers and never will be. You're also a brilliant neuroscientist but you've surrounded yourself with coders and not other neuroscientists in the last few years. Use the findings you already have, forget about copying the brain and use the actual brain."

"No, that would be a huge setback, all that funding wasted so far and I'd have to get a new team. I couldn't possibly."

Henry was determined to put this idea to the back of his mind. It would be like starting from the beginning.

CHAPTER 8

"So that's when the project took off?" asked Joe.

"Yes, Annie was absolutely right, as usual. I was so blindsided from the success of the computer to computer transfers that I was a stubborn fool and carried down the same path that led nowhere for five or six years. It took a while, the funding ran dry and I let some staff go. Annie supported us for a while but with all the groundwork I'd already done, the breakthrough came much quicker than either of us anticipated.

By targeting areas of the brain responsible for behaviour and memories and extrapolating these genes, I was able to implant them into the donor's brain. After a while, they developed and took over the donor's existing brain. Again, it took many experiments until the test subject survived. In the beginning, neither specimen survived; then one of the pair survived with minimal brain damage before I found the method to keep the donor rats alive without any sign of brain damage or immunorejection. The recipient rat was the one not kept in isolation.

The method I used meant this rat always died of brain damage but only after I made the transfer to the donor rat. But finally, the brain of the recipient rat existed within the donor rat's body.

This donor rat originally kept in isolation appeared more confident; it no longer stayed in his dark corner away from the lights. It performed the tasks the recipient specimen performed without itself ever having previously tried. It always took the recipient a few attempts at the task and the maze before they figured it out. The previously isolated specimen could now do it straight away, the cheese they were engineered to hate, they now ate. It was a huge breakthrough."

"Was it your intention for the recipient body to always die?" asked Joe.

"Not really, but then I thought, who would want to transfer their brain into another body unless they were dying? Therefore, the sole purpose of my project from that point was to help the terminally ill."

"So, did you test it on humans soon after that?" asked Joe.

"No, it was another few years before our first human transplant. Once I proved the success of the experiment, my funding returned. I employed staff once again. We progressed from rats to monkeys and then to dogs; dangerous dogs from kennels on the list for euthanasia. We conducted the experiment between sick, dying, gentle dogs and feral, dangerous dogs. When the feral, donor dog became gentle and recognised their owner, I knew I had done it."

"Okay, so the first human transplant was Dean Hunter?"

"Not quite the first. I wasn't allowed to test on the general public but the government at the time was eager to see if it worked human to human. The first experiment on humans was between prisoners: a death row prisoner and a terminally ill prisoner. Both men consented without receiving financial compensation or any other incentives. I guess they knew they had nothing to lose..."

CHAPTER 9

Henry barely slept the night before. Today was the day. The make-or-break day. The day which potentially shaped his future career. If anything went wrong, if the experiment didn't work, or if both patients died, he was likely to lose his financial support from the government. Today was the first time he was conducting his experiment between two humans.

Annie was in the car with him; she clutched his hand and didn't say anything. She knew how nervous he was. Today was also the first time Annie ever came into work with him. She signed a non-disclosure agreement in order to attend the experiment as she insisted on being there for Henry, to offer her support.

He'd met the patients the day before. Both were prisoners – one on death row and the other serving a ten-year sentence. Flown in from America on a private plane.

Peter Marshall had been on death row for ten years for the murder of his newborn child. He shook his son to death during a fit of rage attributed to smoking marijuana coupled with a temperament that was always on a short fuse. His daily life was made a misery by the guards who were all fathers and by whispered threats from other prisoners. Mostly, his life was made miserable by the incredible guilt he felt. He loved his son and couldn't believe what he'd done. When sentenced to death, he accepted his punishment and often considered taking his own life. However, when this strange request of a scientist looking for volunteers for a body transfer programme, he felt he had nothing to lose. As the donor, it meant certain death. Peter was ready to die and thought this might be his last chance to make amends. Yes, he was only saving the life of a fellow prisoner, but if successful, the project would be rolled out to the public. Due to him, the experiment could potentially save many lives.

The recipient was a prisoner by the name of Dante Lopez; currently serving a sentence for armed robbery. Almost at the end of his sentence, he received the devastating news that he was dying of Cirrhosis due to undiagnosed hepatitis going back many years. In prison, he changed and now near the end of his sentence, he was determined to lead a different life to that of his youth. But his prognosis altered these plans, until he received the request from Dr Marlow. Just like the other prisoner, Peter Marshall, he too had nothing to lose.

Henry thanked both patients for the opportunity they were giving him and spoke of their bravery. Bravery for undergoing a procedure never undertaken before in humans. Henry couldn't make any promises on the outcome but was optimistic. Peter Marshall didn't care; he'd lost the will to live a long time ago. Dante Lopez was more hopeful. Henry allowed the two patients to meet each other. Annie questioned if this was a good idea. He thought so; it meant Dante would know what he would look like afterwards and to offer reassurance to Peter. Peter wanted to know he was helping out not a hardened criminal but a changed man.

The two prisoners weren't the only ones who needed reassurance. Annie put her arm around Henry as they watched the two patients from outside the operating theatre.

"I can't believe this day has finally come," he said.

"Me neither. I'm so glad to share it with you."

"What if something goes wrong?"

"Shush. It won't. I have every confidence in you. It never failed in the dog experiments. You're one hundred per cent sure otherwise you wouldn't be doing this. It's just nerves."

Standing in silence for a few moments, they let the patients continue their conversation. Henry was in no rush and the conversation appeared to relax the men. Before he was about to enter the room, Annie reminded him to take a deep breath and remain calm.

Pushing the door open, he stepped in and the room appeared to shrink. Everyone stopped what they were doing and looked at him. This was it; his big moment. He couldn't let these people down; his staff and two patients. Annie was right, if he wasn't one hundred per cent certain, he wouldn't be undertaking the operation today. This thought eased the butterflies. He straightened his shoulders to portray the look of a man completely sure of himself. For the final time, he asked the two prisoners if they still wanted to go through with it – it wasn't too late to back out. Stony-faced and silent, they both nodded. Again, he reassured them; there would be no pain as they would be anaesthetised. He signalled for the anaesthesiologist to come forward.

"Any last words?" he asked the two men.

"See you soon, I hope," joked Dante.

"Tell my ex, I'm sorry," cried Peter.

This brought a tear to Henry's eye as it suddenly hit him, he would be the executioner. It would be his responsibility to take a man's life. The two faces, now fast asleep, looked peaceful and innocent. He felt his nerve go and looked towards the window where Annie was watching, alongside some government officials. Her eyes spoke to him, offering encouragement and urging him to proceed. It was now or never. He closed his eyes for a moment, steadied his nerves and let the professional inside take over.

The staff unveiled the heavy, cumbersome machinery; covered up until now so as not to scare the patients. Attached were numerous leads and buttons; only Henry knew what everything was for. To Henry, it resembled a medieval torture device. Once he proved the operation a success, he'd improve the machinery to make it streamlined and portable. In the meantime, this was the design – ugly and uninviting, but it worked.

Henry hooked the patients up to the two life support machines plus the necessary wires and tubes from his machine. Once satisfied all was exact, he inserted the two large needles required for the transfer into each brain. The silence was overwhelming as everyone held their breath when Henry programmed the transfer. All he could do now was stand back and watch it work. On the outside, to the spectators, it didn't appear as if anything was happening. But as Henry watched the screens with the scans of the patients brains, he could already see the changes taking place.

The first step, via the needle, was to kill the neurons in the donor's brain, apart from the brain stem. At this stage, the patient was now in a vegetative state, never to recover. The second step was to isolate the same neurons from the recipient and transfer them into the donor's brain. Once complete, Henry turned off the life support machine of the recipient patient. Dante Lopez's body was now the one in the vegetative state. Henry administered the fatal injection into Dante's disease ravaged, brain-dead body. This lifeless body was sent to the incinerator. Dante Lopez would hopefully now live within Peter Marshall's body. All they could do was wait for the new Dante to wake up.

It was the longest hour of Henry's life. They all mulled around outside the recovery room. Questions were asked. Would there be any pain? Would

there be any brain damage? How long would recovery take? Would Dante remember everything?
Would he have any thoughts or feelings from Peter
Marshall? Henry thought he knew all the answers
but so far he'd only experimented on animals and
they couldn't talk back. This would be the first opportunity for reliable feedback.

The nurse called Henry into the room when Dante
stirred from his medically induced sleep. The small
welcoming party were all eager to see Dante but
Henry kept them out of the room to ensure privacy.
He felt Annie squeeze his hand as he left them behind. Only he and the nurse stood by the bedside.

Dante woke up and looked around. Please be okay,
hoped Henry.

"Dr Marlow, did it work?" asked the patient.

Henry breathed a sigh of relief as there were no
obvious signs of brain damage. He asked the patient for his name and date of birth. Although
this was Peter Marshall's body, Henry expected to
hear Dante's name and date of birth. The answers
were correct. Henry and the nurse smiled at each
other across the bedside. So far, so good. After a few
more questions and some checks, it was clear the
operation was a complete success. The government
appointed doctor knocked on the door, requesting
updates. Henry beckoned him over, keen to prove
to this man the success of his operation. The doctor
asked his own questions.

"How do you feel?"

"A bit sleepy and my head hurts but apart from

that, I'm fine."

He too checked some of Dante's personal details. Dante gave all the correct answers.

"¿Puedes hablar espanol?"

"Sí, claro."

With that, Dante continued to converse excitedly in his native Spanish.

"English, please! My school Spanish is limited," joked the government doctor.

The atmosphere in the room lightened as everyone laughed. Dante apologised and reverted to English. Peter Marshall couldn't speak Spanish, yet here was his old body, now fluent.

Dante confirmed he knew nothing of Peter's life; all his memories and thoughts were his own. He felt no overwhelming sense of guilt, which was Peter's constant emotional state. After the excitement, Dante was left to recover in peace. The witnesses and Henry met in his office. Annie cracked open a bottle of champagne and toasted Henry.

No one could quite believe such a complicated procedure could take so little time with so little recovery.

"The man's just had a brain transplant or should that be a body transplant? And I believe he could walk himself home straight after. Unbelievable!"

Henry took little credit. The ease of the operation and the recovery was due to the rapidly evolving technology. It meant any major surgery was much less invasive than a couple of decades ago. It was rare for a patient to undergo major incisions these days.

"Nevertheless, I do believe it's due to your genius too," said Annie.

Henry thanked his wife. It was finally coming together.

After the celebrations, Henry excused himself and took a long walk along the river. Peter Marshall had committed an evil crime but he wasn't a completely evil person. Henry, now an executioner, had to think about whether this was something his conscience could allow him to continue with.

"I guess it was, judging by the number of experiments you've undertaken," said Joe.

"Yes. The first time was the hardest but as colleagues pointed out, they would have been executed eventually. At least I was saving a life in return and possibly alleviating the prisoner's conscience."

"So that was the first human to human transplant?" asked Joe.

"Very much so. This experiment was carried out in secret. The government didn't want it documented just in case it went wrong. But they were supportive once I proved the transfer was safe. That's when the idea formed of using a donor from prison. That was my biggest regret of the experiment – I could only transfer the brain into another living body. It meant donors were rather lacking. However, the government at the time were excited about the prospect and a law was passed to permit prisoners to donate their bodies; this was quickly followed by other countries following suit. The only proviso was the prisoner had to be on death row, sign a consent form and receive compensation. We couldn't be seen to profit from someone's death or look as though a vulnerable person was put under undue pressure; even if he was a criminal," Henry explained.

"So yes, Dean Hunter was the first member of the public to receive the operation. He was a dying patient of Charlie's and Charlie begged me to save him. Charlie had been his family doctor for a number of years. They'd tried everything. He had a two-year-old son and this resonated heavily with Charlie at the time as he'd just become a father. He was the perfect donor as well; educated and law-abiding with a young family. The government gave me the go ahead and that was the first 'official' brain transplant. We followed his progress for years; this provided the company with the first case study of not only the effects of the actual procedure but the effects of how a person copes in a different body…"

CHAPTER 10

Dean Hunter

Dean Hunter woke up from his operation feeling groggy. As he opened his heavy eyelids, the first thing he did was bring his hands towards his face. He viewed these unfamiliar hands through his new eyes. They were somewhat bigger and rougher than his own. Dean was a teacher before his illness took hold. He taught history at a secondary school near his home in Cheltenham. These new hands belonged to that of a labourer, not a teacher. Dean scrutinised the coarse skin and calluses on the hands; they felt dry. He clenched his hand into a fist; the veins popped up from underneath the skin on his wrist. Considerable muscle formed on his upper arm as he clenched the fist. This new arm felt stronger than his old one. A tattoo on his forearm caught his attention. Dean never had one before - he didn't care for them. This one was an intricate drawing of a child's face.

"We can take care of that if you like. Some laser surgery and you'll never know it was there," said a voice next to Dean.

This voice interrupted Dean's thoughts; he was not alone. Looking up, he saw his doctor, Dr Gregson, standing next to Dr Marlow. Dr Marlow was the pioneer of the procedure Dean had just undergone – The Marlow Project. In an attempt to sit up, Dr Marlow placed his hand on Dean's arm and told him to relax.

"Take your time, Dean. You've been through a complex procedure and we want to run a few checks with you if that's okay?"

Dean nodded. Dr Marlow took his blood pressure, examined his eyes and performed other small tests. When Dr Marlow peeled off Dean's blanket, Dean saw his new body for the first time. It revealed a taller, more substantial frame than Dean's original body. Dean swore under his breath. Dr Marlow smiled at him as he pricked Dean's legs and feet and asked if he experienced any sensation.

"Yes, I can feel everything," Dean confirmed.

"Good, now, can you tell me your name and date of birth?"

In a daze, he answered; "yes, it's Dean Hunter. I was born 4th April 2010."

"What's your wife's name and do you have any children?"

"My wife is Lucy and I have one boy called Jonny, he's two. Can I see them?"

"Yes, in a little while. We will have to administer some further tests but the transfer appears to have proven a complete success," Dr Marlow confirmed with a wide smile.

Dr Gregson gave him a slap on the back and stared at Dean.

"Dean I can't believe it worked. I'm astonished...you're actually cured! How do you feel?" Dr Gregson asked.

"I have no idea; I feel disorientated. I mean...I feel like me and there's no pain but this body is so unfamiliar. How the hell do I get used to this?" Dean asked as he touched his face. "Can I get a mirror?"

Dr Marlow passed a mirror and advised him to take his time. Dean closed his eyes before lifting the mirror towards his face.

"You'll have to open them eventually," encouraged Dr Gregson.

Dean took a deep breath as he opened his eyes.

"NO!" he shouted when he saw the reflection of his new face for the first time. He threw the mirror across the room and climbed out of bed. His legs beneath him felt like jelly, so he grabbed hold of Dr Marlow for stability.

"Come, come," soothed Dr Marlow as he helped Dean back into bed. "I know this is a complete shock but please remember why you did this. The alternative was unthinkable, wasn't it? Besides, you've inherited a great body; your donor was fit and healthy. It will take time to get used to your new face and body but you will. Eventually, you'll accept it as your own."

"How the hell do I get used to living in a stranger's body? Jonny won't recognise me. I don't even sound like me," Dean asked as he stared in the mirror again.

His old face was smoother, his features – more delicate. He wore glasses; his eyes were blue and his hair was light brown. This face had seen the sun; he looked older even though Dr Marlow assured him the donor's body was about the same age. He had dark brown hair and his chin felt rough with stubble. He had crow's feet around his new green eyes. It wasn't a bad-looking face, some people might say this face was ruggedly handsome but it was so different from the face Dean saw every day. Dean was not a vain man but it was only now he truly appreciated how he used to look. He just wanted his own boyish appearance back.

"Lucy and Jonny will adjust to your new look. You'll have the same mind, the same memories, you'll most likely even have the same annoying habits you used to have. Remember, it's still you. Only the outer layer has changed but deep inside you are the same person; I promise you. Lucy and Jonny will get used to it too. Treat them exactly the same and talk to them exactly in the same way, and they'll accept you. They'll be here in a moment. Are you ready to see them?"

"Is it really me?" he asked.

"Yes, it's really you," Dr Marlow replied.

"Please give me some time on my own; let me get my head around this and then I'll see them. Is that alright?" asked Dean.

"Of course, anything you want. Let us know when you're ready and I'll bring them in to see you."

Dr Marlow and Dr Gregson left the room in high

spirits. Dean knew they were eager to discuss his operation and he couldn't blame them. What they had offered him was a second chance, one that was life-altering. He was the first to go through this operation.

He recalled visiting Dr Gregson six months prior for a simple blood test. During the previous weeks, Dean didn't feel well. All he wanted to do was go to bed. He was also inexplicably losing weight. He assumed it was from a lack of iron or a virus. However, the blood tests were rushed through and it transpired it was cancer. A cancer that spread so rapidly and indiscriminately throughout his whole body, he had only a few months to live. As much as technology and medicine had improved over the last twenty years, they still hadn't discovered a cure for cancer.

This devastating news was a shock to Dean and Lucy. Neither could stop crying, especially when Jonny asked why they were crying so much lately. The thought of not seeing Jonny grow up was unbearable. Dean tried pulling himself together for the sake of his family as he made sure his life insurance was up to date, along with all his other financial obligations. He wanted to make sure his wife and son were looked after, even if it was just financially. He took sick leave from his job but knew he would never return. They even took a family holiday together and tried to make the most of Dean's last few weeks. Gradually, he felt himself becoming weaker and weaker as his body deteriorated.

One afternoon as Dean slept on the sofa, Dr Gregson paid an urgent home visit. A new exciting, pioneering procedure required terminally ill patients as guinea pigs. It was called, 'The Marlow Project,' named after the scientist who discovered this procedure. As a leading expert in the field of neuroscience, Dr Marlow discovered a technique to transfer part of a human brain into another body. Dean recalled hearing Dr Marlow's name on television and wondered who on earth would ever benefit from this breakthrough? And now, his own doctor suggested he would be the one to benefit from this breakthrough.

"Dean, in my opinion, you are the ideal subject. The experiment is only permitted if the host body is dead and the brain donor is dying. The government doesn't want experiments between two healthy humans. Huge lawsuits might arise if anything goes wrong. Dr Marlow is looking for young, terminally ill people who possess sufficient mental capacity and who are willing to take a chance. He's an old university friend of mine and is brilliant. The experiment has already been performed successfully on several people behind closed doors. Yours could be the first official operation. Is this something that might interest you?" urged Dr Gregson.

"No, I think that sounds crazy!" Dean replied. "For starters, where the hell do you find dead bodies? Will Dr Marlow dig up corpses from graveyards?"

"No, of course not, they'd be too decomposed. The transfer would effectively take place in a living body as we can't bring the dead back to life yet."

Dean interrupted, "but you said the government only allowed dead bodies?"

"Yes, or bodies about to die. We're talking about prisoners facing capital punishment. Some have agreed to donate their body – in effect, only their brains are executed. The prisoner's body is kept alive while the transfer takes place and then the recipient body dies once the transfer is complete. In exchange for this, they will receive substantial financial compensation which their families automatically inherit. If there's no family to speak of, or if they didn't require payment, then their remaining time in prison is made as pleasant as possible."

"So let me get this straight; you want to transfer my brain into the body of a mass murderer?"

"More or less," confirmed Dr Gregson.

Dean shook his head as he recalled that conversation in his living room only one month ago. It was Lucy who begged him to do it; they had nothing to lose. He would be dead soon enough and at least this way, if it was a success, they could preserve his old memories and even make new ones. Jonny would still have a father and Lucy would still have a husband. The thought of living in a stranger's body was disturbing for Dean but the thought of never seeing his family again was heartbreaking. The idea of losing his family far outweighed living in a stranger's body, so he chose life. And now, here he was lying in bed at Dr Marlow's clinic, recovering from his operation.

Dean took a moment to compose himself. He pressed the call button; he was ready to see his family. The door opened slightly and Lucy popped her head into the room. Encouraged by Dean, she entered the room and approached his bedside with trepidation. Jonny wasn't with her.

"Hey stranger," she said.

"Hey you," he said nervously as he wasn't sure how she might react to him.

"Say something, something only we know?" she asked.

Dean paused to think.

"Remember our honeymoon in Fiji? I got stung on my privates on the first day, so we played Scrabble all night. We've never told anyone about that?"

Lucy laughed.

"I'd forgotten all about that! Oh my goodness, it's you, isn't it? It's really you? This is so weird, " she said, as she approached him and caressed his face and inspected him.

"Yes, it's strange," he confirmed. "And yes, it's me, I think…I feel like me; I have my own thoughts, all our memories. I feel no different inside."

She stroked his stubble and laughed about how he might be able to finally grow a beard.

"Joking aside Lucy, can you live with me? Won't it be like letting a complete stranger into your house? I have no idea what this man did in his life but it must have been something terrible to deserve capital punishment?"

Lucy reassured him; "it doesn't matter what this

person did before they died. It's your brain that controls this body, not his. This body isn't responsible for the actions of the previous owner. His brain or mind controlled his actions and now that criminal brain is dead. It's your body now. You can have a haircut in your usual style, shave and buy larger clothes, identical to your old ones. You can put on your aftershave and even wear your old glasses without a prescription. That way, you'll smell the same. You'll be familiar. Don't worry about Jonny either, he's only two. He'll adapt, we all will."

His wife's optimism and calmness surprised Dean. He conveyed this surprise by telling her how amazing she was.

"Trust me, the alternative was unthinkable. Now I don't have to plan for a funeral, mourn my dead husband or explain to our two-year-old why he no longer has a daddy. I was prepared to do anything to make sure that didn't happen."

Dean knew that with the support of his wife, he could learn to accept this.

"Where's Jonny? Can you bring him to me?" Dean asked.

Lucy nodded and left the room to fetch Jonny, who was waiting outside with his grandparents.

Dean took another deep breath and felt relaxed for the first time. If Lucy could get aboard and accept the situation, so could he. He had a second chance and wasn't wasting it by questioning the ethics and strangeness of it all.

CHAPTER 11

After a couple of months, Dean became acquainted with his new body. Stronger and taller, he now lifted heavy items or opened jars that previously took more effort. He became familiar with every inch of his body and so had his wife. The first time they made love was a little odd. Lucy felt inhibited as though she was being unfaithful. So Dean gave her full consent to have sex with this body whenever she wanted. Although they laughed about it, he often had to reassure her that his body was just the vessel and the old Dean was still inside. Just as she reassured him in the hospital when he first woke up from the operation. In the beginning, it brought them closer together as his reassurances consisted of reminiscing about old times, to remind Lucy he was the same man.

Dean's new, muscular body gave him more confidence. It required maintenance so he joined a gym to lift weights, determined to maintain the muscular frame and not let it turn into fat. His sex life improved; it was fine before but Lucy definitely seemed keener once she became used to the new-look Dean. Occasionally, he had some issues with that but as he was also benefiting, he didn't say anything.

Jonny, his son, at first was a little shy and nervous around him. He'd ask where his daddy was but it didn't take long for Jonny to accept him. This new person knew exactly the spot where he liked to be tickled and knew all about Jonny's favourite toys and cartoon characters. He even knew the same funny voices and jokes although they sounded a little different. In no time at all, Jonny accepted that daddy had a new body and as Jonny was only two, he'd soon forget Dean's original appearance.

Dean and Lucy often discussed the life of this body before death row. Dr Marlow insisted the new owner should know nothing about the donor; it might affect them negatively or alter their behaviour. Maybe Dean would dwell on the past crimes of the donor. By not knowing names or crimes, it meant increased difficulty for someone to track the donor down. Perhaps a family member would want to see the donor body again and become attached. Unsavoury characters from the past might make an appearance, unable to accept they weren't technically the same person.

The only clue they had was this donor probably had a child. Why else would he have an etching of a child's face on his arm? This tattoo made Dean and Lucy feel uneasy; some poor child out there was probably missing his daddy – no matter what he had done. Dean had the tattoo removed. Not only were tattoos considered old-fashioned; he didn't want to see that poor boy's face every day, even though he knew it was an important link to the old owner's life.

Dean was also due to return to work in his teaching role. Since a young boy, he'd always wanted to be a teacher; he had a soothing manner and explained facts clearly and concisely. The old Dean was a patient man and loved the challenge of encouraging his pupils to love learning. The idea of moulding and shaping young minds who were the future was Dean's motivation for going to work. Before his illness, he stayed at work the latest. Determined to be a head teacher one day, he had to put the extra work in.

However, the new Dean lost this motivation, only doing the bare minimum at work as he wanted more free time. Now as a member of a gym, he felt the need to work off this new-found energy. His extra confidence led him to talk to more people and his popularity increased due to his new appearance. People treated him differently. They recognised him from news reports as the first successful donor, which led him to become a mini-celebrity in his small town. Encouraged to produce blogs and to account for his daily activities, he quickly made fans. At first, he shied away from this as he enjoyed his fairly quiet life. But before long, he revelled in the limelight and receiving freebies such as exotic holidays and luxury products. His life was suddenly more interesting than that of the old sensible teacher, Mr Hunter. People were fascinated by him and women contacted him, sending seductive pictures of themselves. It wasn't long before Dean succumbed to the newfound attention and met up with his 'fans.' It also wasn't long before Lucy found out. Initially, Dean made excuses but the excuses faded so he told Lucy to accept him for whom he was now. This was his second chance at life and he had sampled a rather different existence to the one before and he wasn't willing to let it go.

"Do you think Dean's fall from grace could be attributed to the effects of the old brain?" asked Joe.

"Absolutely not, it was all Dean's fault; the old Dean, I mean. He never received that level of attention before and he let it go to his head. He had this new, muscular body and it gave him confidence and he experienced something he never had before – women throwing themselves at his feet. No, his marriage breakdown was due to Dean's decision to have multiple affairs. I don't believe it was due to any essence of the old owner of the body nor the neocortex of his brain," insisted Dr Marlow. "Besides, he never did anything illegal. Just immoral; infidelity is not a crime. He was intelligent enough to get the consents approved before he succumbed to his affairs. Unfortunately – as you might remember – the media illegally accessed his consent forms, and there were rather a lot of them. Once his wife Lucy knew the full extent of his infidelity, she left him and they divorced."

"Do you know where Dean is now?"

"Yes, according to Charlie, he's living life as a recluse. The fame, followed by divorce and notoriety led him to some dark moments and he's suffered since with depression which led to a drinking problem. Last time I spoke to Charlie, he was helping Dean deal with his alcoholism."

"Did you know anything about the donor?" said Joe.

"Yes, I always had full disclosure. His name was Adam Hill. I believe he was from America. He was a serial rapist and had a wife and child and wasn't a suspect until his DNA eventually caught up with him."

"How did the wife feel about him donating his body?"

"At that point, she was disgusted by him and didn't want a reminder of him left on the earth. But we reassured her she would never run into him in the street as the recipient lived in another country. She was offered a generous compensation package and banned from disclosing what happened to the body. We couldn't run the risk of a relative of one of the victims coming after Dean for revenge."

"But he was an active blogger – the world knew his face. Anyone connected to Adam Hill would have recognised him?"

Dr Marlow agreed mistakes were made early on in the program. For it to be successful a certain level of anonymity was required.

"And you don't think there was any correlation

between this guy being a rapist and Dean not being able to keep it in his pants?" asked Joe.

Dr Marlow shrugged; "I would say the increased testosterone level in the body obviously increased Dean's sex drive, but it's the brain that controls whether or not you rape someone or if you have an affair. That part of Adam Hill's brain was dead, so I firmly believe the part of the rapist was dead. Dean chose to have affairs; he didn't handle the situation well. In hindsight, I should have adjusted other aspects of the body like his testosterone levels but as with any test subject, you never know what will happen. As I said before, Dean did not commit any crime. Who knows, maybe he and his wife would have divorced regardless, there is no way of knowing."

Joe decided to let it lie. Dr Marlow would never admit to any failure of his experiments in the early days and he hadn't come to interrogate him. He just wanted the full story from the expert.

CHAPTER 12

Henry became a household name at the same time as Dean. Joe recalled the time vividly.

"I was about twelve and remember seeing you on the news. I told my dad we didn't have to worry about dying any more – we could all get new bodies. We joked about it at school and made lists of what type of body we wanted. My best friend Billy wanted a girl's body so he could stare at his boobs all day. I think I wanted to be a famous footballer."

Dr Marlow laughed. "Yes, I remember the discussions and reports about 'The Marlow Project.' Lots of jokes were made and controversy always surrounded the project. Some people thought prisoners would be taken advantage of and pressurised into the procedure by their families – who stood to gain a considerable amount of money."

Henry recalled the obsession with watching the news programmes and following all the reports and social commentary in the earlier days. Annie encouraged him to tear himself away from it and ignore the media attention. During an appearance on a show, he hoped to educate the viewers – only prisoners scheduled to die were used. The majority of the population agreed that if this was the only way to save their loved ones, then yes, it was better than nothing. But there were some who petitioned against the project. Quite a few were from religious sectors who thought it was an abhorrence of mankind; it was against God's will. Henry argued if that was the case, then no medical intervention should ever be permitted if anyone got sick. What he was doing was no different, it was still medical intervention.

Other more radicals protested that it was against human rights. Henry and the Government were taking advantage of the prisoner's guilt. Good, he argued; they'd committed terrible crimes and maybe he was helping them assuage their guilt by volunteering on his project. He emphasised that he too, wasn't comfortable with the current arrangement and if somehow he could use dead bodies with donor cards or clone the bodies, then that would be preferable. In the meantime, this was how it had to be and he promised the public he'd work on ways to improve his project.

"I expected garden parties with the King; invites abroad on glamorous yachts and drinking champagne for breakfast. But once I got my first taste of fame, I didn't like it. After my TV appearance, I received death threats, suggesting that I find out what it's like to donate my body. Nothing to take too seriously – I knew the threats were from deranged people. A small band of protesters also appeared outside the clinic on a daily basis. One day, I was pelted with eggs. I received so many negative comments from trolls so I kept away from social media. I thought, 'if this is fame, you can keep it'. So I shied away from the public eye to keep myself and Annie as private as possible. I turned down offers of appearances, tours and interviews. In the first year, I was advised to hire a bodyguard but once the fuss died down, people forgot about me. Eventually, I didn't require a personal bodyguard but I made sure security at the clinic was ramped up. The safety and security of my patients was paramount. Luckily for me, the Russian civil war started around that time so the news and the public turned their attention to that instead."

"Yes, lucky," said Joe.

Joe apologised for his sarcasm but Henry wasn't offended; he knew Joe understood what he meant.

"So fame didn't live up to your expectations?"

Henry agreed.

"I remember when you were pelted with eggs. Your picture was displayed everywhere. I've never seen anyone look so angry," said Joe.

"Wouldn't you be angry if you got abused and pelted with eggs too?" asked Henry.

Joe supposed he would.

"Going back to the case studies, you initially meant for the recipient never to receive any information about the donor?"

"Yes, I consulted a team of psychiatrists and

decided it could be potentially damaging to their well-being. But after one of my recipient's experiences in the early days, I decided to change this policy. Hannah Ford was uneasy about her situation and in her head, she imagined details far worse than what they actually were. I had no choice but to put her at ease..."

CHAPTER 13

Hannah Ford

Hannah arrived home from her life-saving procedure. She didn't know whether to feel grateful that she still had her life ahead of her or sad because when she looked in the mirror, she didn't like what she saw. Admittedly her old body had been ravaged by an incurable illness. Her hair had fallen out; she was skin and bones and her once milky complexion began to take on a greyish hue. Before her illness, she was pretty. She had thick, shiny blonde hair and healthy rosy cheeks. Hannah was tall and excelled at sports but at twenty-one, she found out she was dying. The disease took hold at a rapid rate and she and her family weren't prepared or ready for her death. So when the offer of a second chance came along, she and her family jumped at it.

Hannah was the perfect subject; confident, educated and considered mentally strong. Dr Marlow believed she could handle the transformation despite her youth. The donor body was also a woman in her early twenties who had led a difficult life. As there was a shortage of female donors, there weren't many options and Dr Marlow was keen for his test subjects to be diverse. Dr Marlow warned Hannah that this donor was a drug addict in her former life. Due to that, she had made some bad decisions which led her to death row. He assured Hannah that the donor had already been through 'cold turkey' so Hannah wouldn't feel any of the effects of drug withdrawal. She would however, be left with a body, badly ravaged by the effects of drugs. Dr Marlow promised Hannah, that with time and possibly some cosmetic surgery, they would be able to negate the physical effects.

By this point, Hannah was desperate. The thought of leaving her parents and little brother heartbroken by her death was the worst thing about the illness. She couldn't do that to the people she loved most in the world. Besides, she was at university studying engineering and didn't want all that time and effort to have been for nothing. Although she didn't have a boyfriend at the time, she did one day want to get married, have children and a career. There was still so much left in life to do. She was keen to see how it all turned out.

Now, looking in the mirror and seeing the reflection of her body that was supposedly around the same age as her, doubts crept in. Instead of a second chance of life, all she saw staring back was a ghost. Who'd give her a job or even ask her out? In the mirror, she saw someone who looked nearly as old as her mother. Would this body even last long enough to pursue her dreams?

Dr Marlow assured her there were no long-term effects. The donor's brain was the most diseased part of her body, but the damaged cells from that brain were dead, replaced by Hannah's healthy cells. All other internal organs were checked out and Dr Marlow insisted he would never use a donor that didn't fit his strict criteria.

Hannah was now shorter, much skinnier, her brown hair was dry and thin, she had terrible acne and even some scarring around her face, inevitably caused by picking at the acne. Her teeth were a mess, brown and slightly see-through due to enamel erosion. Before the transfer, the disease left her weakened and bedridden. Hannah assumed she would now feel fit and strong as she used to but she was still so lethargic that it was a struggle to get out of bed most days.

At the time, she tried to find out more about her donor's life, but the doctor insisted it was confidential information. This was necessary to protect her and the donor's family. All he told her was this donor was compatible. If only she had pushed harder for more information but she assumed he knew what he was doing. She told Dr Marlow of her concerns but he made her feel ungrateful and shallow as he reassured her that this body would become strong again. These worries were just superficial.

There was a knock on the bedroom door; it was

Hannah's mum and they sat on her bed together. Her mum stroked her hair; they could make her pretty again. It required time for the body to repair itself from the damage caused by drugs. It was up to Hannah to expedite that progress by eating healthily and taking regular exercise to build up the muscle tone. Other issues such as scars and teeth were cosmetic and could easily be dealt with by surgery. Hannah had a cry on her mum's shoulder and promised to try and accept the situation.

Just then her little brother, Adrian, popped his head around her door; "sorry for calling you ugly earlier, I didn't mean to upset you."

"That's okay, Adrian. It was a shock to all of us."

She remembered the look on everyone's face at the hospital when they saw her for the first time. Her mum and dad were stunned, only her tactless twelve-year-old brother spoke up as he couldn't hold back his revulsion when he saw her.

"I'd rather have an ugly sister than a dead one..." he continued.

"Adrian, stop now!" demanded their mum.

"It's okay," Hannah said, "I'd rather be ugly than dead too. And you're right, we can work on my appearance. I can get my teeth fixed, sort out my hair and skin and tone up. We'll all get used to the way I look and then I can carry on with my life."

"That's my girl, now get some rest," her mum ordered as she gave her a kiss and tucked her into bed.

As the months went by, Hannah relished the challenge of physically improving her body. At first, she could barely run up the stairs without feeling as though she would collapse. But slowly, she built up her stamina. by jogging, swimming and going for long walks with her dog. Even her skin cleared up; she had no desire to pick at the gross acne scabs as her previous owner did. Funded by the Marlow Project, she received the cosmetic treatments she was promised. Her teeth were fixed – now the owner of much better teeth than she had before her illness. Her scars were removed by the latest laser surgery. With an improved diet and some treatments, her hair grew and became thicker. Her skin was no longer pasty white but tanned from the long dog walks. Her eyes brightened up and she was now able to wear makeup, looking less like her mum's older haggard sister and more like a twenty-something, much to Hannah's relief. Not as pretty as before, she looked good enough and with her new teeth, she now had a pretty smile. There were no lines around her eyes when she smiled, not like her old face. Hannah had laughter lines because she'd had a nurturing, loving childhood. The house was always filled with joy. She thought it unlikely that the donor ever had much to smile about.

On the outside, she was more like her old self again but couldn't help think about the life of the girl before her. What was she like? What was her childhood like? Did anyone ever love her? What the hell did she do to end up with the death penalty at such a young age? She blocked out these feelings but nightmares kept her awake. Nightmares which involved murdering people or being murdered herself. Soon, she became too scared to go to sleep.

Hannah couldn't confide in anyone; she didn't want to worry her parents and her old friends now treated her like a stranger. Understandably, they were disturbed when they first met her again but promised nothing would change. It had. Gradually, they became distant. When she walked down the street, she felt uneasy as people knew she was the girl in the stranger's body. They were fearful of this unknown. Did this body still have murderous tendencies? This paranoia made people wary of Hannah.

As the experiment was still in the early stage, there was a huge media frenzy. Preferring to keep a low profile, she rejected offers to tell her story. Strangers nudged each other and pointed; others called her Frankenstein or a freak. Payments were offered to anyone who got a picture of her. Some tried to rile her, make her angry. She never took the bait, knowing they did this to try to make it look as though the experiment didn't work.

Due to the lack of support from outside the family and the scrutiny from the press, this led to Hannah becoming withdrawn and reclusive; only going outside to exercise or walk the dog. When she did leave the house, she disguised herself with a hoodie in case she saw someone who recognised her. She did some research but none of the facial recognition apps recognised her. Not everyone registered for this app, concerned with privacy issues. Prisoners were also not registered for facial recognition. This was a good thing; otherwise, she could easily be tracked down by the donor's family, although they had signed an affidavit before the transplant to guarantee never to track down the body. Even with this assurance, the nightmares increased.

Concentrating was difficult and while her mum thought she was studying too hard, she was in fact just sat at her desk daydreaming. Daydreaming about what this unknown person had done. Were the nightmares true? Were they remnants left in the donor's brain or was it just Hannah's overactive imagination? She dreamt some truly awful things in the night and heard lots of screaming. She woke up in cold sweats screaming out; 'help me!' Was it Hannah who wanted to be helped or the other person? Such thoughts made Hannah feel as though she was going crazy.

Her parents became concerned as Hannah spent more time in her room; she was like the moody teenager from years ago – only much worse. Her mum kept in constant contact with Dr Marlow to update him, but he only ever assured her that it would take time to adapt. Around a year after the procedure, Hannah's parents demanded to see Dr Marlow so he could see for himself how Hannah was coping. They'd only met in person once before so they travelled to London to see him at his office. It took a great deal of patience and persistence to get an appointment; Dr Marlow was always busy.

He was pleasantly surprised by Hannah's transformation.

"Hannah, you look truly wonderful. I heard how hard you worked to look this amazing. I was concerned but you've proven me wrong. This is so encouraging for our current and future patients who have concerns about their physical appearance. I'm sorry I haven't been in touch as much as I would have liked, but I'm so busy. As you know plenty of people have incurable diseases and now we have marvellous successes such as yourself, the world is now taking an interest and I'm in demand," he boasted. "So what can I do for you?"

Hannah took a deep breath; she needed to know what happened to her donor. She talked about her nightmares and how she was going mad.

"Initially, I sort of accepted it. I was distracted by improving my appearance and tried not to think about it. But as time has gone by, I couldn't get her out of my head. I need a name. I need to know what she did. Are my nightmares actually her nightmares?"

Dr Marlow reassured her it would be impossible for her dreams to be anyone else's. Her dreams were caused by the sensory part of her brain, not the donor's brain.

"Dr Marlow, I'm slowly going mad and I want to know all about her. I dream of killing children. I dream of being raped. Most nights I wake up thinking I've had my throat slit. Am I walking around in the body of a child killer?"

Hannah burst into tears and held her head in her

hands. Her mum sobbed quietly too and stroked Hannah's back.

"Dr Marlow," said Hannah's father, "you can see that it's tearing her apart and it's breaking our hearts. We can't do anything for her. We don't know what to say and I think it's damn irresponsible for you to expect such a young woman to handle this without adequate aftercare. You've left us to our own devices to deal with the fallout and the mental anguish. Don't get me wrong, we're eternally grateful to still have Hannah with us but there's been no consideration to her mental state."

"Mr Ford, I'm sorry it's been so hard for Hannah. I'm just technically the surgeon; I have no real experience with psychology. Correct me if I'm wrong but I was led to believe that a counsellor has been provided for the past year?"

Hannah verified she had initially attended all the sessions but wasn't getting anything out of it.

"The counsellors are out of their depth with no knowledge of how the operation affects individuals. How on earth are they expected to know anything? This is unknown territory for everyone concerned. And she couldn't tell me the only thing I wanted to know; who was she? Please, Dr Marlow, if she did the awful things I dream of, I need to know. I need to come to terms with it."

Hannah was begging but she didn't care any more; she was desperate.

Dr Marlow paused for a minute.

"Would it help if I confirmed that what you're

dreaming about is worse than what actually happened?"

Hannah shook her head. She was resolute.

"As I'm already thinking the worst and you don't tell me, the nightmares will continue and will probably turn into other hideous scenarios. I'll go mad if I don't know."

He paused. "Okay, as you've rightly pointed out, we're in uncharted territory. I'll tell you what I know."

Dr Marlow proceeded to tell Hannah that the donor was called Mary, who was twenty-four years old. She'd had a terrible upbringing; absentee parents, in and out of children's homes. Mary had been in trouble with the law from an early age, shoplifting and eventually soliciting. She developed a drug problem which led her to become a prostitute. During drug-fuelled psychotic rages, she killed three of her clients before her capture. With her history of criminal behaviour and lack of remorse, she was sentenced to death. The courts were becoming less lenient and refused to take into account her background or her drug problems.

"Wow," said Hannah. "I feel so sorry for her. What a dreadful life."

Dr Marlow nodded in agreement.

"Does it make you feel better knowing the truth?" he asked.

"Yes, I think so. I prefer knowing that she killed grown men rather than a child. Did she have any kids?"

"No," confirmed Dr Marlow.

That was a relief to hear.

"Am I twenty-five or twenty-two? Have I now got a long history of sexual partners?"

"Hannah, you're still twenty-two as you have only been alive for that many years and no, you don't have a long history of sexual partners as you've never experienced it. You can only be judged by the choices and experiences that you as Hannah have made and not Mary's choices. Mary is dead."

With this reassurance, she left the office in a stronger state of mind than when she walked in an hour earlier.

CHAPTER 14

"**S**o what effect did the knowledge have on Hannah?" asked Joe.

"It helped. The nightmares eventually dissipated. She could now talk to her counsellor more effectively by having one scenario to work through, rather than the multiple scenarios of Mary's life that Hannah concocted in her head. Hannah got back on track. She gained her qualifications, moved away and got a job where no one knew anything about her. Last I heard, she was married with kids."

"So then you allowed all future patients the right to know what their donors had previously done?"

"Yes, I had never considered the psychological effects. These patients were my test subjects. I wanted the procedure to be successful and then I could move on to the next person. I never really thought of the long-term effects. But seeing how broken and desperate Hannah was, I knew I had to take on more responsibility for my patients. So I kept in contact with everyone and I offered the option of providing information about the donors.

Some wanted to know and others thought it was best not to know."

"I guess all the patients went through the same trauma, especially since you didn't have a huge selection of death row prisoners?"

"Yes, in the beginning, we had to make do with a small supply. Most people thought it was disturbing to donate their body; even if the financial reward was attractive. It was similar to the old-fashioned donor cards. Many people were happy to tick the box to donate their organs but not their eyes, some considered it a little creepy."

"Speaking of eyes," said Joe, "wasn't one of your successes originally a blind person?"

Dr Marlow smiled as he remembered Jacob Smith.

"Yes, in the early days most patients accepted the fact they would probably receive a downgrade in physical terms but in some circumstances, the donors received a considerable upgrade such as Jacob who was born blind. As well as being blind, he became terminally ill in his mid-twenties. He was one of the few patients who woke up laughing and joking once the anaesthetic wore off. His main concerns were the colours in the room and what his girlfriend actually looked like. Did she match the way he had imagined her? Her eye colour was blue, but he never really knew what that meant, only that blue was the same colour as the sky. It was a joy to see someone appreciate all the little things in life that we take for granted. It certainly made me want to slow down and enjoy the finer details. Such as the flowers growing in my garden or the beautiful brown eyes of my son Alex or the sandy coloured hair of my daughter Esme."

"Do you have any pictures of Alex and Esme? I've never seen them," asked Joe.

"Yes, of course," he said as he turned on his screen and showed Joe numerous family photos. He swiped to the most recent pictures of his family. "Gosh, how time flies. Here's Alex trying to look cool; he's thirteen now and Esme is eleven. She's the bossy one. We've preferred to keep them out of the lime-light. They've received a bit of flak at school about what I do but they've always handled it well. If anyone teased them when they were little, they simply threatened them with exchanging their brains for the body of a toad or a worm," Henry laughed. "I know I shouldn't laugh and I honestly never encouraged those sorts of threats but I always found it quite amusing. At least the kids knew how to stand up for themselves and I couldn't be prouder of how well-adjusted they are. Okay, enough of my gushing about my children. Where were we?"

"They're beautiful," remarked Joe as Henry closed his computer. "So, you were telling me about Jacob Smith and his upgrade. You also had more success stories like Jacob? Such as paraplegics and transgenders inheriting bodies?"

"Yes, that was the most rewarding side of my job. There was Jacob who was blind his entire life and suddenly he could see. He married and is now a guidance counsellor for blind children. Then there were a couple of terminally ill paraplegics who existed in a prison which was their bodies for most of their lives. Their reactions were amazing; they could walk, touch, express themselves. I always tried to get the neediest to the top of the list in the early days when the operation was free.

Most terminally ill grown-ups at least had a good life, unlike people such as Anna Jones, who had been in a car accident as a child which resulted in paralysis from the neck down. She and her family truly appreciated it. Her family always worried about who would take on Anna's care once they were gone but then they found out Anna would actually die before them with a hereditary disease. It seemed so unfair; she'd had no luck in life. Once I saw Anna's criteria, I made sure she went to the top of the list. Now Anna can take care of herself. She's travelled around the world to make up for lost time. It was wonderful to see her walk out of that clinic once she got used to having a functioning body.

We also had a terminally ill transgender patient. The current sex reassignment surgery is fantastic but it's painful, arduous and sometimes the results are unsatisfactory. Yet, my one patient who was reassigned from a female body to a male body was absolutely delighted. Plus, you can never guarantee everything will be in working order with the traditional surgery."

Joe smiled as Dr Marlow's face lit up when he talked about his success stories.

"One thing that always bothered me, Dr Marlow;

did the donor's family or victims ever come looking for them? You've overseen over a thousand transfers but I've never heard of anything like that happening. I'd have thought maybe a loved one would long to see their son or daughter again, even if it was just to snatch a glimpse of them or even to talk to them, even though they knew it wasn't really them?" asked Joe.

"Yes, we've experienced a couple of incidents like that. As you know, out of respect to the donor and the recipient and after seeing the effect the media had on chasing patients such as Dean and Hannah, we managed to negotiate a media black-out, until now of course. They weren't allowed to show pictures or name names. So family and friends of the donor didn't know who took the skin or where they lived. Skins are now what some people casually call the donor body but I don't think I'm too enamoured with that name.

The recipients needed to adjust to their new bodies and it's a difficult process for most. So we ask them not to involve themselves in social media in their new 'skins.' They can keep their old profile if they insist on networking. The donor family and recipients also have to sign a contract which prevents them from trying to track each other down. In most cases, the donor's family are more than happy with their settlement and many have disowned that donor because of the terrible crimes they've committed. As far as the rest of the world was concerned, the prisoner on death row was executed as normal."

"Tell me about an incident where the rules weren't followed?" asked Joe.

Henry thought for a moment. "There was Damien Cole as I recollect. He had an interesting back-story..."

CHAPTER 15

Damien Cole

Damien was lying in bed stroking the soft, smooth skin of Helena; his first-year psychology student. He enjoyed seducing the most naive of his students and Helena was definitely this until she got to know him. It amused him the way Helena became flustered when he singled her out in class or asked her to stay behind. All he had to do was look at her for a few moments and she blushed or dropped her papers on the floor.

"Remember the first time you met me Helena?" he asked.

She smiled and turned around in bed facing him.

"Yes, of course. I was warned you were handsome and all the girls fancied you like rotten. But you took no notice of me for weeks."

"I spotted you straight away and thought you were the most beautiful girl ever to walk into my lecture theatre."

"But you barely spoke to me; you'd talk to my friends and exclude me."

"Only because I thought I might give myself away

when I looked at you. This isn't something I've ever done before, Helena. I've never cheated on my wife and I never thought I would do so especially with a student. But there was something between us. Did you feel it too?" he asked as he kissed her.

She immediately agreed and they made love again.

Afterwards, he stroked her hair and apologised but she'd have to leave through the back door. He explained his wife was due back soon and he didn't want any of the neighbours to see.

"I'm so sorry, Helena; you deserve much better than sneaking out of back doors. You deserve to be wined and dined and treated like a princess."

"I understand, Damien. I knew what I was getting into. When can I see you again?" she asked eagerly as she got dressed.

"Soon, my love. I'll message you. And remember, not a word to anyone, not even your best friend. I'd lose my job and never be able to see you again," Damien reminded her.

She agreed and left the house through the back door. It was always the same, the first year students were desperate not to mess up the arrangement, so they kept quiet. It got trickier when they graduated from college as he always promised to leave his wife and they could be together as they were no longer students. If they insisted on Damien living up to his promises, he'd tell them his mentally unstable wife threatened to kill herself if he ever left. Soon enough they moved away from college, forgetting about him.

The more clingy ones were the most trouble-some. Already, he had to kill two of them from his current college in order to keep his dirty little secret. It might become obvious if any more students from the college went missing. Fortunately for Damien, neither of his victims were psychology students, so the police didn't question him much. Nor did they manage to coordinate their searches across states, where they might have learnt of a few more missing girls where Damien had previously taught. He'd also done a pretty good job of hiding their bodies. No corpse had been found yet. But he had to remain careful. He enjoyed the kill but he enjoyed the sex and adulation more, so he preferred to keep the girls around. The kill only occurred when threatened.

Damien relaxed and had a beer. Merissa wasn't due back for two days. She was a pharmaceutical sales rep so she travelled around a lot. Her job was perfect for Damien as it meant he could see his girls whenever she was out of town. He'd just lied to Helena about his wife returning soon, the earlier she left the more time he got to spend with someone else. His girls required a lot of attention otherwise they might be tempted to do something stupid. He unlocked his safe, which contained his disposable phones, one for each girl. He currently had four phones which was quite a juggling act. Hmm, he thought, who had he been neglecting of late? It had been a couple of weeks since he had seen Cassie so he sent her a message to come over, in her sexiest underwear. She responded immediately and told him she was on her way. Damien laughed to himself; these young girls were all so eager to please.

Within twenty minutes, Cassie arrived and she was pissed off.

"Hey you, what's wrong?" Damien asked as he pulled Cassie inside for a kiss.

"I haven't heard from you in about a month," she complained.

"Two weeks, I think. I'm so sorry my love. Merissa's been home and I haven't been able to get away."

"No, it's been a month. When are you leaving her?" demanded Cassie.

"Cassie, wait until you finish college, it's only six more months. Then I'll leave Merissa and we can be together. I can't risk her finding out and reporting me to the college. I'll lose my job; my career will be in ruins and I'll never be able to find another job. Then you'll have to support an old bum like me for the rest of your life," Damien smiled at Cassie as he drew her towards him and kissed her.

"But I'm twenty-one-years-old, it's frowned upon but not illegal," she said.

Damien was getting bored with this conversation and regretted asking her over.

"Sorry, it's standard practice these days and it's in my contract. Do you want to stay or not?" he asked.

"Yes, of course I do," she said.

"Then stop worrying and come to bed," he told

her. And shut up, he thought.

Afterwards, as Cassie lay sleeping, Damien wondered if he would have to kill this one. He now remembered why he hadn't contacted her for a while; she'd become clingy. He imagined his hands around her pale, delicate neck, it should bruise easily; the thought excited him. With the lightest touch of his hand, he stroked her neck. Just one quick squeeze and it would mean the end of her increasingly annoying presence in his life. Unfortunately, he couldn't risk it. Three missing girls from one college would be too much, especially since Cassie was a student of his. He decided he'd have to keep a close eye on her to make sure she didn't do anything stupid. He rolled away and let her sleep. Maybe he could talk Merissa into moving away again.

As far as Merissa was concerned, Damien became bored easily and liked to change job every two or three years. She was adaptable as her job meant she had to travel around the country so it didn't make much difference to her where they lived. Neither of them were particularly close to their families, so it was easy to pack up and start again. Damien had excellent references; he knew he was a great lecturer and always excelled in job interviews. Merissa often joked he could charm the pants off a nun. He probably could. Well-built, handsome and persistent, women always gave into him. On the outside, he was charming, kind and self-deprecating. On the inside, he was twisted and evil. Sex and killing dominated his everyday thoughts.

His marriage to Merissa was a way to help control his urges and provide an alibi. He valued his job and life. So he was determined never to be caught and sent to death row. Having Merissa around also meant some semblance of normality. Merissa was beautiful, kinky enough and not too demanding. Neither of them wanted children so the set up was perfect for him. And she was away often enough and never suspected him of doing anything behind her back. Damien was just the handsome college professor who was happy to wait for his beloved wife at home. He often wondered if Merissa got up to anything while she was away. Everyone deserved to have some fun, no matter what their preference.

Lost in his thoughts, he momentarily forgot that Cassie was in bed with him and felt a sudden urge to get rid of her. He woke her up and told her to leave immediately because Merissa was on her way back home. Cassie was not impressed and Damien thought he'd have to think of a way to either finish with her or to dispose of her body without arousing suspicion. He promised to call her soon and said they would be together, forever in six months as he made her leave through the back door. After Cassie left, he headed into town for some uncomplicated fun.

After that weekend, when he'd got a bit carried away in town, Damien decided it was definitely time to move away. He would find out what teaching positions were available, choose the best location and persuade Merissa. He had to stop being so greedy and restrict himself to one or two girlfriends at a time. As he was pondering his move, Cassie approached him in the corridor.

"I need to speak to you urgently."

He smiled and mentioned her current coursework – in case anyone overheard – adding, "not here Cassie. I'll contact you."

He walked away. Cassie was a liability; he had to finish with her. If she didn't take it well, he'd simply kill her. As he fantasised about ways in which to kill her, he passed Helena in the corridor. He smiled at her and she coyly looked away and smiled towards the floor. Sweet, shy Helena. She wouldn't hassle him or say anything to anyone. Why couldn't Cassie be more like her? The next evening, he arranged to meet Cassie in an empty street, miles out of town. She had to take two buses and walk quite far out to meet him.

She complained once she sat in his car; "why didn't you just come and pick me up? It's taken me over an hour to get here."

Did she always complain this much? Damien wondered.

"Don't worry, I'll drive you back. I was out here on business and we can't risk anyone in town seeing us," he told her.

He hadn't decided if he was driving her back or not. That all depended on what she had to say for herself.

"I'm pregnant."

Damien raised his eyebrows. Dumb bitch.

"That's wonderful news, Cassie."

She looked surprised; "I thought you'd be furious?"

"Why would I be furious? I get to kill you now," he smiled at her.

"What?" she said with a nervous giggle.

"You silly, little thing. You think I'm joking, don't you?" he said as he put his hands around her pale, soft neck and enjoyed the look on her face as he squeezed the last breath out of her body.

He sat back and savoured the moment.

He then drove to his new favourite woods, three hours away and buried her body, where the other bodies were buried. It was two am by the time he returned home. Merissa was fast asleep so he took a shower and threw his clothes away.

A few days later, the police began questioning him about the disappearance of Cassie. Thankfully, she hadn't told anyone about their relationship or her pregnancy. They found her phone and knew she had a secret boyfriend but no one knew who he was and they couldn't trace the phone. Damien had already burnt it. He was quite pleased with himself and began to plan for his and Merissa's next move. However, a few weeks later there was a knock at the door and Damien was ordered to submit his DNA for tests.

CHAPTER 16

A hiker and his dog discovered the site of Cassie's corpse. The police conducted a DNA test of her embryo and matched it to the DNA of Damien. They quickly found another three burial sites of his other victims; the two missing students and another reported missing woman last seen at a local bar in Damien's town. Once they realised it wasn't a one-off, they investigated missing people from the other towns and colleges where Damien had connections. In the end, Damien confessed to where he buried all the bodies, hoping it would be enough to plea bargain his way off death row but it wasn't. To his dismay, he was sentenced to death. He called his wife; she wanted nothing to do with him. She never attended his court cases or spoke to him again, although, the lovely Helena wept for him in the courtroom every trial day. The sweet, silly idiot, he thought when he saw her. But he didn't like being alone and apart from his lawyer, nobody came to see him. So he reached out to Helena and begged her to come and visit him. At first, she was unsure but as he knew she would, she eventually came to visit him in prison. It was good to know that he could still use his charm. He cried to her and told her how much he loved her and how he had been set up; he wasn't capable of doing the things he had been accused of. Somehow she believed him; like a junkie, she kept coming back to visit and beg him about appeals and conjugal visits. Sometimes he despaired at her stupidity but she amused him and prison life was dull, especially for a serial killer. As a serial killer, he was isolated and didn't mix with the main prison population. Isolation never suited Damien.

One day, he viewed a short film on body donation for terminally ill patients. The film explained the special opportunity given to death row prisoners; to right their wrongs before they died and to live a more pampered lifestyle while waiting for their recipient to die. Damien wasn't interested in righting his wrongs but he was interested in pampering. He was bored; this was an opportunity to make some demands. Besides, he was far too handsome to die. It would be good to prolong his life even through someone else's eyes. Maybe an opportunity to escape when the transfer took place would arise? Or for the operation to fail? He could pretend it worked; how hard would it be to pretend? There was nothing to lose; he would die in prison anyway so he may as well make the most of it. The next day, he signed up for the program. Merissa would receive some compensation for her husband's body and Damien even managed to wrangle some conjugal visits in his terms and conditions.

During these visits, a desperate Helena told him how much she loved him and how she didn't believe he was guilty. For Damien, he was tempted to have one last kill; he had nothing to lose. But instead, deciding to string her along, he told her about his body donation. This was against the rules so she promised not to tell anyone. As time went by, Damien convinced himself that the operation wouldn't succeed. So he concocted a plan with Helena to meet him near the clinic when it was his time; once he knew the date for his execution. Neither the public nor reporters were allowed to view executions, so as far as the outside world was concerned, Damien Cole would be dead. Executed within the prison system; not sneaked out onto a private jet and flown to the UK for his body donation. Helena agreed to fly out beforehand, find the clinic, stake it out and wait for him. She would then follow him to his new home so they could be together again. Damien wasn't sure if he really wanted Helena to know where he was but he found the planning exhilarating and it was always good to have a backup plan.

One morning, a few months after signing the contract, he was warned to make the most of his last few days as they were to be his last; he was scheduled to fly out the following week. The recipient was close to death. Damien knew nothing about this recipient but if the operation did succeed, he hoped this person would be worthy of him. If the operation failed, he hoped the recipient had a hot wife as well as lots of money. He could pretend to be the recipient for a while before moving on. During the final conjugal visit with Helena, he told her to book her flight; he was leaving the following Friday. She kissed him goodbye; she couldn't wait for them to finally be together. Damien began questioning her sanity.

He called Merissa one last time to say goodbye but she wouldn't take his call. Instead, he left a message that he hoped the money would be of some comfort and he missed her. For the rest of the week, he ordered whatever he wanted to eat and enjoyed some good wine and movies. He felt pretty relaxed whatever the outcome.

Damien flew to the UK on Marlow Enterprise's private jet. The feeling of being out of prison was enjoyable even though he was handcuffed up for the entire flight. After the flight, he remained chained to two armed security guards in a blacked out security van. Chances of escape were out of the question. It took over an hour to arrive and as they approached the clinic, Damien looked around to see if he could see Helena but there were too many cars to be certain.

Once inside, he was escorted to his room and uncuffed. The room was disappointing, just like a hospital room without windows. However, there were some minor luxuries such as in-room entertainment. He used the projector in the room to fake a beautiful view on his wall and pretended to be looking out onto the tropics.

"Do I get room service?" he asked his guard.

"Don't push it, this is so much more than a scum bag like you deserves," said the guard.

"I'm doing a valuable public service and don't you forget it. Treat me with a little more respect, otherwise, I'll back out and everyone will know who's to blame."

Damien enjoyed toying with the guard although he had no idea if backing out was an option. The snarling guard clenched his teeth, desperate to say something but decided against it. The guard left but not before Damien asked him to bring him some food and wine. He ran a bath and relaxed, determined to enjoy his last final days.

Later on, the famous Dr Marlow paid Damien a visit to thank him for his participation.

"What have I got to lose?" he asked Dr Marlow.

"You'd be surprised, most death row inmates refuse point-blank to volunteer. They think it's either disturbing or it will mess with their soul," said Dr Marlow.

"I think it's too late to worry about my soul," Damien replied.

"Indeed," agreed Dr Marlow.

"So Dr Marlow, what are the chances of an unsuccessful operation?"

It was unheard-of but he wanted to get it from the horse's mouth.

"There's no chance the operation will fail. It never has and it never will," confirmed the confident Dr Marlow.

Damn it, thought Damien. He wondered if crazy Helena would chase the recipient around – he hoped so. It would be entertaining, although a shame he would miss it.

Damien asked for details about the recipient. Dr Marlow agreed; there was no harm now as prisoners were not allowed contact with anyone outside the clinic. Damien was donating his body to Edward Morton; a British man – the same age as Damien – forty-one. Currently, a curator of a museum but he came from old money, which enabled him to pay for the operation. Edward was married with one daughter. Dr Marlow showed Damien a family photo of Edward, leaving Damien rather unimpressed. Edward was a plain-looking man with glasses, a weak chin and absolutely no redeeming physical qualities. His wife wasn't much better either. They were a mousey, boring-looking couple.

"He gets to have my body!" said a bemused Damien. "What a waste. Although his wife is in for a surprise."

Dr Marlow laughed, surprised at how someone could be so at ease with their imminent death.

"Well, he's considerably wealthy if that's any consolation to you?"

"Pah," shrugged Damien. He knew it didn't matter anymore.

A couple of weeks later, it was time. Damien lay on the operating bed, reflecting back on his life. In general, he'd enjoyed it; his job, the girls and the killing, not necessarily in that order. It was such a shame to be caught in his prime. He could have continued for another couple of decades if he'd aged well.

Were there any last words? Damien considered this before he went to sleep. Only that he regretted killing Cassie because this led to his capture, not his brightest moment. As the anaesthetic took hold, he wondered if there would be any essence of his mind left behind.

CHAPTER 17

"**E**dward, wake up."

A soft voice roused Edward out of his deep sleep.

Laura, his wife, was looking down at him, holding his hand.

"Is that you, Edward?" she asked.

That was usually the first question visitors asked. Edward sat up, looking confused and asked for water.

"Did the operation not work?" he asked.

Laura laughed and patted his hand; "Edward, believe me; it worked."

She held out the mirror for him as he stared at himself and shook his head in disbelief.

"I'm a rather handsome brute."

"I'll say," Laura nodded enthusiastically.

Edward asked about their twelve-year-old daughter Annabel, who was waiting at home, eager for her father's return. The couple hugged and thanked Dr Marlow over and over again. After a few days of recovery, Edward was ready to go home. As they exited the car park, Edward stopped the car. He got out and looked towards the sky. Laura asked what on earth he was doing.

"Look, Laura, the blue sky, the sounds and the people passing by. It's wonderful!"

"Edward, you can barely see the sky it's so cloudy, it's just noise and grey buildings."

"Look around and breathe it in, Laura. I'm never taking anything for granted again. I'm determined to appreciate everything and everyone. I never thought I'd see the cold, grey streets of London again but it's charming. And I will never take you or Annabel for granted ever again."

"You never did, darling," Laura insisted. "Come on, let's go home where you can appreciate some actual picturesque scenery, such as the orchids, the birds and the rolling, green fields."

Edward agreed and sat back in the car with a huge smile across his face. Holding hands all the way to their country estate, they talked about the things they wanted to do together as a family. The drive was less than two hours out of London and once they got off the motorway, there were fewer cars around. The approach to their home was through some windy, narrow roads.

"Edward?" said Laura. "I'm sure that red car has been behind us all the way from the motorway."

Edward looked behind but it wasn't close enough to make out a description of the driver.

"It's just a rental, nothing to be concerned about. It's probably a tourist who's staying at the hotel," Edward told her.

The Mortons lived in a beautiful part of the Cotswolds, which attracted many visitors. Near to their home were a couple of luxury hotels. Nevertheless, Laura watched the car and once they turned into the drive of their own estate and saw the red car drive past, she could relax.

"It's gone," she informed Edward.

Edward wasn't paying any attention to his wife; he just gazed at his large country house in wonder.

"I never thought I'd see it again," he sighed.

Just then, the front door opened; Annabel ran out to her mum for a hug. She stood by her mother for a few moments, too scared to approach the stranger standing next to the car.

"Daddy?" she asked.

"Squidgins?" He held out his arms and she ran straight into them; only her father called her that.

When she was little, she loved her pet name 'squidgins' but as she got older, she asked her father to stop calling her that. But on this special occasion, she didn't mind. Especially since she remembered how poorly he was when he left for his operation. The three of them went indoors and had a huge celebratory meal with his extended family.

As Edward and Laura lay in bed that night, she asked how he was feeling. He told her how uneasy he was made to feel by their family and friends that evening. Although everyone had been accepting of him, they had all stared at him throughout the evening. Laura consoled him and reminded him that it wasn't just Edward who had to accept the new body but so did everyone else around. It was a huge adjustment for everyone, especially his parents.

"Oh Laura, you are the voice of reason. I love you so much," he told her.

"I'm worried we don't suit each other any more. You're quite chiselled now compared to the old Edward. Maybe that's another reason everyone was staring at you?" Laura confided.

"Really?" pondered Edward.

He'd never been considered handsome before, so never experienced that level of attention.

"Well, Laura. I think looks wise we're now more compatible. I always thought you were way out of my league."

Laura cuddled up to her husband, glad of the reassurance.

"I know we've been talking about all our future plans; places to visit and what we're going to do but there's one thing I want most of all," he told her.

"What's that, Edward?"

"Another child. My imminent death made me think, what if you died too? Annabel would be alone without any siblings. I foresee my future with grown children and grandchildren. What do you think?" he asked.

Laura agreed; she always wanted another child and suggested they start trying immediately.

In the morning, Edward woke her up. She sat up with a fright at the stranger looking down at her.

"It's just me," Edward reminded her.

She apologised, feeling foolish for being so jumpy. As she eased back into bed, she reminded him it would take time to get used to his new appearance. He agreed, admitting to staring at himself in the mirror for about half an hour before she woke up.

After breakfast, Edward decided to go for a stroll in his extensive garden, to gather his thoughts and take in all the things he thought he would never see again. He studied the trees, bushes and birds in a new light. He bent down to smell the flowers, something he hadn't done for a while. It was all taken for granted before.

"It's a beautiful garden," said a voice, which made him jump.

Edward turned around and came face to face with someone he didn't recognise.

"Do I know you?" he asked.

"I don't know, do you?" the young woman asked.

Just at that moment, Laura approached them and put her arm around her husband.

"Hello, can we help you?" she asked.

The young woman smiled and apologised and told them she was utterly lost and trying to find her way to the local village. She noticed the gate open to the house and saw Edward pottering in the garden and she hoped they didn't mind her coming in.

"Of course not," replied Laura. "You're from America?"

"Oh yes," she replied. "I'm just visiting an old friend in the UK and checking out the quaint towns you have in this area."

"Well, you won't get any more quaint than our little town," Edward told her.

She giggled nervously and stared back at Edward a little too long. Edward coughed nervously and looked towards his wife who just smirked back. Laura gave the girl directions, who thanked them and left.

"My god, is that what I have to put up with from now on?" asked Laura as she playfully punched Edward in the arm.

"What do you mean?" he asked.

"She couldn't take her eyes off you, didn't you notice?"

"I wasn't certain. I thought maybe I had something in my teeth."

"No, she was definitely staring at you. Will you run off and leave me for a twenty-something?" asked Laura.

"Good grief, no. She's young enough to be my daughter. What on earth would we talk about? You're the only woman in the world interested in my artefacts."

They both laughed and went back indoors.

After a week, Edward was itching to get back to work. He had been off on sick leave for a few months and was eager to go in sooner rather than later, in order to allow his colleagues to adjust to the new-look him. As he approached his building, he breathed a sigh of relief to be standing outside his beloved museum. He never thought he would see it again. The butterflies in his stomach took hold as he entered and headed straight for the office area. His ID card still had his old picture. Edward sighed as he saw it; it would have to be replaced, erasing even more proof of his old self.

"Can I help you?" someone asked as he entered the staff room.

It was Hugo - Edward's boss.

"Hugo, it's me, Edward. I'm starting back today."

"Ha! Would you look at you? Of course, I knew you were coming back today. I just thought you were a member of the public who lost their way."

Hugo approached Edward and stood within a couple of inches of him, staring while circling around him.

"I just don't believe it. The marvels of modern medicine. Wouldn't you think it'd be easier to find a cure for cancer than transfer your brain into someone else's body?" Hugo asked.

"Well, it was just part of my brain but yes, that would have been preferable," Edward replied as he watched his boss eye him up and down. "Stop it, Hugo, you're making me feel like one of the exhibits now."

Hugo apologised and gave Edward a hug. Some of the other staff members entered the room and Hugo announced Edward's presence. They all welcomed him back, asked how he felt and stared at him longer than necessary. Some even touched him.

"You know you wouldn't normally stroke me and touch my face. Please stop, it's unnerving," Edward told them.

"Sorry Edward, but it's so weird. I've heard about the operation but I've never met anyone who's been through it before," said one of his assistants.

"You don't look like someone who's been on death row. You look like a television actor," said another assistant.

"I've not been on death row, just this body. Please remember that."

They were all curious about the donor and what crime he had committed but Edward had agreed, as per the contract, not to divulge that information. He had no wish to either. He didn't want people knowing he was in the body of a serial killer. As soon as the donor signed the contract, all images of them were deleted from newspaper articles or from the internet. Unless someone was following the Damien Cole murder trial at the time, it would be unlikely anyone he knew would recognise him. As far as Edward was concerned, none of his friends or family followed any murder trials in the USA.

"I bet we suddenly get more interest in ancient Egyptian artefacts," Hugo piped up.

"Why?" Edward asked him.

"Well, you're suddenly more handsome...Not that there was anything wrong with you before."

"Yes, so I've been told," Edward sighed as he looked at himself in the mirror again.

He was used to not having attention; he liked not having any attention. Now this face attracted lingering looks and gawks. Once everyone got used to him and realised he was still the same old boring

Edward, then hopefully his time in the spotlight would be over. He thought it best to leave the staff room so they could chatter amongst themselves and get it out of their system.

He took a tour of the museum to familiarise himself with any changes that had taken place since his sick leave. As he stepped into the foyer, he marvelled at it all. This place was where he had spent the last fifteen years; it was his second home. Members of the public milled around without a care in the world; their lives so ordinary compared to his now. He felt jealous of them. He made his way around all the exhibits, before finally getting to his. It had taken him years, coordinating and negotiating for this collection. Not only was it was the largest in the museum, it was also the largest Ancient Egyptian collection in Europe. He stood back, appraised it and thought about the pieces he still wanted to get his hands on. Edward's thoughts were interrupted by a familiar voice asking him what he was thinking about. It was the girl from his garden the previous week.

"You're the tourist who was lost. What are you doing here?" he asked.

"Don't pretend you don't know," she whispered as she stepped forward and flung her arms around him and kissed him.

He pushed her away.

"What the hell do you think you're doing?"

"I've been dying to get you alone since I saw you. But you're always with that woman."

"That woman? You mean my wife?" he asked bemusedly.

"Don't be coy with me darling. We're supposed to be together," she said.

A cough interrupted their conversation; it was Hugo.

"Am I interrupting anything?" he asked

Edward was relieved to see his boss standing there.

"No, I think the young lady is under some misunderstanding," he told him.

Edward walked away with Hugo, leaving her standing alone.

"My god, Hugo; is this what's it like to be 'hunky'? Do women just throw themselves at men like me?"

Hugo laughed out loud.

"Honestly Edward, I wouldn't know."

Edward hid in his office for the majority of the day to avoid any more bizarre encounters and to catch up with his work. He called Laura and told her about the crazy American girl. She agreed, her behaviour was odd and assumed she must have taken a shine to him when they gave her directions. Laura warned him to look out for her. If she approached him again, they'd report her to the police. When he left the museum that evening, to his dismay, he spotted the girl waiting for him outside.

"Have you been here all day?"

"Yes, darling, I've been waiting for you. I know you can't talk to me in front of your wife or your colleagues. But no one's here now. Talk to me now."

"About what?" he asked.

"About us and when we can be together, silly," she replied.

"Look, I think you're getting me mixed up with someone else."

As he said that, it dawned on him what might be going on.

"What do you think my name is?"

"It's Damien of course."

Edward suddenly felt nauseous. Contacts of donors and recipients were never supposed to know about each other.

"How did you find me?"

"You told me to wait for you, remember?"

This was all too much to absorb so he invited the girl for a coffee to explain everything. In the coffee shop, she kept touching him and was confused why he needed an explanation. He moved his chair further away from her and explained he wasn't Damien but she refused to believe him. So he asked her to remind him again about what she was doing here.

Her name was Helena and she had an affair with Damien before he was caught. Damien was in love with her and was planning on leaving his wife as soon as Helena graduated. Then he got arrested and sentenced to death. He begged her to visit him and explained how he was set up. She knew Damien would never do the things he was accused of. All the other girls who came forward about having an affair with him were liars. They were part of some conspiracy to frame Damien. Damien was convinced the experiment wouldn't work, it was obviously crazy so she was supposed to find him in the UK, where they could finally be together.

Edward tried to make it clear to Helena that the experiment did work and that Damien was gone. The only thing that remained of Damien was his body but the personality and feelings were Edward's.

"You'd find me rather boring compared to Damien," he insisted.

"I don't believe you. I know you have to lie, otherwise, if they find out the operation didn't work they'll put you back into prison. Don't worry, I won't tell anyone."

His frustration increased with this girl. It was apparent she needed help but he wasn't the one able to help her. Edward stood up to leave and told Helena his wife would be wondering where he was.

Helena's pretty face scrunched up into a snarl as she shouted at him in front of the coffee shop; "don't you dare walk away from me, Damien. I've been waiting for you for over two years. You promised to leave your wife for me!"

The customers in the cafe stopped what they were doing and stared at the couple. Edward had never felt so uncomfortable in his entire life. He explained to the people listening in that the girl had him mixed up with someone else. No one believed him and some woman told him he ought to be ashamed of himself. Edward quickly made his way out of the cafe to his car with Helena chasing after him and shouting. He drove home back to Laura, to tell her everything.

"I'm not cut out for this drama. I wish I'd inherited the body of someone less attractive and not some sex-maniac, lothario serial killer."

Laura found it quite amusing and reminded him that most donors would have come from complicated lives. She suggested they call Dr Marlow in the morning to explain their predicament, so this is what he did. Dr Marlow apologised, explaining the process meant only family members were supposed to know about the donation. They signed a waiver that they wouldn't come looking for the recipient who had inherited the body or to tell anyone. He promised to get to the bottom of it.

The next day Dr Marlow paid a visit to Edward's home to explain exactly what happened. Unbeknown to Dr Marlow, Damien received conjugal visits from his girlfriend, who was not part of the contract. Dr Marlow professed his anger that the prison allowed this. After the donor signed the contract, he should have only been allowed contact with people who had signed the clause. Helena Thomas was not part of the process and shouldn't have had any contact with him. Dr Marlow could only guess that Damien obviously told Helena about the operation during their illicit visits and led her on to believe the operation wouldn't succeed. He remembered Damien's disappointment when he confirmed there would be no chance of the operation failing.

Dr Marlow and his partners agreed to track down Helena, explain that she was misled by Damien and she too would be offered substantial compensation in return for her silence. Laura and Edward were relieved and after Dr Marlow confirmed that Damien had no other contact with anyone else, the Morton's agreed this was the correct course of action.

"Please, just find her as quickly as possible. I don't feel comfortable with her hanging around, she's deluded," Edward pleaded.

Dr Marlow assured him he would. Before he left he apologised again on behalf of Marlow Enterprise and let Edward and Laura know that if they needed anything else, not to hesitate and call him. He was always happy to help his patients.

"What a lovely man," Laura commented when he left their house.

"Yes, I just hope they're able to talk this Helena girl into leaving us alone."

That night Edward felt uneasy, like someone was watching them from outside, although all the security cameras confirmed otherwise. It was just paranoia. Luckily the next day, they received a message from Dr Marlow confirming they'd found Helena. She was staying nearby and his business partner had already visited her with the contract. Apparently, she was open to negotiation. She now understood the operation was successful. She'd take the money and keep quiet. Edward breathed a sigh of relief and made plans to go back to work.

CHAPTER 18

After a few days at work, everything was almost back to normal; no Helena and people were adapting to his new-look. Until one evening he returned home and to his surprise, Helena was sitting in his living room having a cup of tea with Laura.

"Close your mouth, dear; we have company," Laura reprimanded him.

"What the hell is going on?" he asked.

Helena stood up quickly and held her hand out for a handshake.

"I'm so sorry about my behaviour, Mr Morton. I'm totally embarrassed. I was misled, you see? I honestly thought you were Damien."

He shook her hand and told her to forget about it.

"Should you be here?" he asked.

"No, I know it's against the rules but I was still in the area and I wanted to apologise in person. You won't tell will you?" she asked.

Laura stood up and promised not to tell. Edward frowned at Laura; he was not as comfortable with the situation as she was. Laura just shrugged back. A little while later, Helena finally left.

"What the hell do you think you're doing letting her in?"

"What's the harm? She's truly embarrassed and now she feels better. She seems quite sweet, just a bit naïve, I think."

"Naïve is not the word I would use. Crazy, perhaps? She still wanted the man even after she knew he had a string of lovers and murdered the odd one here and there if it took his fancy!"

"Oh, shush. He was obviously a master manipulator. I feel sorry for her. Her parents died when she was young, she was brought up by her grandmother who also died before she went to college. She had to work incredibly hard to get a scholarship and I think she was lonely," said a defensive Laura.

"Fine, I just don't want to see her again."

Unfortunately for Edward, they saw an awful lot of her over the next few weeks. She remained in their village with a job at the local pub. According to Laura, she had fallen for the charm of the village and felt she had nothing to go back home for. She even had a new boyfriend. Still, Edward felt uncomfortable around her as he thought she gazed at him in a strange way, so he found excuses not to go into the village. Laura made him promise not to tell Dr Marlow that she had settled nearby. Begrudgingly, he agreed as Laura seemed determined to take her under her wing as some sort of mother figure.

Not long after the operation, Laura found out she was pregnant. Both were delighted and kept the news quiet until the traditional three-month safe period. News filtered throughout the small village quickly and the Mortons received many congratulatory calls. Annabel was delighted to finally get a brother or sister and promised to help out when the baby arrived. One evening as the family settled down to a quiet dinner, the doorbell rang. It was Helena with a huge bouquet of flowers, champagne and a small bottle of non-alcoholic sparkly wine. Laura invited her in as the two women gushed about the baby news. Helena insisted on toasting the couple. Afterwards, Edward excused himself and went to bed early. He didn't want Helena in the house and vowed to tell Laura as soon as she managed to get rid of her. Edward must have fallen asleep for when he woke up it was morning and Laura was fast asleep next to him. She stirred as he got up for work.

"You stay in bed," he whispered to her.

She smiled and opened her eyes; "that was a lovely gesture by Helena, she's such a nice girl. Everyone in the village thinks so."

"Even so, I don't want her here. She shouldn't be here and she still looks at me in that way," Edward told her.

"What way?" Laura asked suddenly interested as she sat up in bed.

"Like she wants me…sexually," Edward muttered.

"I really don't think so, you probably caught her off-guard but she said you and Damien couldn't be more different. She said it was more Damien's charm rather than his looks."

"So, you're telling me I'm not charming?" he asked, slightly insulted.

"Only to me, my dear, and that's all that matters isn't it?" Laura asked.

Edward agreed and cuddled his wife before he left for work. She was right; women wouldn't be attracted to some married, promiscuous serial killer if he was without charm, no matter how good-looking he was. He decided to forget about Helena, she seemed harmless and was friends with his wife, not him. They didn't have anything to say to each other; to her, he was just an old boring museum curator, so she was easily avoided.

That evening when he returned from work, Laura went to bed early with a slight fever and a cold. The next day, he made her promise to stay in bed and relax. When he offered to call a doctor, she refused, insisting it was just a common cold and she didn't want to drag the poor doctor all the way out to their house. She was still feverish when he arrived home from work so she promised she would definitely go to the doctor the next day if she didn't feel better. Laura was fast asleep when he went to bed that night and she felt a little clammy. Edward would be glad once she saw the doctor the next day. He switched off his alarm that night, deciding to stay at home the next day and look after her.

After a good night's sleep uninterrupted by the alarm clock, Edward woke up well rested. He stretched and wondered if Annabel was already up. He turned; facing the back of Laura's head. He reached over her to check her forehead. It was so cold. Edward turned her around, she didn't stir. Her face was pale and her lips had a blue tinge. An uneasy feeling took over. He gently slapped her on the face to try and rouse her, but nothing.

He grabbed her by her shoulders and shook her; "Laura, Laura, wake up!"

All he could say over and over again was 'oh my god, oh my god.' He had no idea what was going on. Just then Annabel burst into the room.

"Daddy, what's going on?" she asked.

"Get out!" he pointed towards the door.

He didn't want Annabel to see this, but it was too late as she ignored him and walked over to the bed, she covered her mouth and burst straight into tears.

"Please, call an ambulance now," he insisted. "Now!"

As she placed the teary call, he continued trying to revive Laura. Annabel attempted to wake her mummy but nothing happened. It seemed to take forever for the ambulance to arrive. Edward cursed himself for living so far away from the town with the hospital. By the time the ambulance arrived, Edward and Annabel hugged each other and cried uncontrollably. They covered Laura's stretchered body and told Edward there was nothing they could do; she had been dead for a few hours.

When the police arrived, they asked some questions and Edward explained she only had a cold and fever. He didn't believe it was anything more serious. He broke down in front of them when he told them he should have insisted on her seeing the doctor. Instead, he just went to work yesterday as normal while his wife lay dying in bed. The police tried to comfort him and told him there was nothing he could have done. Laura's death appeared to be due to natural causes but it wouldn't be officially confirmed until the autopsy took place.

The next few days went by in a blur for Edward and Annabel. The villagers were supportive; checking up on them and bringing home-cooked food. Helena made herself invaluable around the house as Annabel had taken to her just as much as Laura had. Edward was grateful to Helena as he couldn't cope with Annabel's grief; he could only deal with his own. When Helena insisted on staying for a few days to keep an eye on Annabel, Edward took her up on the offer. She gave him some sleeping tablets to help him through the night. One morning when he woke up, he remembered the vivid dream he had the night before. He dreamt of a naked Helena on top of him. He was so disgusted with himself that he was dreaming of another woman so soon. That morning, he could barely look her in the eye as she smiled sweetly at him over breakfast and asked if he had slept well. Later on in the morning, when Helena had taken Annabel out for a walk, Edward received a visit from the police.

"Sorry to bother you, but we've had the autopsy results and we thought you should know," the officer told him.

Edward invited them in; he didn't want to think about autopsy results, this meant now he had to somehow plan her funeral. How did one go about planning funerals for the love of their lives? He wouldn't know where to start.

"So Mr Morton, we know exactly how she died," said the officer again.

"Yes," agreed Edward. "Pneumonia?"

Pneumonia was the initial diagnosis and this is what Edward expected to hear. The officer shook his head.

"How was your relationship with Mrs Morton?"

"What? What do you mean? She was my wife. I loved her, she loved me. We were expecting another child," Edward told them.

Edward sat down; he felt unsteady when he realised this conversation was going in another direction to the one he was expecting.

"Mr Morton...," the officer said slowly, "your wife was poisoned."

Edward stared at the officers in disbelief.

"No, she had a cold, she was sick," he insisted.

"She had polonium in her system. She had ingested enough to kill her but it would have taken a couple of days for the poison to take effect," the officer confirmed.

"Why would she take poison?" Edward asked in his confused state.

"We don't think she did knowingly, we think someone murdered her," the officer said bluntly.

"We have a warrant to search your house now," he told Edward as he showed him the warrant. "This will now be dealt with as a murder investigation as we look for evidence."

Edward tried to stand up but the officer pushed him back into his chair.

"Please stay there and don't touch anything," he ordered as the forensic team entered the house.

Just then Helena and Annabel returned from their stroll. Both looked confused by the presence of the police. Annabel ran over to her father as the officer asked Helena for details of who she was. He told her to sit down and not to move once she had answered his questions.

Edward could hear the house being turned upside down before eventually one of the forensic team entered the living room holding up a bottle. He announced this had traces of polonium even though it had been washed out before being placed in the recycling bin. Edward's body went cold throughout as he looked at the bottle and recognised it as the bottle for the alcohol-free champagne that Helena had brought over less than a week ago.

CHAPTER 19

"Of course, I didn't put two and two together earlier but Helena Thomas was the skin for Anna Jones, the paraplegic?" said Joe.

"That's right," confirmed Dr Marlow. "She was convicted of first-degree murder on two counts, Laura and the unborn child. She was sentenced to death and volunteered for the programme. Helena didn't fight for her cause too strongly. I believe she could have received a lesser charge due to insanity but she thought somehow she'd end up with Damien if she took part in the programme."

"Poor Edward Morton. What became of him?" asked Joe.

"Obviously, he was angry and threatened to sue the company for failure to uphold our secrecy clause. It might have ruined us but he didn't want the world knowing and he didn't want to get Annabel involved. Also, they knowingly invited Helena into their home after they had known who she was. So he accepted an out of court settlement and moved away. I never heard from him since. I've never forgiven myself for the lack of duty of care. Again, it was a learning curve so we had to adjust our t&c's. There were no more conjugal visits or any contact with anyone else outside of the contracts involved. We had to minimise exposure and transparency. The exchange doesn't work well socially if too many people know about it."

"You also benefited from the crime as you got another donor. What did Edward Morton think about that?" asked Joe.

"He wasn't ever supposed to find out but I suppose he will if he reads this interview in your newspaper."

"Don't you think the family of the victims deserve to know or at least be prepared in the event of accidentally coming face to face with the recipient?"

"No, definitely not. You saw what happened with Helena Thomas. We had to maintain the utmost secrecy to ensure these events didn't happen again."

"So as far as the world was concerned, the company was a success and we never learnt about any of these errors. You became rich after that?" asked Joe.

"Ha, not quite," replied Henry. "As you know, scientists, in general, have never been highly paid – always relying on funding. I too relied on this funding in the early days and paid myself a small wage. I was offered money for interviews and even personal operations but for me, it was never about fame or money. It's always been about the challenge. My goal was to perfect the current procedure and maybe one day improve the constraints of it. I knew I would never rest until I achieved it all.

Annie practically supported us financially while I spent time in the lab. Once I got my breakthrough and we followed through with successes; I assumed the Government would increase the funding which would lead to worldwide contracts with other governments.

However, it was never about the cure as the large pharmaceuticals dominate the medical industry and governments rely on their bribes...sorry, I mean funding. There was also the question of lack of supply, mainly due to the pressure from human rights groups which meant we couldn't get the approval to force death row prisoners to donate their bodies. Plus the amount of compensation we were paying out especially for Helena Thomas, the Government didn't feel as though it was getting value for money. Despite my one hundred per cent success rate, the Government backed away financially and I had to come up with another way to continue my project.

I was close to my office manager Felix Carter at the time. He worked with me for about three years at that point. I never wanted to be involved with the business side – it was too time-consuming and distracting, so I hired Felix. I remember the first time I met him; he was a confident young man when he came in for his interview. Felix was in his mid-twenties, rather dapper and supportive of what the company was about, unlike other candidates who were slightly conservative. I could only work alongside people with open-minds as we were dealing with quite a controversial project. With his confidence, he'd make a good spokesperson and was competent in the business side of matters. When the experiments started to succeed, my funding was increased initially. I'm not a money man or an accounts man so I needed someone reliable to run the company for me and handle the money whilst I got on with what I was there for. Felix was a good fit. I felt comfortable around him and he gave me the impression he knew what he was doing plus he came with great references from previous employers. Then, we found out the news that the funding had been cut and the company would fold unless we could find other investors and quickly. As I said before, I'm not a businessman so I had no idea where to start. That's when I met James Talbot for the first time..."

"God damn it, Felix! How could they pull the funding at this stage?" Henry shouted as he threw his tablet on the floor.

"Be careful with the tech," Felix said, eyeing up the smashed tablet on the floor. "We can't afford to replace it anymore."

"I know, I know. But look around, we've got this entire building set up. How do we afford to run it all? How will we be able to pay the prisoners and their luxuries? They'll never donate their bodies for free. And our staff? I've worked so hard to train everyone up. They're relying on their jobs."

"Don't worry, Henry, this is a highly publicised operation and I've been putting the feelers out there. We have some interested parties willing to invest in the company. Leave it to me and I'll find the right people."

As Henry didn't have any contacts, he gave permission for Felix to make some discreet inquiries. These inquiries led to a meeting with a single investor who stood out from the rest. Well-known within the finance community, James Talbot was a successful businessman with a diverse investment portfolio. It was a few days later when Felix invited Henry and Annie for dinner to meet this potential backer. James was a wealthy man by all accounts who'd amassed a fortune through real estate and the stock market.

The dinner took place in an exclusive restaurant which usually required reservations months in advance. James, with his connections, was able to pull some strings, no doubt to impress Henry. The Marlows glanced at each other as they entered the restaurant. Impressed was an understatement. The opulence and atmosphere inside exceeded both their expectations.

"I could get used to this," whispered Annie.

Henry squeezed her hand in agreement. Although they weren't exactly on the breadline, they'd always been careful with money. Nights out and trips away had previously been with a mid-range budget in mind.

They spotted Felix with whom they presumed to

be James, already seated at the table, deep in conversation. To Henry, the two men seemed to be hitting it off and looked like they complemented one another, in terms of appearance. Both were well-dressed in expensive suits and were good-looking men. James was obviously older than Felix, more like Henry's age but Henry already felt like the odd one out. Even though he wore his best suit, it was just one he had purchased a few years ago from the high street. He brushed aside the thoughts of this superficial inadequacy. James was here to impress him as he was the one desperate to invest. As they approached the table, Felix and James abruptly stopped their conversation and James stood up to greet the two newcomers.

"Dr Marlow and Mrs Marlow, thank you for meeting me. I've been following your company with quite some interest for a few years. It's amazing what you've achieved. You truly are a pioneer," James said.

Henry, familiar with all the compliments by now, politely thanked him.

"So, why do you want to invest in my company?" Henry inquired, once they had ordered.

"It's an exciting time for you. But I think by being government-funded, it's held you back. You need to look at the bigger picture and expand. With my help, we can lobby for the mandatory donation of all death row criminals throughout the world. You can't do that by yourself. With my backing, you can expand. You can employ more staff and concentrate on even more breakthroughs, such as helping to save the lives of terminally ill children, which is something you've expressed an interest in before?"

Henry nodded. James had obviously done his homework.

"Also," James continued, "by expanding, we can reach out to the entire world and help the neediest. We can also make a lot of money out of this. Not that money is my main concern – I have plenty already. I want a fresh challenge and to be part of such a unique project. Please consider my offer. I promise not to interfere in the day to day running of the company. You and your staff will be able to carry on as normal."

Henry promised to consider his offer as he told James about his hopes and concerns for the future of the company. Hopes of increased donors in the short term and eventually a breakthrough that didn't rely on donors. Concerns about when the company went private, that the operation may only be available to the wealthy. His potential investor agreed with his concerns and promised that together they could come up with a solution. This put Henry's mind at ease and the four of them had an enjoyable dinner. James insisted on picking up the bill and Henry promised to be in touch.

After dinner, Henry and Annie went for a walk.

"Well, what do you think?" Henry was eager to find out Annie's take on the situation.

"I think he's stupidly rich and he said he wouldn't get involved in the day to day running of the business. Everything should remain the same; the only change is that you'll have James Talbot as your backer and not the government," said Annie

"True, but he seems pretty smooth. Do you think we can trust him?" asked Henry.

"I don't think you have much choice. Felix said he was the only investor willing to invest the amount you need. The company will close if you don't. Besides, he's out to make money. There's nothing wrong with that and you won't have to beg for funding every six months."

No more begging for funding. He hated the preparation and the meetings he had to attend. This interfered with the job he loved doing most – being in the lab.

"Don't you think he and Felix seemed a little too chummy?" Henry felt some of the conversation that evening went over his head on the discussion of tax liabilities and balance sheets.

"They're businessmen, that's all. That's what they know. They wouldn't begin to understand the technical side of what you do. Don't feel so inadequate. Besides Henry," Annie continued, "I don't think I can continue to be the main breadwinner for a while."

"Why's that?" he asked.

She rubbed her stomach and told Henry she was expecting their first child.

Henry picked her up and kissed her. "That's the best news ever," he declared.

And with that, he accepted James Talbot's offer.

The public funded company was now a private limited company, Marlow Enterprise. Felix and Henry were also partners in the company. Now Henry could relax; James was confident of the business model and assured Henry he'd never have to worry about money again. He could go on to have a multitude of children who would be well looked after if anything ever happened to Henry.

"So that's how Marlow Enterprise became private and it coincided with you starting a family?" asked Joe.

"That's correct and at the time it seemed right. With the extra cash injections, we bought better machinery which I programmed to practically run itself, although I was the only person able to programme it. I'm sorry to say, I've always been a control freak. I wanted to be the only person able to perform the actual operation until the time was right to pass on the reins. Once the machines were improved and fully automated, I didn't need to do as much research as I previously did. It meant I could spend a little more time away from the clinic and enjoy it with Annie and the kids. Not long after Alex was born, Esme followed. Life was good. My little family were the most precious people in my life. I'd forgotten how it felt to be part of a family unit since mine was destroyed all those years before.

During those years, business was steady. Supply of donors were low but demand was high which meant we could charge a hell of a lot of money for each operation. It was unfair that only the extremely wealthy could afford it so with my extra spare time when I wasn't at home with the kids, I spent it in the lab experimenting. Alongside geneticists and other scientists, we investigated ways to clone the body of the dying patient so we wouldn't have to rely on prisoners but alas, that failed me. I believe it will be possible one day but I lacked the dogged determination of my youth so, in the end, I decided to concentrate on Marlow Enterprise as it stood and my family."

CHAPTER 20

"**S**o how did you get along with your new investor James?" asked Joe.

"Fine, at first. He did what he said he was going to do – invest in the company and let me get on with my work. Felix ran the business side on a day to day basis. We didn't see much of him as Marlow Enterprise wasn't his only business interest. The three of us met up at quarterly board meetings to catch up..."

"Hi, Henry. How are Annie and the kids?" asked James.

The three partners were in the boardroom to talk through figures and forecasts. Henry was always happy to talk about his beautiful family. He told them about Annie's new, exciting job which concerned the health of the entire nation. She was creating the website responsible for collating all information gathered from individual health monitors, which in a few years, hopefully everyone would be wearing. Alex just started school and Henry told his two partners how he secretly thought he might be a genius. He could already read by himself and was proficient in the piano. As for Esme, she was walking and talking and continually asking questions.

Henry noticed Felix typing on his phone, not listening.

"Sorry. Were you just being polite? I get carried away with talking about the kids and Annie."

"Not at all. I think Annie's great and you're obviously proud of your kids. I think they both sound like a chip off the old block. What do you think, Felix" asked James.

Felix stopped what he was doing and looked up at the two men.

"Yes, they're adorable. Great kids."

Henry promised no more family talk - both James and Felix were single men. Single men weren't that interested in the aspects of family life. Although Felix was keen to eventually settle down and have children one day, he wasn't looking for anything serious at the moment. James was the same age as Henry and had no interest in ever settling down and having a family. He was a womaniser, and keen to stay that way.

Henry didn't know James on a personal level at all and received his information from Felix. Both Felix and James lived in the city and met up regularly. Henry lived in the suburbs and after a long day at work, the only thing he wanted to do was go home. Felix often filled Henry in on the antics of James - which usually involved visiting the best clubs and restaurants and going home with a beautiful, different girl most nights. This easily impressed Felix but Henry was less impressed. As long as James kept investing his money in the company and didn't interfere, that's all Henry cared about.

They discussed business – the figures weren't looking good. Although they charged a small fortune for each operation, James worried this wasn't enough. He pointed out the huge overheads of running this London city centre operation. The rent and rates of the building were extortionate as well as the running costs of the equipment. Money paid to the prisoners as well as their security costs and the Marlow Enterprise's private jet were eating into any profits. And although the public didn't show as much interest any more, the staff of Marlow Enterprise still received threats and protests outside the building every day.

"These people are making us look bad. I believe they're having a direct influence on our supply. The word gets back to prisoners via their visitors, who persuade them not to go through with the operation. We need more donors to keep afloat. I can't keep pumping my money into this without any payback," said James.

This worried Henry. He hoped the money side of the business would sort itself out once James got on board but it had been five years and James was losing patience.

"What are you suggesting, James?"

"Let's join forces and lobby more urgently to make it mandatory for death-rowers."

Henry sighed; he'd been trying this unsuccessfully for years. James sensed the despondency in Henry but promised with his money and connections and Henry with him, it was worth one last shot. Henry agreed.

A few days later, Henry sat with James in a private members bar waiting for their contact to come along. Henry fiddled with his cuff-link as they sat in uncomfortable silence. Henry normally lobbied from the privacy of his office, messaging various people to see if he could persuade them to push his law through. James lobbied from members bars like this, wining and dining and schmoozing. Neither had been successful.

"I can't believe we haven't joined forces before? I think we'd make a formidable team, what do you reckon?"

Henry reckoned he wanted to get out of here as fast as possible as he gulped down his drink. This was not his scene.

"What will happen to my company if we can't change the legislation?" asked Henry.

"Our Company? Well, it won't be viable if we don't have any donors. Unless we can think of another way, it will fold," said James.

Henry knew this and it broke his heart. To James, it was just another business venture. To Henry, it was his life.

After the meeting with the lobbyist, James felt optimistic as they walked out for a taxi. Henry, less so.

"Should you be bribing the lobbyists? That's a lot of money you offered?" said Henry.

James patted him on the back and told him that's the way business worked. With James' bribe and Henry's passion, the lobbyist felt he could get the change reviewed at the very least.

"Are you coming out for a night-cap, Henry?" offered James.

After seeing the way James handled business, he didn't want to spend too much time with this man. Henry declined and joked about how James already corrupted Felix on their wild boy's nights out and didn't want the same to happen to him. James laughed and promised to be in touch soon.

"Don't worry, old chap! I never give up on business. Especially ones I've invested so heavily in," James shouted out of the cab window.

Was that a good or bad thing, wondered Henry.

"So you and James were never friends?" asked Joe, showing Henry an old picture of him and James laughing and joking in the street.

"Never. Whenever I spent time with him, I felt uneasy and just pretended to like him at first. It was only ever business between us."

"And you never did get the law changed?" asked Joe, putting the photo away.

"No, James' optimism was short-lived. I spoke to him a couple of months later and he confirmed that his huge bribe didn't work. No one was keen to change the status quo. Too much opposition remained concerning the project and James said it was likely to fold within the next six months. Then things went from bad to worse..."

The phone rang in the middle of the night. A sleepy Henry took the call and immediately woke up when he heard Marlow Enterprise was on fire. He shot out of bed and dressed quickly, telling Annie the news. He called his business partners and Felix was already at the scene when he arrived.

"I spoke to the fire service. They think it was deliberate. Probably our loyal protestors," Felix told Henry.

"Oh my god, did the night staff get out? What about the patients?" he asked.

Felix didn't have an answer.

Henry looked around but couldn't see any sign of the staff. There should have been at least two security guards on duty as well as one donor, his security detail and one patient, and their night care staff and possibly one of the patient's family members.

Henry dashed over to speak to the chief firefighter, who confirmed no one had left the building.

Henry staggered over to the kerb and threw up in the street. His company was up in flames and people were dead. James eventually turned up and the three men stood in silence as they watched the fire brigade put out the fire.

"You must have thought it was the end of 'The Marlow Project?'" asked Joe.

"Yes, but at the time, my only concern was for the

people in the building. Ten people were killed that night. Including the patient who went in thinking they were getting a second chance. Instead of a second chance, he and his brother were killed, as well as the staff and the donor prisoner."

"It worked out well for you in a twisted way?" asked Joe.

"Yes, in a very twisted way," Henry sighed.

"It was a deliberate attack. So we received a substantial insurance payout. One of our regular protesters had managed to shut down all the security cameras and break in. She planted a bomb. I assume her intention was to get the staff and herself out. However, a fault was found on the detonator and it went off too early, instantly killing herself and everyone else inside."

"Her group have always denied any knowledge of this planned attack," said Joe.

"Of course they would. They'd be on death row if they admitted to any part in her plan. Whether she acted alone or if her group did ever know about it, we'll never know. After the explosion, I wanted to walk away. I took some time out and I assumed James would want out too. Instead of taking this opportunity to back out, he was rather excited. With the insurance money, we could get brand-new premises in a cheaper area, just on the outskirts of London, near a small airfield. Away from the city, we wouldn't need as much security. Sympathy steered away from the protesters towards us. James was optimistic that with much lower overheads, we could find a way to encourage volunteers."

CHAPTER 21

"So you had new premises, new equipment but there were still too many people dying and not enough donors?" asked Joe.

"Exactly, the rise in technology has left fewer people committing crimes as they know they will be caught. It's only the desperate or psychotic who commits crimes. I also firmly believe that this rise in technology has led to increased cancer rates. Yes, we can combat a lot of it now with earlier detection and improved treatments but we're all surrounded by technology twenty-four hours a day. Our whole houses are controlled by it; we're surrounded by screens twenty-four/seven in some cases. Yes, no one smokes any more, people drink less and obesity is on the downfall, yet cancer rates are on the up. We have cleaner energy so less pollution. But everything is touch screen and automated and everyone has a seventy-five per cent chance of contracting some form of cancer. Another scientist has recently had the breakthrough with genome designer organs where a diseased organ can now be successfully 3-

D printed and replaced. But do we know what the long-term effect of that is, with people having foreign objects implanted into their bodies? This is all so new to us; I can't help but think that the problems are addressed in the short term but not in the long term. Will it be similar to fifty years ago with Botox injections for cosmetic reasons? The body couldn't cope with the toxins and this led to a new form of cancer.

And yes, it's great that we all have our own health monitors that we wear every day to warn us of risks of disease, but again, is this additional technology increasing the problems?"

Just then, Henry's health monitor buzzed. He laughed and apologised to Joe.

"Sorry, that little outburst caused my blood pressure to increase. Rant over," he promised.

"But you were always a huge advocate for advancements in technology. When did you start seeing it as a bad thing?" asked Joe.

"It was about ten years ago, when my wife received some bad news. She surrounded herself with technology, day in and day out. We were among the first people to wear Annie's health monitors…"

Henry arrived home after a busy day at work. There was so much demand for his skins and so many improvements still to go to make sure the process was as seamless as possible. The operations had now been successful for a number of years but idiosyncrasies were still found that had to be dealt with such as individual hormonal adjustments for each operation and as a perfectionist, Henry worked hard to address every detail. Annie insisted he came home early tonight, so he promised to read the kids a bedtime story. Annie was home more for the children than Henry as she chose to work from home, so this was an unexpected treat for the kids. After he had tucked Esme and Alex into bed and turned off their light, he went downstairs to unwind with Annie. She already had a bottle of wine open and was halfway through it when he sat down with her. Her eyes were red, as though she'd been crying so Henry asked what was wrong. Annie burst into tears and handed him her health monitor. The readings were in the red, which meant a medical emergency.

"What the hell?" he asked.

Annie shrugged her shoulders and told him that only last week, the monitor advised her to go for a scan.

"Why didn't you tell me?"

"Oh Henry, you're always so busy and it wasn't showing an emergency reading. I've been so tired lately and catching the odd bug here and there. The scan was just checking my immune system. I assumed it would advise me to change my diet or take extra supplements. But the reading came back as urgent. I went in today while the kids were at school. I have pancreatic cancer."

"What?" Henry's eyes immediately filled up. He couldn't believe what he was hearing. His logical mind took over and he immediately reassured her. "But your health monitor caught it in time, right? So we can treat it?"

Annie shook her head; "it's not that simple. The main purpose of the system is to alert the user of any future complications they might be exposed to. I had a very low chance of getting pancreatic cancer, so I never looked for early possible treatments. Like your experiment, I guess it's not foolproof yet and it still misses vital clues. It's a pretty good predictor but it's not one hundred per cent yet. Especially when it comes to such a progressive form of cancer. There's often no warning for pancreatic cancer."

"So what are you saying?" Henry asked but he didn't want to know the answer.

"Obviously, I'll go for all available treatment, but the prognosis isn't good," she replied.

"What's the prognosis?"

"A year with treatment, maybe a little longer," she smiled sadly at him.

Henry let the tears run down his face as he held onto Annie's hands.

"You obviously know what I'm about to suggest," he told her.

Henry always had it in the back of his mind that if anything did happen to anyone close to him, he would without a shadow of a doubt, get them to participate in his project. However, he never considered this would ever happen to someone he knew, especially Annie, who was healthy and active. She was also a huge advocate of the new health monitors. If there was ever a slight glitch in any of her readings, no matter how small, she would re-adjust her diet and lifestyle immediately and stick to it. Unlike Henry, who regularly got warnings for his cholesterol and blood pressure. He would eat properly and try to take a bit of exercise until they got back to their normal reading and then slip up again.

"Yes, of course, I've thought about it. When you started, I always said I'd rather just die peacefully. But faced with the dilemma of actually dying and never seeing Esme and Alex again, then yes, it's definitely something I would consider," Annie told him.

Henry felt some relief. He was worried for a second that she'd refuse. Prior to this, she joked about it and said it was a bit 'icky.' During drunken conversations with friends, they spoke about the worst part of having the operation. Such as flossing their teeth and experiencing someone else's bad breath, ear wax, or snot and the worst was always wiping someone else's bottom. Henry remembered those evenings and Annie was always the one to think of the worst experiences with a new body.

"You're prepared to go to the toilet with another body?" he asked jokingly.

Annie laughed and wiped away her tears. "I did it for our two children. I'm sure I can get used to it. Besides, I'm been thinking of getting a Japanese toilet. Honestly, who wipes their own bottom these days!"

Henry agreed immediately and they hugged.

They also promised never to talk about the subject of bottom-wiping again.

CHAPTER 22

As time went by, Annie attended all her appointments, followed every fad diet and holistic treatment she could read up on. However, her vitals never improved. In the beginning, apart from feeling tired and losing her appetite, she really wasn't that ill but gradually, she spent more time in bed. They hired additional help for the children and eventually, Annie didn't even want to work any more. As soon as Henry learnt about her illness, he went straight to James and Felix and recommended Annie as a recipient. She was educated, intelligent and still young enough to be considered.

Since the privatisation of the company, the procedure had become prohibitively expensive. Only the super-rich could afford it. Henry and James still lobbied in an attempt to make it mandatory for all death row prisoners to donate their bodies, but human right groups had so far opposed it. Just as in the beginning, prisoners had to give their permission for their corpses to be used in the operation. They still got a generous pay off which they could give to friends or family in their will. However, it was not the government paying the prisoners off any more, it was the private recipient. It disturbed Henry to hear rumours of some clients engage in a bidding war for the younger fitter bodies. Henry preferred to keep out of this unscrupulous side of affairs and stick to working in the laboratory.

One rule that he insisted on, otherwise he wouldn't approve the operation, was bodies had to be of a similar age. There was no point in giving a sixty-year-old man the body of a twenty-year-old man or vice versa. It would be disturbing if the brain deteriorated rapidly and a thirty or forty-year-old person experienced dementia and was then a burden on their family for many years to come. Or if suddenly, the parent looked as young as their grown-up child. He also knew this would keep the bidding down slightly. There weren't enough willing donors, so he didn't want an older person who had already lived their life to be in competition with a twenty-year-old who had yet to really experience life.

His partners unanimously agreed that Annie went to the top of the list. After all, he was the creator. He or his family were worthy recipients. They even agreed to waive the compensation fee for Henry; it would come out of the company's profits. Henry's news came at an unfortunate time as Felix's mother suffered a stroke and Felix took a few days off. This added to Henry's tension as it was Felix who had all the details of the potential donors. Finally, when Felix returned to work, Henry was relieved to find out that for once they actually had a surplus of donors. This was unusual, especially when it came to female donors as there weren't as many on death row. For once, Henry was pleased to know there was so much evil in the world. Some of these women on death row were even similar in age to Annie which made them eligible to become Annie's donor.

Henry took their details to show Annie a few days later at home. At first, Annie refused to look at them. The thought of selecting a skin seemed to confirm her imminent death. And no matter what the prisoners had done, no matter how heinous their crimes were, they usually had one thing in common; most death row prisoners lived terrible lives and that's what led them to death row. She couldn't help but feel sorry for them, especially women. Henry had to be persuasive. He reminded her that willing donors were snapped up from buyers all across the world, usually immediately and no one was ever given this much choice. His partners agreed, Annie would be allowed a few days to make her selection before they let buyers bid on the other prisoners.

So eventually, when the kids were in bed, they sat down on the sofa and Henry uploaded the files. The large screen lit up the wall in front of them and displayed the first prisoner. She was a black American woman who looked slightly younger than Annie. She talked as though she was taking part in a job interview, up-selling herself; demonstrating she was fit, healthy and had never taken drugs. Although having never completed her education, she was sure she would have done well. Henry whispered to Annie that education was unimportant.

"What did she do?" asked Annie.

This information was not in the short film as the prisoners were encouraged to make themselves look good for the potential buyers, nor were their names given. The company wanted to keep this as impersonal as possible. Once the transaction was complete, recipients were given the donor's name. It was now down to them if they wanted to find out more information about their donor. As far as the world was concerned, the prisoner would have been executed as normal. Only next of kin and the recipient would know the truth.

"Do you really want to know?" asked Henry.

Annie nodded.

"She killed her two husbands and three boyfriends that we know of. She hated men. Unknown paternal father. Abusive stepdad. Nicknamed, 'The Black Widow.'"

"Very original," Annie sighed.

She tried not to imagine why this woman hated men so much.

"So would you feel comfortable sharing a bed with someone who kills all of her lovers?"

"Yikes, it might cause a few sleepless nights," Henry joked.

Annie laughed too and hit her head gently.

"Henry, we can't laugh. Look at that poor woman selling her soul. She's probably desperate to help her children or her mother. Who knows? She's pretty attractive but I think it would be harder to get the children to accept me if I'm a different colour. I think I'd prefer to get someone closer to my look."

They both agreed and moved onto the next one.

The next candidate looked hopeful, her skin was clear and her hair was blonde like Annie's. This one had potential; she looked healthy albeit slightly overweight. She spoke to the camera as if she was taking part in a documentary. She spoke of her normal upbringing, her qualifications and her career as a compassionate, caring nurse.

"She seems like a good fit, don't you agree?" asked Annie.

"Yes...I suppose so," agreed Henry.

"Why the hesitation? Out with it, what did she do?" Annie asked again.

"Annie, they're all on death row. None of them are innocent, do you need to know? Are you choosing them based on the level of crime or by their looks?"

"Tell me, Henry," Annie demanded.

"OK, she killed her heavily pregnant friend, by cutting out her unborn baby and running off with it as she had discovered a few years prior that she couldn't have children. She still doesn't think she did anything wrong and that she would have made a better mother."

"Oh my god, how horrific. No way. Next one now please, Henry."

Henry sighed. To have options was probably not a good thing. Annie swiftly skipped the woman who had murdered her child as revenge for her boyfriend leaving her and the one who left her child to starve to death as she was so out of her mind on drugs that she forgot about her.

"People are so evil; I was never supportive of the roll-out of the death penalty in this country but quite honestly, I think I agree with it now. We can't have these people on earth; no matter how awful their childhood was."

"Well, hopefully when your company's health monitors are rolled out and made mandatory, then not only can we prevent more deaths and increase health. Eventually, it should also spot different brain patterns. People like this can be stopped from ever having children and can be heavily monitored."

Henry was pleased when Annie got her company to consider looking into the monitoring of people's brainwave patterns and behaviours. The health monitors at the time were at stage one and the purpose of stage one was people's general health. Stage two in the future would be monitoring the cognitive behaviour of the brain; Henry had ambitions to become heavily involved in this.

"Hear, hear. Right, the last one, please. Otherwise, it will probably have to be 'The Black Widow.' I just can't be in the body of a child killer."

The final candidate was well-spoken, slim and cold. She was thirty-six, so just a few years younger than Annie.

Annie nudged Henry and asked if he felt a bit scared of staring into her eyes.

"Yes, she's a sociopath called Lucinda Willis. She manipulated her new lover into murdering her rich husband so she could inherit everything. But remember, behind those cold icy eyes is a cold heart. With you, that frosty stare will be replaced by your warmth. Are you choosing her?"

"Yes, I think so. Can you guarantee I won't become a sociopath?" asked Annie, who knew the answer before she asked it.

"Yes, you won't become a sociopath. The donor will be brain-dead; there will be no trace left of her. I can't guarantee how it will affect you mentally but that will happen with any skin."

"Why does she want to donate her body? I assume the rest of the family inherit the dead husband's fortune?"

"Simply because she's a narcissist and believes she's too beautiful to die."

"Do you think she's beautiful?" asked Annie.

"I don't believe anyone with such an ugly soul can ever be beautiful. But you can make her beautiful."

Annie took a deep breath and confirmed she had made her choice.

"What now?" she asked Henry.

"I'll let Felix know and he will 'reserve' her for you. It means you are guaranteed her body and no one else can take it unless you change your mind of course."

"It feels so clinical, like we're picking out a new car or something just as impersonal."

"I know," Henry agreed, "but like everyone else in this situation, I just tell them to think of the alternative. And these people aren't innocent. They do deserve to die; mistakes don't happen anymore."

Annie gave Henry a hug and said she just wanted to go to bed and have a cry in private. Henry felt his eyes well up. Getting permission for Annie to become a recipient and the selection process had made him briefly forget that Annie was dying. He sat in the living room alone and poured himself a whisky. He turned off the damn health monitor; it always notified him when he had too much to drink.

CHAPTER 23

"**S**orry to hear that. What a difficult time; it must be hard for you to talk about," said Joe, noticing a slight tremor in Henry's normally composed voice.

Henry agreed.

"So this was around the first time that you realised something was going on?"

"Yes, I felt foolish when I realised I didn't know what was really going on in my own business."

Henry continued to tell Joe the story...

Within five months of Annie selecting the skin, her body gave up fighting the disease. She was frail and couldn't keep any food down and spent most of her time in bed. The children were devastated to see their mother in such a fragile state. Henry insisted it was time for her transfer to the palliative care at his clinic. Likewise, the prisoner would be transferred to a secure but comfortable room at the clinic at the same time. Henry promised to stay with Annie throughout the whole process, leaving Annie's parents to stay with the children. It was an emotional goodbye and they thanked Henry for giving their daughter a second chance. Like Henry, they didn't care about the implications of what was happening; they just weren't ready to say goodbye to her. Annie took one last look in the mirror before Henry led her downstairs.

"Bye bye old body. It was nice knowing you," she whispered.

"Do you want me to carry you down the stairs?" asked Henry.

"No, just let me lean on you. I want to remember how awful I feel and how much pain I'm in so I don't regret going through with this."

Henry understood; saying nothing as he helped her into the car. He selected his clinic for the destination. Annie rested her head on Henry's shoulder as the car set off in self-drive. The journey completed in silence.

Henry put Annie into bed. The room was decorated with personal items from home to make it appear familiar. Since the privatisation of the company, the room had become luxurious. It resembled a decadent hotel room, not a hospital room. More for the benefits of the loved ones rather than the patients; they were usually too sick and medicated to appreciate the luxury. A second bed was set up in the large suite which Henry never imagined he would ever use. He tried making himself comfortable once Annie fell asleep and decided to watch an old film in the hope that it would take his mind off the situation. There was nothing he could do until the prisoner arrived the next morning. He just prayed to himself that the doctors had the timings right and Annie would last until morning.

Once before, a delay in getting the prisoner to the clinic on time meant the patient died earlier than expected. They failed to keep his brain alive and had simply lost the patient. His family were devastated as they never got to say their final goodbyes and the prisoner was rightly disturbed as they had been prepared to die that day, only to be told it would have to be another time. As a result, Henry always made sure patients came in a few weeks before, as well as the prisoners.

After a restless night, Henry made his way out of the suite, ensuring not to disturb Annie. Until he saw the prisoner assigned to her own suite, he wouldn't be able to relax. The doctor on duty assured him that Annie's vitals were stable. There was enough of a comfort zone between now and the very last moment when the operation could be performed. Henry knew this but still couldn't help but feel agitated.

Felix, finally arrived at eight am. Henry was pleased to see him; practically greeting him at the reception and urging him to check on the logistics of the prisoner. Felix offered his condolences and told him that there was no movement yet on the tracker as the prisoner was allowed a lie in this morning and would be transported as soon as she woke up.

"Relax, Henry. It's a short flight."

"I just want her here. I want to see her and make sure she hasn't changed her mind."

"She hasn't changed her mind; I would have heard otherwise. Let me get to my office and call the prison for an ETA. Just go and spend time with Annie and try not to worry."

Henry agreed; the prison had only heard the evening before that the transfer was to be made. Henry knew he was being unreasonable, expecting them to transfer Lucinda Willis immediately.

The morning went by slowly; he checked on Annie and made sure she ate something.

"You've got to calm down, Henry, you're making me even more nervous. We've got a couple of weeks left, haven't we?" Annie tried to reason.

Henry left Annie to have a nap before going to Felix's office again. It was nearly eleven and there was still no movement on Lucinda.

"Call the prison now, please Felix," Henry begged.

Felix agreed and made the call; he spoke quietly and left the office. Henry instinctively knew something was wrong and followed Felix out of his office. Finally, Felix hung up.

"I'm sorry, Henry; I don't know how to say this but..."

Henry interrupted; "she's changed her mind, hasn't she?"

"Yes, I'm afraid so," replied Felix.

"She can't; she's signed the contract!" yelled Henry.

"It's not binding until the money has been transferred, that only gets transferred once the prisoner is here in this facility and signs off for the final time."

"Why? Why has she changed her mind now? She's known about this for months."

Henry burst into tears due to the frustration of the situation but he didn't care that he was crying in front of Felix.

"Please, we've got a couple of weeks at the most. Who else is left?" Henry begged.

"I'm so sorry, Henry; I'll get the status of other volunteers. I have no idea why she changed her mind. She didn't give a reason. You'd better go and let Annie know and I'll get back to you later. We'll find someone. Don't worry," Felix reassured him.

Henry slowly made his way back into Annie's suite. She was awake and instantly knew something was wrong as Henry couldn't help but break down in tears again. Henry explained how the donor had changed her mind and they couldn't do the operation without her consent.

"That will teach me for opting for the prettiest sociopath," Annie laughed as she tried to make light of the situation.

"Felix said he'll find us someone else," Henry told her.

"Okay," agreed Annie, without much conviction.

Soon after Henry broke the news to Annie, Felix came to visit them.

"It's no good Annie, we have no available female donors. They've all been claimed," Felix explained.

"What about the other four donors we saw, are they all taken?" Henry demanded to know.

"Yes, you know about the shortage in supply, particularly with female donors."

"Let me go and see Lucinda Willis and talk her round?" Henry begged.

"You can't do that; it's strictly forbidden for the recipient and their family to meet the donor," Felix said.

"But I would have seen her in the operating room!" Henry shouted.

"That's not the same as meeting her," Felix replied coolly. "I'll do some touting, offer her more money or find someone else."

"We haven't got time!" Henry shouted again.

He felt so angry at the coolness from Felix. He needed more urgency from his colleague. "This is not just any old patient. This is my wife. My Annie!"

Then he heard sobbing; they both stopped talking and looked at Annie.

"Bring me home. I just want to see my babies for my last few days," Annie said quietly.

Henry sat next to her on her bed and took her hand; "Oh, Annie. I'm so sorry. We can't give up. The children think you're coming home to them. They've accepted you'll have another body; they don't care about that. They just want you. Please stay here, you'll get much better treatment than at home and you'll be more comfortable. The kids can come and see you every day. I'll keep them off school if that's what you want. I'll think of something, I promise. Have I ever let you down?"

Annie shook her head but said: "Well...all those dinners you were late for?"

"Apart from those dinners?" he asked.

She smiled and said no. Henry held her for as long as he could and she agreed to stay. Both men left the room to let Annie rest.

"You see how much she means to me, you've got to help me?" begged Henry.

Felix promised to do everything he could.

A few days passed; there was still no luck in finding a donor.

"I'm sorry Henry. No one wants to do it; especially in such a short time frame."

Henry knew this would happen. Once the donor agreed to the procedure, he lived in relative comfort for the rest of their death row stay. Henry insisted on this as he wanted them to be comfortable and healthy in time for the operation. It also deflected additional criticism from the human right groups. Anyone accepting the offer now, wouldn't get to enjoy the comfort for long.

"What about offering more money? I'm willing to give up all of my savings?" Henry offered.

"No, we've upped the offer. We've reached out to all the death row female prisoners and offered Lucinda more money too. But no, nothing."

"How about a male prisoner? We could borrow the skin for the short term before someone else comes along and then do another transfer?" Henry was grasping at straws by now.

"No way Henry, even if Annie was willing to go along with that idea, we have no idea if a second transfer would be successful and it contravenes the current laws. The transfer must be between the same sex – unless transsexual – and of a similar age. You know all of this."

Henry sat back in his chair and looked up at the ceiling. He was out of ideas and completely desperate. The kids had been visiting Annie but she was slowly becoming hysterical over the thought of never seeing her family again. Henry couldn't help but feel responsible for her mental anguish. He was the one who promised her another chance. He was the one who convinced the children that everything would be alright. If it hadn't been for him, Annie and the children could have used these last few months to come to terms with her death, instead of just a few days.

That night he lay beside her in bed, listening to her short, shallow breaths as she slept. He would lose her soon and there was nothing he could do about it.

His phone buzzed; a message from Felix asking Henry to come and meet him at a nearby bar. Henry sat up immediately. Did Felix have new information? He messaged he'd be there as soon as possible. He dressed, crept quietly out of the room so as not to disturb Annie and quickly made his way to the bar.

Felix was already there, sitting down in a quiet booth in the dimly lit bar. He ordered Henry to sit down.

"You want a drink?" he offered.

"No. Tell me why you've asked me here?"

"I need to talk to you away from the office; without a record of this conversation and no witnesses. We're just two work colleagues having a drink. Order one, Henry."

Henry selected a drink from the screen and within a minute the waitress brought it over. Felix didn't speak until the waitress left the table. He looked around and in a hushed tone, told Henry he had a proposition.

"Go on," encouraged Henry.

"As you know, I've been putting the feelers out for female volunteers for Annie. Earlier this evening, I was approached by someone offering me a willing volunteer. Someone desperate for money for her family."

"Who approached you? Is this woman on death row?"

"I can't tell you; I've been sworn to secrecy. But this woman is a civilian. She's not a prisoner," Felix told him.

"Then no, I won't be responsible for the death of an innocent woman. Annie would never go for it either."

"Think about it, Henry. Annie wants to live; this woman wants to help her family and this is the only way she knows how. She's not from this country. She's from some war-torn state in Russia and her family are starving. With this money, they can escape and start a new life. Without the money, they will probably all die. Yes, you'd be indirectly responsible for one woman's death but isn't that better than knowing that her entire family will die because they are so poor, they can't escape. Trust me, she has no life at the minute."

Henry knocked back his whisky. "I need time to think about it. I need to check with Annie first."

"There's no time; Annie could die within days and this family could be killed at any moment. The contact is currently in place to get them out. You need to make the decision now."

"I don't know. What would you do?" asked Henry.

"I'd look out for the person I love most," he replied.

Henry stared at the drinks screen on the table, his hand shook as he ordered another one. He told Felix to go ahead.

Felix left Henry so he could go and make the arrangements and he would see Henry and Annie in the morning. Henry made his way back to the lab and he sat next to Annie. He looked at her from the glow of the monitors currently keeping her alive. She was deteriorating rapidly; now so pale, she had aged so much in such a few weeks. He stroked her forehead and thought of their children as he convinced himself that he was doing the right thing.

When she woke up the next morning, Henry was still at her side looking at her. He hadn't managed to doze off.

"What are you looking at?" she smiled at her husband.

"I've got some good news, Annie," he said, trying to sound positive.

Annie tried to sit up but couldn't quite manage it.

"We found a willing donor; she'll be here soon," he told her.

"Really?"

He nodded.

"Tell me about her?" Annie asked him.

"I don't have the details yet. It was all last minute but she should be here today. As soon as she gets here, we'll start the procedure."

"But what does she look like? What did she do? How old is she?" Annie asked.

"Shush my love; save your energy. I don't have the answers at the moment," Henry calmed her.

"Find Felix," she whimpered as she slipped back into sleep.

Henry rushed off and ran into Felix in the corridor.

"Is she here yet?" he asked.

"Yes," confirmed Felix. "I can see from the central monitor that Annie's vital signs are in rapid decline. We have to do it now."

"Can I meet the woman first?"

"No, we don't have time; this is urgent. I'll send the nurse along to prep Annie, you go with her. Keep her company in case she wakes up. Go back, Henry."

Henry knew Felix was right and daren't delay the operation any longer. He couldn't risk Annie dying before they got her to theatre. He stayed by her side until it was time; he wasn't needed for the setup today. Usually, Henry micro-managed the entire procedure but today he surrendered control. The operation was completely automated by now and the staff had been extra prepared today. The only thing required from Henry today was his code to operate the machines.

Henry was the only one with the code. With his expert knowledge, he had set up an unbreakable firewall so no one else could have access. Over the years, the company had been in talks with various governments and overseas companies to sell their product. So far, talks always came to an end when it came to money. Money wasn't the main issue for Henry; he wanted to ensure all bugs, laws and any ethical issues were all ironed out before they could roll the product out across the world. His partners were more concerned with the amount of money they could make and were holding out for more. In the meantime, Henry didn't trust anyone and made sure he was the only one who could perform the operation.

By the time they got to the operating theatre, the other patient had been prepped and anaesthetised. Henry was disappointed not to thank the woman for her tremendous sacrifice.

"She wanted to get it over and done with," explained Felix.

Henry nodded, it was understandable. In a way, he felt relieved not to meet her alive. It would have been too upsetting.

Henry made sure everything was in place before activating the machine. He held his breath, half expecting something to go wrong. It didn't. The operation was a success and all they had to do was wait for Annie to wake up.

CHAPTER 24

Henry and Felix agreed to keep the truth from Annie. This way, she wouldn't be complicit in the crime and the fewer people who knew, the better. Together, they worked on a background story about the donor. Henry demonstrated how to produce a fake prisoner report. This report would not only tie up with their company records, it also meant if Annie did any checks on her donor, this is what she would see.

When Annie woke up, she went through the usual array of emotions Henry had seen his previous patients experience. For once, Henry got to experience what it was like to be the loved one of the patient. Most family's emotions ranged from relief to euphoria in the clinic – that the operation had been successful. It was at home where this relief turned into wariness before becoming acceptance. Seeing Annie alive; he too went through this feeling of relief. It didn't matter to him that his wife was now unrecognisable.

He warned Annie what to expect and she decided

to look at herself as quickly as possible. Luck had been on their side. With blonde hair, blue-eyed and of similar age to Annie, the donor was not dissimilar to their original choice. Annie's new skin appeared healthy but of course, no medical checks had taken place. Henry hoped the donor didn't suffer from any underlying diseases; he didn't want Annie to suffer again.

Henry led Annie to the full-length mirror, where she gazed at herself for a couple of minutes before speaking.

"This feels better than I expected. I'm still me and I feel healthy. Please tell me about her?"

Henry explained she was a last-minute donor who was offered a lot of money. She had served many years for her participation in a large drug's cartel in Eastern Europe. The payment went to her family, who could now leave the country and have a better life.

"So she's not a killer or sociopath?" asked Annie.

"Not that we know of, although the drugs she was pedalling would have probably been responsible for multitudes of deaths. We'll never know." Henry felt uneasy for lying to his wife, this was the first time he ever lied to her.

They took pictures of her to show the kids before introducing the 'new' Annie. Annie adapted to her new skin remarkably well; by being so close to death's door and desperately not wanting to be there, she felt grateful. The fact she looked completely different didn't concern her one little bit.

Their children also adapted remarkably quickly; Henry knew that was due to Annie's calm and collected composure. They immediately felt Annie's old love and warmth once they met their new-look mother. Henry couldn't help but be proud of his family and how strong they were. Once Henry ran all health checks, which confirmed Annie was healthy, he could finally relax. Henry confided his relief to Felix.

"We were lucky; I just hope we did the right thing. I expected the skin to be malnourished or in much worse condition?" Henry told Felix.

"They still had rationing in her particular state of Russia, so I think she was fed. I got the impression she was on the verge of starvation. Don't think too much about it, Henry; you'll drive yourself mad. Just be grateful we saved Annie in time. So how does it feel to have Annie in a new skin?"

Henry had been so busy since the operation, he hadn't given it much thought. It didn't quite feel real but he remembered how desperate and sad he felt only a few days before. How would he manage without her and what he would have told the children, dominated his thoughts. Now he was just relieved.

"I'm so happy. We've been given a second chance and I don't care how Annie looks or sounds. It's still her," Henry said.

"You're pretty lucky; she's not unattractive?" Felix nudged Henry.

Henry hadn't given this much thought. To him,

the old Annie would always be the most beautiful woman he ever met. Henry left Felix and vowed to spend as much time with Annie and the kids as he could. Maybe he could even share the code with the board and take more of a back-seat role.

As the Marlow family got used to the new Annie, Henry felt a sense of dread. What if he and Felix were found out? Who was the broker who arranged this and had they covered their tracks properly? Felix assured Henry they had nothing to worry about. The broker had been well-paid and was discreet. The increased funding had been pre-approved by the board and the company was operating as expected. No one would question anything; as far as their records showed or as far as their staff were concerned, there were no anomalies. All Henry had to do, was carry on as normal and put it out of his mind.

"But why did you take such a risk in something illegal?" Henry asked Felix.

This question bothered Henry the most. What they did was a huge risk. It was against company policy and against the law. They were in a unique position so even Henry wasn't sure what the fall out would be if they'd been caught but he knew they would lose the company and maybe even go to prison. Henry understood his motives, but he didn't understand Felix's.

"Henry, we're good friends and I'm so fond of Annie and the kids. I've known you for nearly ten years. You begged me to help and I couldn't stand back and do nothing, that's what friends are for," Felix replied.

Henry shook his friend's hand. "Thanks, Felix, I am forever in your debt."

CHAPTER 25

Although Henry vowed to take more of a sideline role, he found he couldn't quite pass the reins over to a predecessor. Annie teased him about having a God complex. Maybe he did? He was the only person on earth capable of performing the procedure. However, now that Annie didn't require any care and the kids were either at school or preferred to spend time with their friends, he didn't feel the need to be constantly at home. Maybe he just wanted to be kept busy, so he found himself back in the lab, as always perfecting his product.

The procedures continued as normal and he even encountered some of the female prisoners he recalled viewing a few months ago with Annie. Some were rather scary in the flesh and he felt relieved Annie had inherited such a gentle looking face.

One day, he came across Lucinda Willis' profile. She was due as the donor of a rich banker's wife. Henry was furious when he saw her name; he stormed into Felix's office to ask why the hell she was a donor.

"Calm down, Henry. She simply changed her mind, the banker offered her a lot more money than we could," Felix told him.

"She's on death row receiving a generous payment to start with! What does she care how much it is?" Henry demanded to know.

"What can I tell you? She either reconsidered or liked being bargained for. Maybe she just wanted to make sure her family were well taken care of?"

Henry doubted that as he remembered those cold, unfeeling eyes in the film he watched with Annie.

"I'm speaking to her as soon as she arrives!" Henry threatened.

"No way, It would be unprofessional; if you go in with all guns blazing then she might back out again. She's flaky, remember? Imagine if your interrogation causes her to change her mind. Our patient today, Jenna White will probably die. Do you want to be the cause of that?"

Of course he didn't but he had questions. Felix advised him against talking to the Whites as well. Henry remembered how fragile he and Annie felt when she was dying and knew it was not the time to demand answers.

"You got lucky Henry, just be thankful," said Felix.

Henry reluctantly agreed, assuring he'd keep contact with the Whites to a minimum. But he couldn't help but feel angry that he could have lost Annie due to someone else with a bigger wallet. It didn't feel right to him.

When it was time for the operation, he administered the whole procedure stony-faced and cold, without any of his usual bed-side manner. He normally engaged with the recipient and loved to be present when they woke up, so he could note their reactions, but not today. Today, he barely spoke to either patient. He marked off his checklist but didn't ask how they felt. He watched cold-heartedly, more like a bystander, as Lucinda's brain was shut down. Normally he barely watched this part of the process; he was a doctor, he wanted to save lives not end them. Did she really hold out for the highest bidder or did she simply have a change of heart? He would never know. He actioned the operation, left and told his assistant to call him if there were any complications.

Instead, he went home to spend time with his family. He needed to be around his main reminder of why this project was so important to him. It was Annie; they were both getting used to her new-look and now that Annie had a second chance at life she was determined to make the most of it. She accepted her body and appreciated it; as well as appreciating the sacrifice made by the donor. The children had also adapted quickly, hugging Annie on a daily basis to let her know. With her usual sense of humour, she compared the body swap to having a rather drastic new hairstyle.

Henry talked to Annie about the disillusionment he felt with the project. Since the company became private, only the super-rich could afford the operation. This was never Henry's intentions; he always naively assumed it would be on a needs basis but since it wasn't publicly funded anymore, this was no longer an option. Between himself and Annie, they came up with certain solutions which Henry would document and take to James and Felix and see what he could get approved. He was the talent; he held the codes. Without him, the company was nothing. He understood his other two partners were only concerned with money but if they weren't willing to compromise with his demands, he was prepared to walk away. He arranged a meeting with Felix to discuss the documentation and details for the next day.

The next day, he went to work in a lighter mood than in previous weeks. He stopped by the suite of Jenna White to apologise for his lack of attention the previous day and hoped she was happy with the service. Assuming he and Annie had been out-bidden by the Whites, he reasoned to himself that he would have done the same thing. They must have been just as desperate. There was no need to confront them as everything worked out in the end. He would just have to ensure this type of behaviour didn't happen again.

The Whites were more than happy. Jenna told Dr Marlow how she had been bed bound for almost a year while her disease slowly took over her body. She called him a miracle worker and Mr White agreed and if Henry ever needed anything, then to just ask. They were forever in Henry's debt. Henry told them it was all part of the service and wished them luck in the future.

Afterwards, he made his way to Felix's office and to his surprise James Talbot was present.

"I didn't expect to see you here, James. What a nice surprise," Henry lied.

His presence made Henry feel uneasy; he never trusted James and knew they would never be on the same wavelength. James was a money man and nothing else. It was Felix who had persuaded Henry to accept James as they needed his cash injections to keep the company afloat. James had so far kept to his original promise of keeping out of the day to day running of the company. Therefore, the contact between the two men had been minimal; Henry preferred to let Felix deal with James.

"Hi Henry, Felix told me you had some suggestions to make?"

Henry's face flushed as he took a quick glimpse at Felix and felt anger towards him. He was unprepared.

"It was nothing official, there was no need to come in. I wanted to make suggestions as I always do whenever a new problem arises. I wanted to talk to Felix to get his opinion," Henry told James.

"Well, I'm here now. Just get it out in the open and let's see what we can come up with," suggested James.

"I have nothing in writing, maybe I could come back in a few days…"

"No need; spit it out now so I don't have to come back," James urged.

Henry didn't like being caught off guard, but this was his company and he wasn't letting a blowhard like James Talbot sweep his ideas under the table.

Henry recounted how he almost lost Annie, probably due to a higher bid by a wealthier person. He kept quiet about the solution he and Felix had come up with; he knew he could never tell anyone. So he lied to James about how he'd been lucky to find a last-minute prisoner for Annie. James raised his eyebrow at this; he didn't appear to be sympathetic.

Henry continued regardless; "so, my future recommendation, in essence, would be that we don't allow this to happen again. Everyone is set at the same price so there will be no last-minute outbidding and I propose to do some pro bono work. The prices are astronomically high and I understand this is a business but so many decent people are dying out there, it's not right that we only help the rich. If I wasn't the inventor, Annie would have died. She's a brilliant person in regards to her personal and professional life. People like her are much worthier than some banker's wife who shops all day."

James flinched at this. Henry knew nothing about this man's personal life but assumed he had a beautiful, trophy girlfriend at home.

"Your sentiments are admirable Henry, and I would love for you to do some pro bono work so you don't have to waste your time saving the lives of rich, pointless folk; however, you are overlooking some small facts. Firstly, if it wasn't for rich people like me funding this whole operation then 'The Marlow Project' would have folded a long time ago. Annie would not have been in a position to receive the donor and you would have been a widower and your children would have been left without a mother."

Henry squeezed his fist as his heart beat rapidly and his face flushed. He hated confrontation but he was about to explode in front of this odious man. James could sense this and held up his finger to let Henry know he hadn't finished what he was saying.

"Secondly, to do your pro bono work, you need an excess of supply. As you know, we're struggling under the current stipulations in our Term's and Condition's to attract the death row prisoners to donate their bodies. Crime is on the way down and most people on death row don't give a damn about comfort, money or helping their family. They're mostly psychotic, they only think about themselves. Hell, once they know they've signed up to be a donor, they probably only have a few weeks or months left. They could still have years left on death row if they don't sign up as a donor. So until the law changes to make it mandatory, which is what we are pushing for, then we still have our problem of supply in the future. By setting the price and operating for free on some poor, worthy pleb, this company will go bust. Thus, we can't help anyone, is that what you are suggesting, Dr Marlow?"

This is why Henry wanted to speak to Felix beforehand. Instead, he felt the two men had ganged up on him; he was a scientist, not a businessman. He hoped Felix could help with the finer details but at this moment, Felix sat back and failed to defend Henry.

"Of course not," replied Henry, " I just wanted to make some suggestions."

"Well, I assume you're not able to make any suggestions on ways to increase the supply of donors, are you?" James asked. "However, I do. I suggest we use the same method we used for Annie."

"What do you mean?" demanded Henry.

"We seek out private volunteers. It worked out pretty well for you, didn't it Henry?"

Henry looked at Felix and slammed his hand down on his desk.

"How could you? This was between us; you swore you would never tell anyone?"

Felix finally spoke up.

"I'm sorry, Henry, I thought I covered our tracks. I didn't. I had to come clean. It happened so fast that I couldn't warn you."

Henry knew it had all gone too smoothly.

"Yes, Henry. It was up to me to clean your mess, luckily for you, I didn't report you both to the police," James gloated.

"Oh, go to hell, James," Henry knew James never had any intention of reporting this to the police.

He just sensed a huge moneymaking scheme. He also knew what James was about to propose next. After sitting down to listen to James proposals for what seemed like hours, he left Felix's office more disillusioned than ever.

He had been backed into a corner and James knew it and was intent on taking full advantage. Somehow, Henry had now agreed to operate on private donors. Felix and James assured him they'd be able to cover their tracks and would use a fail-proof computer system to fake their criminal records. Henry didn't have to be involved; he could just turn up on the day, input his code and check on the patients and then use the rest of his time coming up with improvements or other scientific discoveries.

James suggested he hand the reins over to them and give them the code so Henry wouldn't even need to be there at all. Although Henry didn't feel like he wanted to be there anymore, there was no way he would ever give up the code now. He had to keep a close eye on them and if he was suddenly to drop off the radar, this might attract the attention of the inspectors. The company was always under scrutiny and if Henry stopped attending the operations this might arouse suspicions. Besides, if it got to a point where they didn't need him anymore, he knew James might try to turn this into a global enterprise with many offices around the world. Where would all the donors come from then? The most important factor in agreeing to go along with this was Annie. He knew he would be arrested but didn't care. He also knew that any operations performed outside of the law might result in the recipient's termination. After all, they had gained the body by illegal means even though Annie had no idea. He hadn't gone through all of this to get thrown into prison and still lose Annie.

He felt he had no choice but to go through with James' proposal. In the meantime, he would lobby for the mandatory donation of death row prisoners, so that it meant poor, desperate, innocent people wouldn't become donors for too long.

CHAPTER 26

Henry became distracted and moody. Annie assumed it was due to disappointment with the outcome of his meeting. Again, for the second time in his life, he lied to Annie. He told her he put forward his propositions only for them to be turned down but got cold feet when it came to resigning. She reprimanded him that he wasn't forceful enough and that he should draw up his proposals again; she would help him this time. Admitting defeat, it wasn't worth it.

"It's not like you to give up so easily," she said.

"I'm not corporate or political and never will be. I can't reason with them."

"Then quit. We have enough money to live on. Let's move to a tropical island," she suggested.

"Nice idea, but I haven't worked this hard to give up on my life's work. We'll get more donors somehow and I'll renegotiate then. Besides, you're willing to give up on your work?"

Of course she wasn't ready. Just like Henry, she too had so much more she wanted to achieve.

"I'm just throwing it out there, just in case."

"One day," Henry promised.

Feeling as though he wasn't in control anymore, a despondent Henry showed up at work the next day. Felix apologised and explained the matter was taken out of his hands once the discrepancy in the system was found.

"This might not be a bad thing. James knows people who can cover our tracks. At least it was him who found out. If it had been someone else, who knows what could have happened. We might have been arrested by now, with Annie's life in the balance too."

"I just don't trust James. I wish you came to speak to me first."

Now Henry didn't feel as though he could trust Felix either.

"Sorry Henry, he literally just found out and I had to spill the beans. But now, we can discreetly advertise for donors. Many people just like Annie's donor are desperate and would do anything to help their families. Why should just the prisoner's families benefit? Why not decent families too?"

Henry didn't agree with crime paying but he didn't want to be indirectly responsible for taking away some child's father or mother. Surely it was better to be poor and loved than rich and without one of your parents? Henry explained this to Felix, but Felix said they were lucky never to know what such extreme poverty or threat of war could do to a person.

As the months passed, the clinic became busier. Henry assumed it was due to these private donors.

The less he knew the better so he asked not to be informed which was which and stopped visiting the donor patients. He didn't want to be deeply complicit if they were ever caught. However, it wasn't actually difficult to notice the difference between the legitimate death row donors from the voluntary donors.

"Dr Marlow, pleased to meet you," greeted a woman with an American accent in the suite as he went to check on the stats of his current recipient patient. He shook her perfectly manicured, gold-ringed encrusted hand.

"I am Eliza Davenport, you are treating my husband, John. We are so honoured to have you performing this operation. Since my husband found out he was terminally ill, we have been beside ourselves with worry. Can you imagine our surprise when we were accepted into the program?"

Henry assumed they weren't that surprised. He guessed they just kept bidding until they were accepted, although he didn't know the details behind each case and didn't want to know.

"It's my pleasure," Henry pretended. "May I ask what you or your husband do for a living?"

He was originally determined not to get involved with these vastly wealthy people but he couldn't help but be curious.

"My husband is in the energy industry; he's a broker."

Of course he is, thought Henry. For years the oil industry had the grips on the world's wealth and delayed years of advancements towards cleaner, alternative energy. As time passed, increased legislation had gone through in the western world to encourage the use of cleaner, renewable energy but everyone knew that in countries such as the war-torn Russian states and some other oil-producing countries that the oil industry still had a hold on those countries. War had prevented any progress in new infrastructures, making them still largely dependent on this rapidly depleting, expensive fossil fuel. The old oil industry now not only had large stakes in renewable sources, they still controlled the old industry making a fortune from both sides no matter what the human cost in terms of war or pollution. Henry doubted if John or Eliza Davenport had many scruples in accepting a private donor.

Henry reminded himself not to be a hypocrite. Not that long ago, he was in the same boat. However, when the donor and the recipient were in the same room ready for the operation, he couldn't help but note the difference between both of them.

John Davenport looked older than his years, despite the terminal illness he had been suffering, he was still overweight and unattractive. His pock-marked, red face with broken veins over his bulbous nose made him look rather unappealing. He was balding yet had hair protruding out of his ears and nose. One of the operating room assistants commented on what a huge upgrade he was getting. Henry glanced over at the 'skin', who was already anaesthetised. His appearance suggested he was quite a few years younger, fitter and much more handsome. Henry had second thoughts about the operation but felt he had no choice; he didn't want his staff to become suspicious. As soon as he was done, he stormed out of the room and barged into Felix's office.

"This is not a damn vanity project! This is supposed to save lives; it's for the desperate. I didn't sign up for this!"

Felix shut the door behind him and tried to calm Henry down as he guided him towards a chair.

"What are you talking about Henry?"

"Have you seen the skin? Our donor and recipient are supposed to be of the same age. And it's strange some young, handsome guy suddenly wants to die for some fat old man?"

"Calm down, please. They're actually much closer in age then you think. We're still roughly following the same guidelines. John Davenport looks older than his age and the donor just looks young for his age. We can't deny a donor because he's good-looking. We have more people to select from. I assume the better-looking ones get offered more money and just because he's good-looking, it doesn't mean he's not desperate."

"So what you're saying is that only the handsome or pretty, desperate ones will be selected and not the ugly, desperate ones?"

"Don't oversimplify it like that. It's still the same story as the prisoner volunteers. There's not a huge queue of people waiting to die for money. John Davenport and his wife got very lucky, that's all."

"Where do we find the donor?" Henry demanded.

"The less you know, the better. Don't you think?" asked Felix.

Henry supposed he was right; he wanted little to do with the selection of donors as possible. When he left the office, he checked the donor's file. It showed his name as Afrim Tahiri, death-row prisoner from Albania aged fifty-six. Obviously, all completely made up; the donor looked more Mediterranean than Eastern Europe and there was no way he was fifty-six, more like forty. On paper, it looked legitimate. The authorities wouldn't question a death row prisoner from Albania as Felix assured him all the prison states in these areas were open to bribery, if it ever came to that. But in reality, it felt wrong. He wondered why this person had volunteered to end his life so prematurely.

A few days later, he watched the recovered John Davenport leave the clinic; he and his wife looked very pleased with themselves.

"He'll upgrade to a newer model, no doubt."

Henry, lost in his thoughts, looked around and saw Felix standing behind him, watching them too.

"You're okay with this?" Henry asked.

Felix just shrugged his shoulders.

"It is what it is. We were caught out so now we have no choice."

CHAPTER 27

"**D**r Marlow, you're admitting you knew some of the 'skins' were illegal from the start?" asked Joe.

"Yes, I never denied that. Unfortunately, I buried my head in the sand and hoped it would go away. But it didn't. The Davenport transfer worried me and I hoped it wasn't a sign of things to come. But the illegal transfers were always serious upgrades, whereas the legal ones were considered downgrades as you would expect. Death row prisoners weren't usually the most pleasant looking of people."

"So how much longer did you go through with it?"

"Too long but some instances made me believe it was still worth it," admitted Henry...

Business at the clinic was booming. Annie commented there must be a huge surge in crime. Henry pretended they had an increase in volunteers from the prisons, as people were getting used to the idea. He was in the clinic performing the operation up to two to three times a week, compared to roughly once a week or before. One case a week, he guessed was legal going by the 'skin.' The others were similar to the Davenport case – obvious upgrades in body and looks. Felix enjoyed the extra business, judging by the new purchases recently made with his bonuses. Notable purchases consisting of a palatial new penthouse overlooking the river, installed with all the latest gadgets and a flash new car.

Henry wasn't interested in the material possessions that Felix appeared obsessed with. Limiting his purchases to a few presents for the family and putting some money to one side towards the costs of university for the kids. Aside from that, he donated most of the money towards scientific research, such as finding the cure for cancer. Determined to carry on as normal, he didn't want to attract too much attention. He spent most of his time concentrating on the genuine cases. In one instance, he even paid for one patient that his old friend Charlie was desperate to save.

"It's good to see you and thank you for your time now that you're the famous Dr Marlow," greeted Charlie.

"Stop it! And it's so good to see you too," Henry said as he hugged his friend.

Charlie moved away to Scotland a few years ago and although they had kept in touch it wasn't the same as seeing each other. Both men had also been incredibly busy with life and progressing careers.

"I'm afraid I've come to see you with an ulterior motive," admitted Charlie once they caught up with each other.

"Tell me?"

"I want to nominate someone for a transplant. I know it's incredibly expensive and only the ultra-rich can afford it now, but I was hoping you might have some influence," said Charlie.

Henry didn't want to admit to his lack of influence over the way his company was run anymore. No longer did it feel like his company. These days, he was just an employee, going through the motions. The passion for his project was long gone.

"Give me the details and I'll see what I can do," offered Henry.

"It's my nephew, Monty. You met him when he was little. Remember?"

Henry did remember; it must have been about fifteen years ago when Charlie's older sister came to visit them in London along with her eight-year-old son. He remembered going to Hyde Park to kick a ball around and feed the ducks with the young boy.

"Is he still football mad?" asked Henry.

Charlie's eyes welled up and he shook his head; "he'd like to be if he could. He was in a car crash. The car was so mangled. It blew up; he suffered seventy per cent burns and will likely never walk again."

"What the hell sort of car was he driving?"

Cars were all self-driven now. There was the odd computer error but it rarely ended up in such a catastrophic accident. Manual driving wasn't permitted anymore. Insurance premiums became too high and the law changed as ninety-nine per cent of accidents were due to manually driven cars.

"It was supposed to be a treat for his twenty-first

birthday. He's obsessed with cars as well as football. He's always been fascinated with the old-fashioned racing cars so his parents bought him a racing day experience. But he lost control; it was stupid of his father to allow him to drive such a powerful, fast car when he had so little experience."

"I'm so sorry Charlie. I remember how fond you were of Monty. What's the prognosis?" asked Henry.

"They think he'll live but his face is a complete mess and his spinal injury is too severe. He'll need care for the rest of his life, but that won't amount to any quality of life."

"The advancements in burn victims and skin repair are remarkable," said Henry, maintaining an optimistic outlook.

"Not good enough yet; his face was melted away, Henry. Any replacements would always just look like a clumsy attempt at a mask."

Charlie showed Henry a picture of Monty's current face. It was disturbing; Henry looked away.

"He's a young boy, just twenty-one and such a nice kid. He can't live like this and my sons worship their older cousin."

Henry agreed, but the recipients had always been terminal before. There was no precedent for someone who wasn't dying.

"Can you help us, Henry?" begged Charlie.

Henry thought of the undeserving people who had been through his clinic lately, so yes, he would help Charlie's nephew.

All patients were voted through the partners now. Henry insisted Felix help; he had to make sure Monty was approved and that a suitable donor would be found, preferably through the correct channels. Henry offered to pay the market rate to ensure Monty wouldn't be overlooked.

"Of course I'll help you, Henry. That's what friends are for. You're a partner in this business and if you nominate a recipient then we'll go along with you. As luck would have it, we do have a young, white male in his early twenties on the books. He was in a gang and was involved in a shooting, including a police officer. He wants to help out his mum."

Felix wasn't concerned that Charlie's nephew wasn't terminal.

"It's serious enough; I don't think any justification is required. Let's get on with it. I'll see when we can get the prisoner in and will let you know."

Henry felt relieved; he didn't want to let Charlie down.

Within a month the procedure was completed without complications. Henry knew it was the right thing to do as soon as he saw Monty stretchered in for the operation. He wasn't a young man anymore with his whole life ahead of him. The body stretchered in resembled a mummified corpse, with no quality of life. Monty and his mother were so grateful.

Charlie and Henry met up for a drink to celebrate and talk about old times. They reminisced of their ambitions and ideals when they were young.

"Was success everything you thought it would be?" asked Charlie.

"No," admitted Henry. "If only I could make the procedure free and have it on a needs basis. You should see the messages I get from distraught parents, spouses or children asking me to save their loved ones. Instead, only the highest bidders get to save their family. I would walk away from it now if I could."

"What's stopping you? Walk away, sell the company. Become a charity to continue funding if you're not interested in personal wealth."

Henry wished it was that simple. He knew he could confide in Charlie, so he told him everything. Charlie wasn't surprised and reassured him he had done the right thing by Annie.

"I can't leave, I'm too invested. At least today reminded me why I still want to do it. If I only get to do one genuine case against ten others, then it's worth it. And it's worth it anyway, all the people in the program are sick, they're all desperate."

"You can always talk to me if you choose not to tell Annie," Charlie told Henry.

"I can't ever tell Annie. I don't want to make her an accessory to the crime if we're ever found out. But thanks for listening to me. It's good to get it off my chest and put it into perspective."

"Anytime, old friend," said Charlie.

CHAPTER 28

"**S**o you accepted the circumstances and went about your business as if every-thing was normal?" asked Joe.

"Yes," agreed Henry. "I justified it to myself. I guess deep down, I wanted to continue my work. I reasoned to myself that we wouldn't go to prison if they found out the donors weren't prisoners. In the worst-case scenario, the company would close or we'd receive a huge fine. I could live with that; it wasn't a crime as the new donors were volunteers. We were still saving lives."

"How was your relationship with your partners, Felix and James?"

"I kept away from the business side of operations as much as possible. I never trusted James Talbot. I couldn't relate to someone whose sole purpose in life was making money. As for Felix, I kept it profes-sional as I still saw him on a day to day basis but it wasn't like before. I couldn't talk to him anymore; he had James' ear. I couldn't trust him. The money went to his head."

"So how long did this arrangement continue for?"

asked Joe.

"The company ticked away nicely for a couple of years. I stayed in line and performed all the operations. There was no question of handing over the code. It was a huge responsibility and we were only small-scale, yet people were already taking advantage. I didn't want one of our clinics in every city in the world. Could you imagine the immense pressure on the desperately poor to become volunteers if laws were relaxed? Besides, I was never asked to release the code. The board seemed happy with the small-scale operation; we could charge a fortune per procedure and remaining small meant less scrutiny and fewer prisoners to fake."

"When did things begin to change?" asked Joe.

"It was three years after Annie's operation. Since the clinic became busy, I could never get away. I'd been asked numerous times to give a lecture in Boston in front of my old alumni and the current students at Harvard. It was an honour to be asked but I never had the time. Anyway, we had a rare few days with no patients booked in, so I took the opportunity to take my family to America to show them around my old university..."

"It's great to meet you, Dr Marlow and thanks for the lecture. It was fascinating and we loved the personal success stories of your patients too," said one over-enthusiastic student.

"It's an honour; I was glad to have such an enrapt audience," smiled Dr Marlow.

Henry spent all day at Harvard, dining and catching up with some old friends. He enjoyed regaling everyone about the success of his company and tried forgetting about the shadier side.

Annie and the kids spent the day exploring the city without him, as the kids didn't want to come - it sounded boring. Due to his work overload at the clinic, he didn't get much chance to spend time with them lately so he rushed back to the hotel. He was just in time to say a quick hello to the kids, who caught him up on their day before the hotel babysitter arrived. Tonight, he and Annie were going out for dinner on their own. Annie had booked a table at an exclusive restaurant in Boston, reminding Henry that he could afford it and she was worth it.

"You're definitely worth it but you're also probably the one paying the bill tonight," Henry reminded her.

Henry had covered all the costs of Monty's operation. Charlie had offered to pay but Henry knew he didn't have enough money; not many people had. Instead, Henry led Charlie to believe that he was able to do it for free. This wasn't the case. Henry didn't want to owe James or Felix any favours so he covered the cost out of his own pocket. This practically wiped out his savings. Annie knew how much it cost but she understood. She would have done the same thing for Charlie too. Luckily, Annie's company were doing pretty well for themselves at the time.

They sat down at their table in the beautifully

lit, old-fashioned restaurant where the staff were charming and attentive.

"Look, not a touchscreen in sight. I much prefer ordering from a real person than a machine," commented Annie. "You can't ask a machine for its opinion."

"Just give it time my dear, I'm sure they'll have that eventually."

They ordered a bottle of red wine to go with their meal but were surprised to receive a bottle of expensive champagne as well.

"We didn't order this," Henry told the waiter.

"No, it's from the gentleman over there," the waiter indicated to a couple behind him.

They were both familiar.

"Oh my god," mouthed Annie to Henry.

It took him longer to register who it was but then it came to him. It was the Whites; Rufus White and Jenna White, the woman who got Lucinda Willis's body instead of Annie.

"That was supposed to me," Annie whispered.

Both Annie and Henry couldn't help but stare at Jenna White.

The Whites raised their glasses towards the Marlows, who sat there speechless. This prompted Jenna White to come over to the table.

"Oh no, she's coming over, Henry," whispered Annie.

Annie knew how much Henry resented the Whites for outbidding them and putting Annie's life in danger.

"Dr Marlow, you obviously don't remember me but you treated me a few years ago," said the woman. "What a small world. Fancy seeing you here. What are you doing in Boston?"

Henry composed himself.

"Of course I remember you; it's just a shock to see you, that's all."

Jenna White turned her attention to Annie and introduced herself.

"Yes, I know exactly who you are," Annie replied quite abruptly.

She shrugged at Henry. Jenna, obviously feeling uncomfortable, apologised for interrupting their meal and walked back to her table, no doubt to tell her husband how rude the Marlows were.

"Sorry Henry, I had no idea I felt such anger towards them as well."

"That's understandable, they nearly screwed everything up for us. But I'm curious. Did Lucinda change her mind or did the Whites outbid us? Felix said he didn't know so I let it go. But now they're sitting there, I could find out?"

"Does it matter?" asked Annie.

"Probably not..." replied Henry. "But damn it, Annie. I want to find out. Let's go over and talk to them. Those rich bastards could have left our children without a mum just because they have more money than us. I shouldn't interrogate them, it would be unprofessional but you bloody well can."

Annie needed little encouragement and with that, she grabbed the champagne bottle and strode straight over to their table. Henry followed right behind as he was worried about what she was planning on doing with the champagne bottle. Luckily, she just sat down at their table and thanked them for the champagne.

"I hope you don't mind us coming over but I wanted to thank you for the champagne, it's a lovely gesture. Please share it with us."

Henry glared at his wife but she took no notice as she poured the drinks.

"Henry, bring our glasses over too," she asked sweetly.

He did as he was told and then sat down with them as they made a toast to Henry.

Henry apologised to Jenna for their apparent rudeness, explaining it had been a shock to see her.

"You've never seen one of your patients after the operation before?" she asked.

After Hannah Ford, one of his first patients, he made sure he kept in contact with most of his patients to make sure they were learning to adjust to their new bodies. It helped with future patients as he could pass on their experiences. He also encouraged the legitimate cases to keep in touch with each other as their experiences were relatively unique and only someone who had been through the same procedure could truly understand. His bedside manner with the Whites had been cold, to say the least, so he was not surprised to think that Jenna assumed he never kept in contact with his patients.

"No, it's not that. It's just the circumstances and

the skin that you inherited," Henry told her.

She looked confused so Annie decided to get straight to the point.

"What my husband is trying to say is that I was supposed to get Lucinda Willis's body."

"Oh, I had no idea. I heard you went through the operation too but wasn't that before me?" Jenna asked.

"Yes, we selected Lucinda as soon as we knew I was dying."

Rufus White interrupted, "I'm not sure what you're implying, but we weren't given a selection. We were only told at the time of Jenna's diagnosis that there was an available donor and that we were locked in unless she changed her mind."

"So you didn't put in a higher bid at any time?" asked Annie.

"No, never; we were told a price and we paid it," Rufus replied.

"Oh...we were under the impression that Lucinda Willis asked for more money but I guess she simply changed her mind when I was dying and then changed it back a few months later for Jenna?" said Annie.

"Yes, that's probably what happened," Rufus agreed. "She must have changed her mind; a death row prisoner would hardly require extra money. But just so you know, we were aware of Jenna's condition for quite a while. We were promised our donor three years before the operation. It was always Lucinda Willis, they told us her name at the start."

Annie and Henry looked at each other, now they were really confused.

"But I sat down with Annie about two years after that, they told me Lucinda was available. We opted for her and were told two weeks before Annie would have actually died that Lucinda had pulled out."

"That can't be right, we had her locked in and contracted to us. She never changed her mind and the procedure went through as expected. Sorry Dr Marlow, but I think you're getting your wires crossed. Maybe you got the wrong name?" Rufus tried to explain.

"Please, can we stop talking about this?" asked Jenna.

The Marlows apologised again and went back to their table.

"My god, we're like vultures, fighting over a dead body. I believe them, so what the hell is going on?" Annie asked.

"I have no idea but I intend to find out when we get home."

Henry couldn't relax for the rest of their short break and as soon as he got back to the UK he messaged Felix to request a quick catch up. It was evening time and Felix suggested they meet in the office in the morning but Henry was adamant, so they met in a quiet coffee shop in the city.

"How was your holiday?" asked Felix.

Henry ignored the question.

"Shut up Felix, I want the truth. Lucinda Willis,

you remember her?" he asked.

Felix twitched slightly as he confirmed he remembered her.

"Tell me exactly what happened and why she couldn't be Annie's donor?"

Felix sighed; "we've been through this before; she probably changed her mind or was holding out for a better offer. I don't know, we don't press the prisoners on their choices."

"Well, I do know. She was never scheduled to be Annie's donor. She was already contracted to Jenna White, who was diagnosed much earlier than Annie. They were told Lucinda would be their donor."

"I don't know what to say. There must have been a mistake," offered Felix.

"We don't make mistakes like that. You don't make mistakes like that; you're meticulous. So Felix, don't take me for a fool. I believe the Whites and not you. Tell me what the hell happened back then and make sure it's the truth otherwise I walk away from the whole project."

Felix stared at Henry for a few moments before speaking; "I don't know if I should tell you or not."

"Just tell me," Henry was feeling impatient by now.

"There was never a female donor for Annie. They were all assigned by the time you came to us," admitted Felix.

"So what the hell was the point of the pretence?"

"To get your hopes up, to dash them and then to make you desperate."

"But why?"

"So you'd come aboard and agree to the private donors," said Felix.

Henry shook his head. This was too much to take in.

"So you knew all along that there was no viable donor for Annie and you built our hopes up like that. How could you Felix!"

"I had no choice. I was forced into it by James and I owe him. He felt the whole operation was becoming stagnant by the lack of bodies. He'd already started delving into the possibility. I was supposed to talk you into accepting private donors but you came to us with Annie's illness. James was delighted at the timing, so he took advantage. I knew how much you loved Annie and wouldn't let her die."

"Let me get this straight - James was in on it all along? You bastards!" yelled Henry, accidentally knocking his coffee off the table. "And what the hell does James have over you anyway?" he asked, although he didn't care anymore.

Before Felix could answer, the waiter came over to clean up the mess. Henry calmed down and told Felix he was out.

"That's the final straw Felix, I'm done. I'll complete our existing obligations as I don't want to let anyone down. But don't get any more patients in. I'm shutting this down. The company will cease trading. It was never meant to be like this. We had ideals, remember Felix, when we first started? How could you let it go so badly wrong?"

Felix just shook his head; for once he had no answer. Henry stood up and left the coffee shop; he felt a huge sense of relief. He just had to figure out how to tell Annie.

Annie was eager to hear what the mix up was about, so Henry sat her down and told her the truth. She was as angry and upset as Henry expected her to be.

"How could you let me take the body of some innocent person? It was hard enough accepting a new body. I thought they were going to die anyway and didn't deserve to live because they did awful things. But someone just desperate for money? That's not right," she wept.

"Annie, you were about to die. I had no choice. I was the one in the room with the kids when we visited you. You were too out of it to notice how devastated they were. You would have done the same."

"I don't know, Henry."

"Please forgive me?" he pleaded.

"Oh Henry, this is such a mess. Do you think you'll be able to walk away?" she asked.

"Yes, don't worry about that. I should have never let it get this far."

CHAPTER 29

As expected, James was at the clinic the next morning.

"What a surprise to see you, James," said Henry.

"Cut the shit, Henry. Felix told me everything. You can't walk away. You're too involved already. Annie is alive because of me. If it wasn't for me, she wouldn't have had a skin," James said.

"Don't pretend you did any of this out of the goodness of your heart. Annie and I are prepared to accept the consequences if you choose to make this difficult for us. All I propose to do is shut the company, quietly walk away and no one will ever find out why."

Henry felt confident. James and Felix were too deeply involved, they would never say anything.

"Really, you want to walk away from your life's work? What about the next time a friend comes to you or even one of your children, in a few years, when they become sick. You won't help them?" asked James.

"Yes, I'm prepared to walk away. My work was never about how much money I could make, it was

206

to help people. I don't want to help some people while other people are needlessly dying just so they can become donors. I'm here to save lives not swap them. I'm out and there's nothing you can do to stop me."

"Fine, leave. I wanted you to remain the face of the company but we can find a better spokesperson. We don't need you; the machines are automated and the code can be infiltrated and changed. It's really not a big deal; we would have done that before if you hadn't gone along with it."

"No," shouted Henry. "There is no way I'm leaving this company in your hands. I dread to think what the pair of you would do to it and how far you would go. It's my name that has the approval to operate. Without me the company will lose its licence," Henry reminded them.

"Very well, you can stay but keep your mouth shut. We'll keep the details away from you but you'll operate as normal," James told Henry in his calm voice.

Henry was becoming tired of repeating himself; once again he refused to go along with James.

James looked towards Felix; "do you want to explain or shall I?"

Felix, who had been very quiet up until now, just sighed; "no, I will."

"Good, let's catch up later," James said as he walked away.

Henry couldn't believe the sheer arrogance of the man but was relieved when he left the room. He looked towards Felix; "there is nothing you can say to make me continue working with that arrogant, piece of..."

"Stop it, Henry," Felix interrupted, "let's take a walk and I'll explain everything."

It was a balmy, spring day as the two men left the building and walked aimlessly down the street in an uncomfortable silence.

"What's he got on you, Felix?" Henry eventually asked.

"It's a long story."

"I'm almost retired, so I've got all the time in the world," Henry told him.

Felix nodded towards a bench on the street; they both sat down.

"Okay Felix, I'll indulge you. Tell me everything," Henry said, wondering what on earth Felix could say to make him change his mind.

Felix apologised and told Henry everything. He admitted to knowing James Talbot before Marlow Enterprise became private; when he was looking after the government funded accounts. Felix always had an eye for the finer things in life and lived above his means. He admitted to being vain and shallow and liked to show off so he wanted the best car, the latest gadgets, the best apartment as well as designer clothes and furniture. Henry was aware of this and it often amused him and Annie how much he was willing to spend on a car or a new suit.

Worst of all, gambling gradually took hold of him. Felix led Henry to believe he could live like this because he had made some wise investments. However, in reality, Felix never had any money to invest – he just couldn't hold onto it. That's when he admitted to Henry that he misused the project funding. He started shaving from the funds, a little bit here and there, just small amounts at first so no one would notice. He faked the receipts of how much all the equipment was and told Henry the project was costing much more than it actually was. Felix knew how passionate Henry was and how persuasive he was in front of the funding committee. So Felix assumed Henry would receive additional funding to cover any shortfalls.

However, when he learnt the company was to be audited, he panicked. Henry was easily fooled by the fake accounts but he wasn't confident in his ability to fool an expert. So he needed to inject the money back into the company. Felix explained how a friend from his gambling circle knew of someone who could help him out. That's when he was introduced to James Talbot. James was only too happy to cover the shortfall in funding. At the time, Felix was desperate so he took it without asking too many questions.

Felix knew the Marlow project was close to a breakthrough so assumed there would be additional funding and when that happened, he expected to receive a large pay rise. James led him to believe that he expected Felix to repay the loan with extortionate interest. However, James never demanded the money back, he told Felix to pay him back when he could. So Felix started to put money aside and tried to keep away from gambling so when James did ask for the money, at least Felix could pay him off in instalments.

When it became apparent the company would have to become private as the Government could no longer fund them, that's when James came back on the scene. Instead of Felix paying James back, all he had to do was vouch for James and arrange a meeting with Henry and then persuade Henry to accept James' terms.

"So you put my company in the hands of someone you barely knew and lied to me about his credentials?" asked Henry. "You're an idiot Felix but it's not my problem. You've said nothing to make me want to stay."

"Unfortunately, it's not that simple."

Felix explained that James' connections went a lot deeper than he initially thought. James' eagerness to invest in Marlow Enterprise was because of its huge potential to launder money. James was connected to the Russian mafia and he saw Marlow Enterprise as the perfect place to clean his money. At first, when the business was legitimate, only small amounts were laundered. The prisoners were offered much lower sums of money than Henry was led to believe. It wasn't enough, they had to increase business and the only way to do this was to increase the supply.

James wanted Henry fully on board; hence the plan to make him so desperate, he would agree to their new chain of supply, who were the volunteers mainly from the Eastern Bloc. So currently, they've increased the business volume which meant their ability to launder more money has increased.

However, it was still not enough and James always saw the company becoming much bigger on a global scale. Currently, James was still lobbying to change the laws to make it mandatory for all death row prisoners to donate their bodies. Apparently, he knew some people he could bribe to hopefully fast track this change but he needed Dr Marlow at the head of the company to provide the legitimacy of the business.

Once the laws were changed, Henry wouldn't be needed any longer and they could go global. There were enough death row prisoners across the world that Marlow Enterprise would offer them an undisclosed amount of compensation towards their family, yet put a larger amount through the books. The same method would also be applied regarding the cost of the operation for the recipient. The globalisation of the company also meant more premises, more staff and more equipment, which meant the opportunities for laundering were substantial and would make James Talbot a formidable player in the world of business.

"Money laundering?" Henry was in shock.

He just thought James was a greedy bastard, not some mafia mastermind.

"And you knew about this? He told you all of this?"

"He's given me the bigger picture of his plans; I've filled in the blanks. And you know what it's like, you get drawn in and then you're in too deep to get out. I never realised he had such grand plans for us. I thought the company would stay small scale but he became greedy and saw the potential. There's nothing we can do to stop him."

Henry stood up and shouted at Felix; "nothing we can do! Like hell there isn't. I've made a few mistakes but I'm not letting you drag me down to your level. I'm reporting the lot of you, now!"

Felix's phone rang so Henry took this opportunity to back away and reach for his phone to call the police.

"Don't do that Henry," Felix called after him. He held his phone up; "it's James on the line. I think you should take it."

Like hell he would, thought Henry. Felix caught up with him and showed him his phone. It was a video call and James was with Annie. Henry hung up his own phone just when the operator answered.

"Hi Henry, I'm just catching up with Annie; we're waiting for you," said James from the phone.

A confused looking Annie waved at Henry from James' screen. "Hi Henry, apparently, you invited James over for dinner tonight?"

She then turned to James and apologised for her husband's lack of manners in not informing her of the arrangement and for the lack of food in the house. He told her not to think anything of it and that he would come back another time. He asked

Henry to stay on the line while he said goodbye to Annie and the kids. Henry waited until he was sure James was out of the house. His heart was racing; he was furious with this man.

"What the hell do you think you are doing turning up at my home?" Henry demanded.

"I just want you to have a think about our current arrangement before you do anything stupid like going to the authorities," James told Henry in his usual cool, calm voice.

"Are you threatening me?" asked Henry.

"I only want to remind you that I know all about you, where you live and who the most important people are in your life. You have such a beautiful family, Henry; your children are a credit to you. I see them having a bright future. It would be a pity if anything happened to any of them."

"You stay away from my family, do you hear me? This is between you and me!" Henry yelled as he clutched the phone tightly.

"No, Henry, this is between me, you and your family now. Toe the line, otherwise, your family will be in danger. And don't test me otherwise I will demonstrate what I can do."

As soon as he finished talking, James hung up the phone. Henry was shaking and he squeezed the phone in his fist before launching it straight at Felix's head. The phone smashed on the floor causing on-lookers to stop and ask if Felix was okay. He waved them away as he clutched his head. Henry grabbed Felix by the collar and slammed him against the wall.

"What have you got me into?" he demanded.

"Stop it, Henry, I'm sorry. I would have never got involved if I'd known what type of man he was."

"Why didn't you just come to me in the first place? I would have helped you?" wept Henry as he let go of Felix.

"No you wouldn't have, I was squandering your funding. You would have had me charged with embezzlement. I was desperate," Felix replied.

"So you've gone along with everything and brought this madman into my company just so your gambling debts were paid off?"

"No, I did try to stop him; I felt uneasy with his level of involvement. When I found out he wanted to trick you into accepting the private donors, I threatened to tell you the truth but he made sure I didn't. He thought you were so sensible that instead of becoming desperate you and Annie would come to terms with her death instead of opting for the Russian donor. I knew how much you loved Annie; I didn't believe you'd simply accept her death without doing everything you could. That day you were waiting to receive details for the potential donors for Annie; I was late because my mother was in the hospital."

"Yes, I remember that. She had a stroke, didn't she?" Henry said as he took his hands off Felix.

"No, they made it look as though she had a stroke. Just before it happened my mum had a visitor from someone who said they were from the clinic. I have no idea who he was but he said he worked with me and she invited him for a cup of tea. Whoever it was, he was the one who called the ambulance and got her to hospital. Then I got a warning from James telling me not to interfere and that next time it wouldn't just be a mild stroke."

Henry turned away from Felix and paced around, clutching his head and muttering to himself. He couldn't believe what he was hearing. If he didn't go along with this, his family would be in danger. But on the other hand, he couldn't keep the company open knowing what James was doing.

"This is madness Felix, do you really want to go along with it a minute longer?" Henry asked.

"Not really, but I've embezzled and my mum's life as well as my own, have both been threatened. I'd rather just keep going as we are. You're still saving lives. You and James have actually been lobbying to make death row donors mandatory. You're working towards the same goal. If you help him do that, then we can stop using the illegal volunteers."

"But he's using the company to launder his money. What misery and death does that money come from? We're not saving lives, we're just re-placing them."

Felix nodded his head, "I'm not doing anything, Henry. Let's just keep our heads down and carry on with business as usual. It's not worth the risk to Annie and the kids."

Henry nodded and relented. He agreed he wouldn't risk the kids and told Felix to let James know he would go along with it; as long as he agreed the long-term aim was to stop using voluntary donors. Felix assured Henry that he was doing the right thing and that he would pass on the message to James.

CHAPTER 30

Henry walked away and rushed home to be with his family. Before he walked through the front door he looked around to see if anyone was watching them. There was no one. Annie greeted him immediately at the door and asked why he forgot to tell her about James and why was he home so late.

"Annie, I don't have time to explain but pack a bag, grab the kids. We've got to get out of here. We're in danger."

"What are you talking about?" Annie thought Henry was joking for a moment but she saw the panic in his eyes. "You're not joking, are you?"

Henry grabbed Annie's hands and told her they had been threatened. He promised to tell her everything once they got to a safe place.

"Oh my god Henry, what the hell?" she started sobbing and he hugged her.

"I'm sorry, Annie, but we have to go now."

He dashed upstairs and grabbed their documentation and threw a few things in his bag. Annie was crying and packing at the same time. She ushered the sleepy kids out of bed and strapped them into the car. They asked where they were going, so she told them they were going on a surprise holiday. The kids were too sleepy to notice how upset their mum was.

"Where are we going?" she whispered to Henry.

He sat back for a moment; he had no idea. He just knew he wanted to get out of the country.

"We'll head for the airport and book the first flight to America. It's a big place and we'll drive to the middle of nowhere. I've had a lot of clients from there who said if we ever needed a favour, just look them up. I think this constitutes a favour."

As he was about to start the car, his phone rang. It was James. He threw the phone out of the window, told Annie to do the same thing and turned on the car. Just then there was a knock on the window. Henry and Annie jumped in fright. He wound down the window and a figure bent down and peered through.

"Are you going somewhere, Dr Marlow?" asked the shadowy figure.

"Who are you?" Henry asked as he felt his voice falter.

"Turn off the car and step outside, both of you," he demanded, as he flashed a quick glimpse of his gun under his jacket.

Henry glanced towards Annie, who looked terrified. She nodded towards him so they both stepped out of the car. The stranger picked up Henry's phone from the floor and made a call. He handed it to Henry; it was James on the line again.

"I thought we'd cleared this up? You can't run away; you're being followed and I mean all of you. I've put tracking devices on your entire family and I know where you are at all times. The next time you try to run away, I will catch you. I will then make you choose which one of them I kill first. All you have to do is carry on as normal. I'm not asking you to get involved in the running of the company. You just have to continue saving lives. We have the same goals. Now, have I made myself clear or do you need a demonstration of what I can do?"

Henry shook his head.

"I can't hear you, Henry," said James.

"You've made yourself very clear," confirmed Henry.

"Good, I'll see you tomorrow at the clinic. Remember, you've been lucky tonight. I have a great deal of respect for you and your work. Don't test me again. Good night Henry and apologise to Annie if we scared her."

James hung up and the stranger walked away. Henry told Annie to put the kids back to bed as he got the bags out of the car. The kids were disappointed not to go on their impromptu holiday. Once they were tucked up in bed, Henry sat Annie down and told her everything. Neither of them slept very well that night.

Henry and Annie agreed that they couldn't risk the children's lives until they could come up with a plan. So far, they couldn't think of anything so Henry continued with his daily routine. He clocked in, performed the operations and clocked out. He barely showed any interest in any of the patients. Felix encouraged him to engage a bit more and to join forces with James to speed up the lobbying. Henry was torn, he wanted nothing to do with James but he wanted to stop the voluntary donors. However, he also didn't want this company to expand or go global as that would play straight into James' hands. In the meantime, he had as little to do with Felix as possible and he barely saw James, who wasn't usually at the clinic. Although James made sure he called Henry every few days to ensure he was still onboard and made lightly veiled threats to remind Henry who was in charge.

As a gesture of goodwill from James, he fixed it so once a month, a patient who normally wouldn't be considered, as they couldn't afford it, were now eligible for the operation. This made the whole situation slightly more bearable. But the downside of this was the huge waiting list of people desperate for their second chance and Henry had to play God and make the decision of who was selected. As a pragmatic man, he would choose the person on the list who was the closest match to the available donor. This at least meant something good came out of the whole awful situation.

CHAPTER 31

"How did you and Annie cope knowing you were being tracked?" asked Joe.

"It was dreadful. We felt on edge all the time. James had been in our home but we didn't know if he'd planted anything there. We checked everywhere but couldn't find any bugs. I even bought equipment to detect for any listening devices in the house, car, office and of course our clothes but I never found anything. Not to say there wasn't anything. You know what technology is like, it's constantly evolving and some listening devices are so minuscule now and can avoid detection. Annie and I decided it was best to assume the worst and that every word we spoke could be heard. It made for difficult conversations; we did a lot of note passing and whispering. We took many long drives in the middle of the countryside for picnics with the children to discuss matters in private and try to come up with plans to escape our predicament. But it always came back to the same thing – the fear of what might happen to our family. I promised Annie she had nothing to be scared of and if we went along with it for the time being, I would eventually think of a way out for us."

"So in the meantime can you tell me about any of the case studies who received the pro bono treatment?" asked Joe.

Henry was surprised by the abrupt change of subject.

"Sure, we had quite a few worthy cases come and go. It gave me the motivation to continue and took my mind off everything else that was going on. Because I got to pick the candidate, I tended to go for people with kids or younger adults with their lives still ahead of them. Anyone with a criminal record was denied, not that they weren't deserving. After all, they may have gone to a great deal of effort to improve their lives. But the list was so long that we had to make cuts. Anyone with dementia in the family was denied. I preferred to go for people who would never be in the position to afford it and who I hoped would still make a difference in the world; even if it was just a small difference. So I focused on anyone who dedicated their time on research of life-threatening diseases, or even volunteers at charities. Wait, did you say your name was Slater?" asked Henry.

Joe nodded.

"We had a Patrick Slater a few years back. In fact, you look familiar. Are you related?"

Joe smiled and told Henry that Patrick was his father.

"My goodness, what a small world," commented

Henry. "How is he?"

"He's doing great. All thanks to you."

"Why didn't you mention it as soon as you met me?" asked Henry.

"I don't know; I guess I wanted to see if you would remember me or if my father would come up naturally in the story. I also want you to remember I'm here on a professional basis and not a personal one."

"I see," said Henry. "Well, seeing as you steered the interview towards your father, let's talk about him. Patrick was a marvellous success story. I'm sure I would have mentioned him eventually. I picked Patrick because as you know he was such a worthy candidate."

The mention of Patrick brought a smile to Joe's face.

"Yes, you remind me of my dad. He was a bit like you in the beginning, an idealist. He was extremely determined, intelligent and wanted to make a mark and to make the world a better place. He studied law at university, just when the law was changing. It was a worrying time for him as the UK originally abolished the death penalty in 1965 but like most countries of the world, had decided to bring it back..."

Patrick Slater

Patrick was sitting his final law exam at Cambridge. It was one of the easiest papers he'd had so far and he was in a hurry to get out of the exam room to check the news. Today was the day that parliament was voting on the death penalty; the decision would be made while Patrick was sitting in this exam. He dashed outside and switched his phone on. Before it turned on, someone shouted out in the corridor that the death penalty was reinstated. He felt so disappointed and hoped they got it wrong. But no, his phone notified him of breaking news. Parliament had indeed voted in favour of the death penalty.

"It's such a step backwards for this country. We're supposed to be innovative and forward thinking. Instead, we're heading back to medieval times," Patrick complained over his pint with a friend at the student bar.

"It's because of innovation and technology that we're in this position. Everyone knows everything now; all the good and certainly all the bad. We're fed every tiny morsel of detail of all the most dreadful crimes committed. People are baying for blood. Enough is enough. Do you really want paedophiles and serial killers walking the streets?" asked Anthony, Patrick's closest friend at university.

It was the rape, torture and finally the slow death of six-year-old Toby Roberts which ignited the latest debate. All the sickening details of this case were published everywhere and you couldn't escape it. People had had enough of sick perverts and they wanted the punishment to fit the crime. Patrick agreed that the perpetrator of this particular crime didn't deserve to live but he just couldn't seem to agree with the death penalty.

"What are they supposed to do with him? Leave him in prison for the rest of his life, courtesy of the taxpayer? It's not as if he'll be dragged out into the streets and locked up in the stocks and eventually have his head chopped off. He'll serve a bit of cushy gaol time and then have a nice sleep. It will be a much more dignified, less painful death than that poor boy," argued Anthony.

"I know, but it's a slippery slope. Yes, I'm not concerned with perverts like the Robert's murderer. But now the law has been passed, where do we draw the line? What crime deserves the death penalty? And you know my biggest reservation; that we send someone innocent to their death. I think even hundreds of executions of the biggest scumbags in the world would be negated by the execution of one innocent person," Patrick counter-argued.

"Unlikely, not with the amount of technology and DNA information we have," said Anthony.

"That can all be tampered with, we're not above corruption."

"Look, we'll just have to agree to disagree. We're celebrating our finals and this announcement could make our careers very interesting indeed," said Anthony.

It certainly did make Patrick's career interesting as he became a prosecuting barrister and found himself arguing in favour of the death penalty on more than one occasion. He still was not an advocate of it but unfortunately, some of the criminals he was prosecuting, were automatically assigned the death penalty if their particular crime fell into the appropriate criteria. Crimes such as aggravated murder, the murder of a police officer, treason, high scale drug-dealing and any offence such as rape or torture of a child automatically qualified, if found guilty.

One of Patrick's cases as a prosecuting barrister involved an African migrant named Samuel Oni, who was found guilty of attempting a large-scale terror attack on Wembley Stadium during a sell out football match. If successful, he'd have killed approximately ninety-thousand people, many of whom were children. His sophisticated bomb and cool demeanour got him past security. He was only foiled when he slowly opened his coat, said a prayer and held out the trigger to set off the bomb. Some eagle-eyed spectators sitting nearby spotted him and managed to wrestle the trigger out of his hand.

Despite being caught red-handed, Samuel always protested his innocence. He said he suffered from black-outs and had no recollection of going into the stadium. He admitted initially showing an interest in the Chewa Delta group before they became a well-known terrorist organisation. Samuel argued that he only attended the early meetings because he loved his country, Nigeria, and thought this group was about uniting Nigeria and making it strong again. Once he realised they were actually a group of extremists, he backed away. Eventually, he put any involvement with the group to the back of his mind and got on with his life. He moved to London with his family where he became a financial analyst for an international accounting firm. He met up with fellow expats from his home country where they would reminisce and talk politics.

It was only when he moved to London that he first started to suffer from black-outs and occasionally a few hours of his day would be unaccounted for. The courts had Samuel's medical records which confirmed he had seen a doctor about his problem, but no medical explanation had been found. The defence brought in their own specialist to check Samuel but again they found no evidence to corroborate Samuel's claims. Patrick argued that Samuel was trying to use mental incapacity as an excuse to cheat the death penalty. The jury agreed and Samuel was sentenced to death. He pleaded his innocence until his final day, where he was executed by lethal injection and the baying public now had their pound of flesh.

The verdict never sat right for Patrick. He saw the confusion and terror in Samuel's eyes on a daily basis in court. This did not match the calm, cool exterior of the person who entered Wembley Stadium that day. Patrick saw Samuel's wife pleading and crying daily at the courtroom. He couldn't help but feel sorry for them, but Samuel was caught red-handed and Patrick assumed he regretted his actions only because he was caught. The thoughts of what could have happened that day if Samuel hadn't been caught made Patrick shudder. But still, he did not believe in the death penalty. Samuel Oni was just a small part of the terrorist cell; if he'd received life imprisonment, then he may have eventually given more information about The Chewa Delta group. Now all his secrets would go to the grave with him.

Some days after the execution, there was breaking news. It was reported that the terrorist group had developed an interesting technique where they had recruited a more modern type of witch doctor; witch doctors with backgrounds in hypnosis. Someone with a guilty conscience within the group had broken ranks and had come forward. This is how they claimed Samuel Oni was tricked into attempting the attack. There were international debates on whether this level of hypnotism could be possible. Patrick immediately knew it was possible. The man in the court was a scared and confused family man, not the international mastermind behind such a heinous plot. Samuel was dead and there was no way to check if he had been hypnotised so he could receive a pardon. The pardon would be little comfort to his wife and child but it would have been better than nothing.

From that moment, Patrick lost all his enthusiasm for prosecuting and making money. Instead, he worked tirelessly as an international human rights lawyer, concentrating on cases concerning the poorest and most underprivileged in society and working endlessly to highlight their plights.

Joe spoke fondly of his father. Even though he barely saw his dad during these years and they often struggled for money, he and his brothers were all so proud of him. Sometimes if his father was abroad for an indefinite period of time, the boys were taken out of school and educated abroad.

"It was interesting to suddenly go from the local comprehensive in London to a makeshift hut somewhere in Africa for our daily lessons. Dad wanted us to experience all aspects of life, not just one where everything was handed to us on a plate. It opened my eyes to the world and I think I got my passion to tell stories from those experiences plus all the stories dad told us about his cases. He was much happier working as a human rights lawyer than as a stuffy barrister in London. He felt more relaxed. Then he got sick, there was nothing that could be done. He wasn't ready to die; there was so much more that he wanted to fight for, but we couldn't afford your operation. I was the one who insisted he put his name down on your list but we knew it was a long shot. Then we got the call, telling us dad had been chosen as a candidate. I had to talk him into it; persuade him to do it for us, as he's firmly against the death penalty." Joe paused for a moment..."I just want to say thank you. It brought the family closer than ever. We all really appreciate what you did for us. And my father, as you know is still out there somewhere defending minorities."

"It was nothing," Henry replied modestly. "I'm just glad that someone so remarkable and with such a high sense of values could benefit from my work."

A silence fell in the room. Eventually, Joe spoke

first and asked Henry if he was okay to continue. Henry agreed. He enjoyed the reminiscing.

"As you know I started resenting the rich recipients. Somehow they always got attractive skins; I felt like I was a plastic surgeon and not a scientist saving lives," said Henry.

"But you were saving lives, these wealthy recipients were all dying," Joe reminded Henry.

"That's what I thought until I met a woman called Amelia Jarvis."

CHAPTER 32

Amelia Jarvis

Amelia appeared to have it all; her son Arthur who she loved more than anything in the world, a beautiful house, plenty of money and marriage to her childhood sweetheart. Yet she was seriously unhappy. She and Teddy had been together for twenty-five years since they were sixteen. She was the shy girl in class and Teddy was the charismatic, confident know-all whom she couldn't stand the first time they met. Initially, she thought him cocky and arrogant. But for some reason, they started to sit together on a regular basis in business studies and she found herself looking forward to this particular class. As a teenager, she'd always felt insecure so when Teddy started to show an interest in her, she took it to mean he liked her as a friend. He couldn't possibly be interested in her in any other way? After all, she saw herself as a plain Jane and he was good-looking.

They started waiting for each other after college and walking to the bus stop together. One day, Teddy asked Amelia out to the cinema. She accepted and when he tried to kiss her, she was con-fused. She thought they were going to the cinema as friends. He couldn't possibly have any romantic inclination towards her? There were much prettier girls at college who'd love to go out with Teddy. He insisted he really liked her and thought she was pretty. It took a while for her to accept his inter-est was genuine and that he did see her as pretty. That was when she could relax and enjoy the start of their life-long romance.

They both went to different universities but missed each other immensely and saw each other as much as possible during the holidays. Once univer-sity was complete, they moved to London together where they both became financial advisors. They enjoyed London life, the parties and exotic holi-days. After about ten years together they married in a beautiful ceremony and invited all their old col-lege and university friends. Amelia and Teddy were still completely in love with each other; people always commented on what a happy couple they made.

Eventually, Teddy became a broker on the stock exchange, in which he did extremely well for him-self. The money was coming in so fast that after the birth of Arthur, Amelia decided not to go back to work. She didn't feel the need. They didn't depend on her money and Amelia enjoyed motherhood. Amelia endured a complicated birth in which she and Arthur both nearly died. Arthur would be her only child, so Amelia and Teddy agreed for her to leave work and dedicate herself to the upbringing of their son. Initially, she and Teddy enjoyed the arrangement and Amelia never previously liking work, now didn't dread her day any longer. Teddy was making so much money that she didn't need to worry about such things any more. She spent time with her baby and had much more energy for Teddy when he came home. Gradually though as Teddy gained promotion after promotion he was at home less and less. Once Arthur went to school and didn't need her as much, she felt increasingly isolated and found comfort in watching television and eating. She told herself she would exercise it off the next day but struggled to find the motivation to do so. Gradually, she gained weight; a lot of weight. Teddy lost interest in her and she lost interest in sex anyway. Her thoughts were consumed by what she would eat that day. Teddy encouraged her to join a gym and offered to get her a personal trainer. She went along with it, but couldn't stick with any plans. Besides, the exercise made her even more hungry. They had an indoor swimming pool and she attempted some lengths but found herself floating around instead, looking up at the ceiling. Teddy worked late and he crept into bed after she went to sleep. Days went by when they barely saw each other.

One night, she suggested they go out for dinner and Teddy reluctantly agreed. She felt judged every time she ate something. She commented on how they ought to make a bit more of an effort with each other as she barely saw him anymore and she missed him. He didn't say anything. She promised to lose the weight but he only rolled his eyes.

"What?" she asked.

"You always promise to lose the weight, yet you do nothing about it," he told her.

"I'll try harder," she promised.

He shook his head; "it's not just the weight. Don't you feel as though we've missed out on life by never being with anyone else?"

Absolutely not; she never felt like that.

"What are you saying Teddy?" she asked.

"I just don't want to go through the rest of our lives never having slept with someone else, or even never having sex again."

"We'll have sex again; I'll make more of an effort. Come home early or I'll wait up for you," she pleaded.

Teddy looked disgusted; "I'm sorry Amelia but I'm not physically attracted to you anymore. I miss the old Amelia who wanted to do things, go places and who took care of herself."

Amelia was shocked. She knew she had let herself go but she didn't think Teddy felt this strongly about it.

"How can you be so cruel?" she asked.

"I'm sorry Amelia but I have to be truthful. I want out. I'll always look after you and Arthur but I'm too young to be in a sexless marriage and I'm really sorry to say but I'm embarrassed to be seen out with you."

An uncomfortable silence followed as Amelia tried not to cry. Eventually, she excused herself and took a taxi home. As she sat in the taxi sobbing, she couldn't believe her life was falling apart. This sent her into a spiral of depression as she barely saw Teddy at home anymore as she stayed in bed eating and crying. When she did see Teddy, she begged him not to leave her; Arthur wouldn't be able to cope without his dad around. He reluctantly agreed not to leave until Arthur was a little older but she had to promise in the meantime to lose the weight by drastic measures. Reluctantly, she agreed to weight loss surgery. At this point, she would have done anything to make sure Teddy stayed with her.

For a couple of years, the surgery helped and with exercise and a controlled diet she managed to keep the weight off. She pretended to be happy as Teddy seemed happier with her and they even started sleeping together again. The talk of separation stopped; she hoped he wouldn't bring it up again. However, this always made her feel on edge so after a couple of years, the effort all became too much. She turned back to her old friend, food, and the weight rapidly piled on. She stayed in bed all day and watched telly when Arthur was at school; the only time she got up was to replenish her snacks. Amelia wanted to be left alone. One afternoon, Teddy came home early and saw what she was doing; she jumped out of bed, trying to hide the empty packets.

"Amelia, I've been nothing but supportive of you

over the last few years but you've done nothing. You've hung around the house, moping about. I caught a glimmer of the old Amelia that I fell in love with when you had the surgery but look, you're back to how you were before. It's not working out, I love you and you'll always be my best friend but I think that's just what we should be from now on."

"No, please don't leave me. You're my best friend too and you can't do this to Arthur. He needs you around," pleaded Amelia.

"Stop using Arthur as an excuse. He needs a mother who isn't a fat slob, lying in bed all day. He needs a mother that's he's not ashamed to be seen with!" Teddy shouted at her.

He packed a bag, told her he would be in touch and left the house.

Amelia sobbed. She couldn't believe he could be so cruel. When Arthur returned home from school, he confirmed his friends made fun of her and he was embarrassed by her. He wanted to go and live with his dad. That weekend, she was all alone in her big house and the two men in her life had abandoned her. She left endless messages with Teddy, telling him how much she loved him and that she was prepared to do anything.

A few months later, Teddy came to see her. She hugged him as soon as he walked through the door. She cried and told him how she missed her best friend.

"I miss you too Amelia. I can't imagine life without you but you've always been uncomfortable in your own skin. You've always had these feelings of unworthiness and I've tried to show you how beautiful I thought you were but now you look like this, I can't do it anymore."

She looked at herself in the mirror and saw how big she'd become and as always saw how ugly she was. She agreed with him and asked what they should do. Teddy mentioned that one of his clients was part-owner of Marlow Enterprise. He'd had a meeting with him a few weeks ago and they got involved in a discussion about body donors.

"I'm sorry Amelia, but I told him I wished I could get a new body for you as you're perfect inside. It was just meant as a flippant remark but James said it was possible. He told me to contact him if I was ever serious about it. I immediately told him no but now I've been thinking about it. It could be the answer to our problems."

"You can't be serious, Teddy?" Amelia interrupted.

"Look, you've always had a thing about the way you look even though you didn't need to and I think that's caused the depression and over-eating. Now that you're so big, you feel there's no way back. How about you get a fresh start? If you look different then you might feel differently about yourself and it might stop the eating. Then we could try again."

Amelia paused and thought about it for a minute; she'd always wished she looked like someone else.

"But aren't the body donors criminals? I might end up with a drug-ravaged body and I thought it was for terminally ill people only?" asked Amelia.

"Yes, officially it is but James said he could do me a favour and get you signed off as a terminal patient. And apparently, sometimes they get lucky with prisoners. We just have to let him know the type of looks we would be happy with and they will let us know when a donor who fits the description becomes available. The more you pay, the better quality donor you get. I'd pay anything to help you. Would you consider it for me?" Teddy pleaded.

She promised to think about it and eventually agreed.

They met with James who was charming and helpful. Teddy wouldn't tell Amelia how much the operation was but she knew it was a vast amount of money. Beforehand, they drew up a list of criteria for the donor. Skinny was top of Amelia's list. Teddy wanted someone who looked similar to Amelia but she wanted to look completely different. Growing up, she always felt plain and pale so she asked for a brunette donor with an olive complexion and to be as beautiful as possible. She knew this was asking a lot but maybe the prisoner would come from a South American country? With this new body, she might become confident and overcome her thoughts of ugliness. Teddy was surprised at her choice but she reminded him that he wanted to sleep with someone different so she may as well look completely different. James assured them, they would have no problems in finding a match. He was right. Six weeks later, she got the call that her operation had been scheduled and was to come into the clinic that week. She had no time to think and along with Teddy they rushed in. The recovery suite was luxurious. She wasn't sure how she would feel afterwards but she told Teddy it could be like a second honeymoon.

A man called Felix asked her to sign some documents. The form stated she had some disease she could barely pronounce, let alone heard of. She had to confirm that she was terminally ill and the clinic wouldn't bear any responsibility if the operation went wrong. She hesitated at signing this, what if something did go wrong? She hadn't thought about that before. Felix pointed out it was standard practice and everyone signed as they had nothing to lose, they were all terminally ill after all. She smiled and agreed. She had no idea if this man knew the truth or not. Teddy gently persuaded her to sign the form. She looked at her husband and just wanted him to be attracted to her again so she signed.

Amelia hoped to meet Dr Marlow as she'd seen him on the news and read up on him. But he didn't come and meet her. This was disappointing as she wanted some reassurances from him. When it was time to go to the operating theatre, she got cold feet. She told Teddy of her concerns but he said it was too late to back out now. He was right; instead, she had a little cry before the anaesthetist took over. As she lay down becoming drowsy, Dr Marlow entered the room. She tried to say 'stop' and that she had changed her mind but the room went black.

When she woke up, she felt relieved. Teddy was sat by her bedside, holding her hand.

Her throat felt dry but she managed to speak; "thank goodness I woke up. I changed my mind; I don't want to go through with it."

Teddy frowned at her.

"But it's too late. You've already had the operation."

"Oh no," she cried as she lifted up her blanket and looked underneath her covers. Even with the hospital gown on, she could see she wasn't in her old body anymore.

"You look great Amelia, don't cry. You just have to get used to it," Teddy told her. "Do you want to see yourself?"

She shook her head and rolled over. She needed more time and wanted to be on her own. Teddy understood and promised to take her abroad when she was feeling better. He owned a few holiday homes located around the world but she hadn't visited them for a while as she always felt like a beached whale. She agreed and told him to check on Arthur at home and come back later. As he left, she felt relieved to be on her own. Her relief was not long-lasting as a doctor came into the room soon after Teddy left. She recognised Dr Marlow immediately.

"I heard you woke up. I just want to check a few things and then I'll leave you in peace."

He prodded and poked her and took some readings. Amelia thought his manner cold for a doctor;

he didn't even ask how she was feeling.

"Very good," he said to himself as he walked away.

"Wait," she called after him. "I just wanted to thank you for letting me take part in your programme."

"Don't thank me; I don't get much say in who takes part any more," he replied gruffly.

She was taken aback by his abrupt manner; he always seemed so nice on the television. All she wanted were some kind words. She couldn't help but burst into tears. Dr Marlow came back to her bedside even though he obviously just wanted to get out of there.

"It's perfectly normal to feel like this," he sighed. "It's a huge change but you'll get used to it."

"But I changed my mind, I didn't want to go through with it. I only did it to please my husband," Amelia sobbed.

She didn't know why she was telling this man but she just wanted to get it off her chest.

"Well, he obviously didn't want to lose you. You surely didn't want to die, did you?" he asked.

"But I wasn't dying, I was just despicable to look at," she told him.

"What do you mean you weren't dying?" he asked as he flicked through her records on his tablet. "Look, it says you had oesophageal cancer and your prognosis was terminal." He directed the screen towards her.

She shrugged her shoulders, "I don't even know what that is."

"It's cancer of your oesophagus. What do you mean you don't know what it is?" Dr Marlow looked confused.

Amelia knew she wasn't supposed to say anything as James reminded her before the operation that her documents were forged. They could get into a lot of trouble if anyone found out but Amelia didn't care any more.

"Doctor, I didn't have a disease. My husband fixed it for me to have a transplant because he didn't want to leave me but he didn't want to stay with me either as I was so fat," confessed Amelia.

"You're lying!" he shouted. "Please tell me you're lying?"

"I'm sorry, but I'm not lying."

"Do you know how many terminally ill people are out there who actually need these donors? You selfish, vain woman!" he shouted at her.

"I'm sorry," she whimpered again. She wished she hadn't said anything. "James said it would be okay; there were enough donors to go around. My husband talked me into it. I was dying inside, I would have probably died soon anyway. According to my new personal health monitor, I was likely to get some sort of heart disease..."

"Enough!" he interrupted as he left the room.

Now Amelia felt terrible. She had gained this body dishonestly knowing someone else should have benefited. Someone who was dying, not someone who was trying to win back her husband. Dr Marlow's reaction brought her back to her senses.

Deep down she knew Dr Marlow didn't know but she felt as though she had to confess to someone. Now was not the time to feel sorry for herself. She and Teddy had manipulated the system but it was too late to undo what they had done. Amelia was determined not to let it all be for nothing. She would make the most of this second opportunity by embracing this new body and treating it with the respect it deserved. She couldn't wait for Teddy to get back so they could restart their marriage.

CHAPTER 33

"Ah, you must have felt so cheated when you met Amelia?" asked Joe.

"Indeed, my discovery, my invention, my cure...whatever you want to call it was being manipulated to satisfy the greed of my partners and to satisfy the shallow insecurities of people."

"So what happened after?"

"With Amelia or with the company?"

"Both," said Joe.

"Well, predictably with Amelia she just reverted back to normal. It wasn't her body that was the problem but her mind. We transferred an unhealthy brain out of a perfectly functioning body into another perfectly functioning body. I spoke to Amelia a few times after her operation as I felt sorry for her in the end. She was pressured into the procedure and had mental health issues which were never addressed properly. She needed a good psychiatrist, not a body swap. Although the transfer helped in the short run, she couldn't overcome her internal issues of never feeling good enough due to her body dysmorphia. Within months, she gained weight again and still saw herself as ugly when she looked in the mirror; even though she had an attractive skin. I intervened before she or her husband did anything else that was stupid and I referred her to one of the top psychiatrists in the world. It took a while but the last I heard she was doing much better. Although she had to mourn the loss of her real body, once she realised what a drastic thing she had done."

"And what happened with you and the company?" asked Joe.

"Well, I went in with all guns blazing but only to Felix. James scared me; I avoided talking to the man whenever possible. Felix wouldn't do anything about it, to him, it was just about getting rich quick. In time, I eventually calmed down. Annie calmed me, she reminded me of the pro bono work and that only truly desperate people would go through with the procedure. It was not as if people would choose a body transplant over a simple facelift or nose job. She was right, so I let it go and continued for a little while longer."

Joe looked down at his notes; "so Amelia Jarvis was actually one of your last few patients. There were only a handful of operations after that?"

"That's right, things got out of control soon after that," said Henry.

"Tell me?"

Henry slumped in his chair and couldn't meet Joe's eyes. He paused for a few moments before recollecting the moment that destroyed his company.

"I was busy in the lab one day and I'd received numerous missed calls from Annie. She left messages to call her, that she needed to speak urgently. So I dashed home, I thought maybe something had happened to the children..."

Henry went to the kitchen and saw Annie pacing around. He asked if the children were alright. She assured him they were fine. Both were at a friend's house after school so wouldn't be back until later.

"I got stopped in the street today," Annie told him.

"Okay, anyone we know?" asked Henry, relieved that it didn't sound so serious.

"No, it's bad Henry. Really bad," she insisted.

Henry frowned; "just tell me."

"I was stopped by a man who looked around my age with a Scottish accent. He was calling out, 'Carolina;' I ignored him and carried on walking. Eventually, he caught up with me and grabbed my arm. He insisted that I was Carolina. I told him he had the wrong person and that my name was Annie. He kept asking if I was sure. Apparently, I'm the doppelgänger of his long-lost wife."

"Did you tell him about the body swap?" asked Henry.

"No, of course not. That would have just confused matters even more. Henry, he showed me a picture of her. It was me. I asked him if his wife was Russian but she was Scottish. She walked out on him and the kids years ago. Apparently, she wanted more in life and needed a break. She told him she would be in touch but he never heard from her again. He went to the police but they weren't interested. As she left on her own accord, they never listed her as a missing person. I assured him I wasn't his missing wife. I showed him my driver's licence and pictures of you and the kids. But I know for certain that this body belonged to Carolina and not some Russian volunteer."

"How do you know for sure, it could be a doppelgänger? They say we all have one in the world," Henry tried to reassure her.

"Because he asked to check my wrist. Carolina had a mole on her left wrist. I had that exact same mole removed, remember?" asked Annie.

Henry nodded, she didn't like looking at it so had it removed shortly after the operation. It left no scars.

"Did you show him your wrist?" asked Henry.

"Yes, the poor man apologised but he looked so confused. I felt terrible lying to him."

"You did the right thing," assured Henry.

"What's going on Henry? Have you told me everything?"

"Of course I have! I thought your donor was a desperate Russian refugee who volunteered her body."

"Why did they lie about her origins? I don't understand anything," Annie demanded.

Henry walked over to Annie and told her he had no idea what was going on either.

"I've got to go and talk to Felix. See what he

knows. Sit tight and I'll be in touch as soon as possible."

"I don't like this!" Annie called to Henry as he left the house.

Nor did he; he contacted Felix when he got in the car and told him to make sure he was available as soon as Henry arrived at the clinic.

Felix was waiting in the car park when Henry arrived.

"What's so urgent?" he asked as soon as Henry got out of the car.

"What do you know about Annie's skin?" he demanded.

"The same as you, she was called Vera Petrov. She was a thirty-seven-year-old and caught up in the Russian civil war," Felix replied.

"Where's her current family now? What happened to them?"

"I have no idea; we don't keep track of the donor family or even contact them personally. It's all arranged through a broker. Why bring it up now; it was almost ten years ago?" a confused Felix asked.

"And the money definitely left the company?"

"Yes, of course. Tell me what's going on," he asked again.

"I don't believe the donor was from Russia or caught up in a civil war. I don't even believe any money went to any family member for Annie's skin."

Henry told Felix all about the encounter Annie had earlier that day.

"Do you think James was lying about where the donors came from?" a worried Felix asked.

"I wasn't sure but I'm beginning to think so. Felix, you signed off on the donors. You must have seen their details or had family details when sending the compensation?"

"Yes, I saw the details but all the donors were fairly consistent. They were poor and from third-world countries or war-torn countries. I didn't delve into them; I just signed off on their profiles and bank transfers. I swear, that's all I know," Felix pleaded.

Henry believed him. "So what do we do now? Is James really hauling dead bodies in from the streets?"

"Unlikely, we'd know about it by now. I'm not sure what happened with Annie's skin but surely there'd be police searches and missing person reports. I just don't believe it. James is evil but is he that evil?" asked Felix.

"Yes! He threatened both our families," Henry reminded Felix.

"What do we do?"

Henry had no idea. He couldn't risk the safety of his family by going to the police or continuing to go along with it. Neither were viable options. He told Felix not to breathe a word to anyone until he thought of something.

Both men walked away from the car park, unsure if anyone was listening to their conversation. Felix asked Henry if he was certain that the Scottish husband believed Annie. From what Annie said, Henry felt as though he believed her.

CHAPTER 34

"So that's when you suspected the 'voluntary' donors weren't actually volunteers after all?" asked Joe.

Henry paused as he recollected that dreadful moment of knowing something far more sinister was going on.

"Yes, there was no doubt. Especially with the proof of the birthmark. A thorough investigation of Carolina's disappearance was launched not long after. The police never caught the scouts involved, but with CCTV, witnesses and the false name from the passport she used, her last movements could be traced..."

Carolina Stewart.

Carolina and her husband had been together since they were sixteen. She became pregnant by accident and their families forced them into marriage. Baby number two followed soon after and Carolina never finished her exams. Eighteen years later, baby number two left for university and now she could finally leave Andy. With Andy, she'd been so bored

L M Barrett

for the last twenty years. He was a good man but had the same office job for the last fifteen years, never progressing. She'd had the odd part-time job here and there but they'd always struggled for money. While her friends went on exotic holidays; the best she could hope for was to drive somewhere within the British Isles. Air travel was too expensive and they had been saving up for the boys to go to university. Both she and Andy were determined for the kids not to follow in their footsteps of leading a life of watching every penny. Carolina's life consisted of working, usually cleaning, watching telly and going to bed early. She and Andy barely spoke anymore; there was nothing to speak about.

Every morning, she woke up hoping something exciting would happen. It never did, until one evening on a rare girls night out. Accepting an invitation from an old school friend she had spent ages dressing up and applying her make up. She looked good, at least she thought so but Andy didn't bat an eyelid when she said goodbye as she left the house. The foreign man in the bar they went to thought so as well. By this time, Carolina was a little drunk and happy to flirt with this stranger. She told him she was celebrating...or commiserating, she wasn't quite sure, her second son leaving home.

She had the house predominately to herself and she didn't feel the need to behave herself any more. All her life she put Andy and her two children first. But now, finally, it was her time. The handsome stranger agreed she needed a bit of excitement in her life and he was willing to give it to her; if she let him. He left her to ponder this along with his number. The way he looked at her, Carolina was under no illusion of what type of excitement he meant.

A couple of days later, she plucked up the courage to call him. They arranged to meet at his hotel; he was in business in Edinburgh for a few days. After a drink in his room, they went to bed. It was a few years since she and Andy had made love and she had no desire for him any more, and likewise for him.

When her handsome stranger invited her on a business trip to Budapest, she jumped at the chance. There was nothing to lose, she told Andy she needed to get away for a few days and if it didn't work out she could simply return. She made sure not to tell her friends where she was going; she couldn't risk burning her bridges.

Dmitri was the most exotic person she'd ever met. He was sexy and brooding. Although she barely knew him, she felt she could trust him enough to go away with him for a few days. The worst that could happen, is he might lose interest in her. All he was offering was a small trip away. She'd never been abroad before. She deserved it; Andy would never get off the sofa and take her away. She was old enough to know that Dmitri wouldn't be interested in a woman like her in the long term, she had nothing to offer him. She knew nothing about life, nor had she any fascinating anecdotes to speak of but in the meantime, she could offer him enthusiasm and some non-committal sex.

The day of the flight, she packed a small bag and left Andy a note. She felt guilty but simply told him she was having time away by herself, making sure not to mention Dmitri. She didn't even need to bring her passport. It was out of date anyway and she never bothered to renew it as there never seemed any point. Dmitri was unconcerned by such small details as he told her he could arrange a passport for her. It would be fun to pretend to be someone else for a change.

They spent a couple of wonderful days in Budapest, staying in a luxury hotel, making love and eating out. Although she had only known Dmitri for a short time, she felt as though she was falling for him and hoped he felt the same way too. On the third night, he had a business dinner with a Russian client and invited her to come along. She was pleased to receive the invite and assumed Dmitri wanted to show her off. This made a change from her life in Scotland. She and Andy were never invited out on business dinners. The most she could hope for was Andy's annual Christmas dinner which usually involved everyone getting as drunk as possible.

That night, instead of the refined bars and restaurants that Dmitri had been taking her to, he took her to a dark, dingy bar down an old cobbled street. They passed beggars and what looked like prostitutes on the way. Carolina tugged at his arm on the way into the bar as she began to feel uneasy. But he patted her hand and told her his client was a little less flashy than his other clients and preferred to meet in less salubrious types of places. Carolina smiled and apologised for making a fuss as they sat down and ordered a drink.

A tall, broad man dressed in black with an unfriendly face walked in and approached their table, much to Carolina's dismay. The two men talked in Russian throughout the evening and looked at her occasionally which made her feel uneasy, especially when they laughed. Dmitri apologised and told her that his client couldn't speak any English but they were only saying nice things about her and that his Russian client thought she was beautiful. He encouraged her to drink more so that she wouldn't get too bored, so she took his advice. She felt herself relax once she became tipsy. Eventually, she asked Dmitri to ask his Russian client what he did for a living. Dmitri laughed and translated this to his client, who laughed even louder. Carolina felt confused as though she was the butt of some joke that she was unaware of.

"What did he say?" she asked Dmitri.

"Well, I told him you were curious about what he did for a living."

Carolina paused to let Dmitri continue. She now had a horrible feeling that he did something illegal for a living and wished she'd never asked.

"He trafficks people for a living," Dmitri told her.

Carolina thought she misheard and asked Dmitri to repeat himself.

"I told you, he's a human trafficker," Dmitri told her calmly.

"That's not funny."

"I'm not joking," he said.

Carolina suddenly felt sick and tried to stand up. The room was spinning and Dmitri quickly pulled her by the wrist to sit back down.

"You've had too much to drink," he whispered. "We'll help you to the car."

She was about to tell Dmitri that she wanted to walk back to the hotel when suddenly everything became black.

Later on, Carolina woke up feeling dreadful. She lay in bed for a moment while she tried to retrace her last steps. She remembered being in a bar with Dmitri and then feeling scared. What was it that she was so scared of? She tried to remember. Suddenly, she sat up with a fright. She didn't recognise the room. It was not her hotel room; instead, it was a dark, small room with a mattress on the floor and a bucket near the bed. The room was dirty and it smelt. She got up and walked to the door but it was locked. She banged loudly and the man from the night before came. He threatened to hit her across her face and shouted something she didn't understand.

"Where's Dmitri?" she cried.

He laughed. A slow, evil sounding laugh as she suddenly remembered why she felt scared the night before.

"Wow, to go from the safety of Scotland into the hands of traffickers. That's horrendous," said Joe.

Henry agreed, although horrendous was probably an understatement of what Carolina went through.

"These people operate in the black market. No one ever knows their true identity. We only know now that somehow she was kidnapped, brought back to the UK and ended up in my clinic. I assume she was drugged most of the way and never got a chance to speak up to anyone. It appears that James brought in some of his own staff, who suddenly went missing when this all blew up. I'm sorry Joe. Can we have a break? It makes me feel sick to think about it."

Joe agreed to come back the next day. Dr Marlow's discomfort was apparent and the man needed some time out.

Joe rushed home to make a start on his first draft.

CHAPTER 35

The next morning, Joe returned to continue the interview. Again, he brought Henry his favourite coffee. Henry apologised for not being able to finish the interview the day before.

"It's understandable, it's a difficult situation. I see you still have protestors outside?"

"Are there? They think I'm the devil incarnate," said Henry.

"Well, they won't, once they read my article. Are you able to continue your story?"

Henry took a sip of coffee and nodded. He felt stronger after a good night's rest and was determined to get his side of the story out there for the world to read...

That evening at home, Henry sat with Annie unable to provide her with any answers.

"She couldn't have volunteered. Her husband would know about it; he would have received the money," insisted Annie.

"Not necessarily. Maybe she wanted the money to go to someone else."

"But why would she be that desperate? She wasn't from Russia. She was just from Scotland."

"I don't know Annie. I just don't know," Henry sighed.

Henry wasn't sure how much more he could take of James and his double dealings. He knew he would have to confront the man. There was no way to avoid that now, especially with Annie contemplating going to the police. He asked her to stop talking about the police; reminding her of the threat of what might happen if they tried to report James. Suddenly there was a knock at the door; this stopped the conversation as they stared at each other.

"Stay there," demanded Henry.

Annie looked terrified as he slowly made his way to the front door. To his relief, it was just a friend of his son. He let him in and watched him go upstairs to Alex's room.

"See Henry," Annie approached him in the hallway. "We can't go on like this. We can't go on not being able to talk freely in our own home and now your company is potentially murdering innocent people. I will not be part of this any longer."

Henry put his hands on Annie's shoulders to try to calm her down.

"We can't go to the police; we're accessories to the crime. We both know your donor has come through illegal channels. They could execute us. And even if they don't, there's no telling what James will do to us."

Henry looked out of the window to see if anyone was watching the house, but as far as he could tell, there was no one out there.

"They could be listening to us now," he reminded her. "Let's sit on this for a couple of days before we decide what to do. This woman's husband believed you, didn't he? So we don't have to do anything drastic yet. I'll think of something, I promise."

Annie reluctantly agreed. She gave in as she felt sick and her head hurt from all the stressful scenarios she imagined panning out.

"But we have to act on this; we need to find out where the other donors came from," she said.

Henry promised he would get to the bottom of it once and for all.

The next day as Henry entered the clinic, the security guard stopped him. Security informed him of a man buzzing all morning, trying to get in and see Henry. No one was allowed in without an appointment and security clearance. Clearance could take up to a week to go through as there were many people who did not agree with what Henry and his team were doing. Sometimes they had protesters outside who were against the death penalty.

Apparently, it was a man called Andy Stewart. The name meant nothing to Henry, but when the security guard mentioned he had a strong, Scottish accent and insisted the clinic knew something about the disappearance of his wife, he realised who it was. Once he confirmed that Andy Stewart was still outside, he decided to go out and speak to him.

Against the advice of security, he went alone. Henry couldn't take the risk of anyone else hearing what Andy Stewart might say. Slowly, he made his way out and saw a man standing by the gate. His hair was greying and he looked tired and sad. Henry introduced himself.

"What can I do for you, Mr Stewart?" he asked.

"I bumped into your wife yesterday. I assume she told you about me?" he asked.

Henry nodded; "yes, she explained to you that she couldn't possibly be your missing wife."

"Yes, I felt daft. I thought I was going mad. Can you imagine not knowing where your wife has disappeared to for the last ten years?"

"No, I can't imagine what that must be like," Henry confirmed.

"She showed me her arm where I was expecting a birthmark and there was nothing there. But she also showed me her driver's licence. I looked her name up on the internet and saw she was married to you, Dr Marlow. Then I thought, there's no way my missing wife and your wife could be the exact image of each other. Not the wife of a doctor who specialises in body swaps. And I saw the before and after pictures of your wife. She's been through it, hasn't she?"

Henry could hardly deny it; it was common knowledge by now, no matter how private he and Annie tried to keep themselves.

"Yes, she has. But our donor was from a Russian prison. We have all the records to prove it. She was on death row."

Henry hoped he sounded convincing. He could hardly admit he now had no idea how they came across his wife's donor.

"Sorry, but I don't believe you. It's too much of a coincidence. I've informed the police. They said I could ask for a voluntary DNA test from your wife. So that's what I'm here for."

"Of course, if it will put your mind at rest; I can show you our records of Annie's original donor?" Henry offered.

He was at least sure the forgery would be good. James would have made sure all the records were in order.

"No, I'm not interested in that. I'm just here for DNA. If you don't provide that, I will go to the news-papers and to the police again. I've already talked to my sons about it; they need to know what happened to their mother."

"Yes, yes. I understand," Henry flustered. "Well, I will speak to Annie and get her permission. She can come here tomorrow and we will provide it for you."

Henry had no idea what he was saying, he wanted to buy some time before speaking to Annie.

"Not here. Bring your wife to this clinic," he told him as he handed Henry a card with another doctor's name and address. "I want to do the test on neutral ground."

Henry tried to control the shaking in his hand as he took the card, he hoped Andy Stewart didn't notice.

"That makes sense and I will speak to my wife and see when she's available."

"Tomorrow, at the latest or I go to the press," Andy Stewart said as he walked away.

Henry marched back to the clinic, he couldn't think straight. What the hell had Felix and James got him into?

"Felix, we have an emergency!" he shouted as he stormed into Felix's office.

Felix held his hands up to remind him to quieten down. He closed the door, making sure no one could hear them.

Henry was breathless as he blurted out the events from outside the office. Felix had no choice but to call James and tell him what had happened; James told both men to sit tight and do nothing.

"James will sort it out; he'll know what to do," Felix tried to reassure Henry.

"That's what I'm worried about. What if he does something to Andy Stewart? His sons know as well. I don't see how we can get out of it!" exclaimed Henry.

"Calm down, he won't do anything crazy like that. He'll get his solicitor involved. Annie can't be forced into giving a DNA test and our records are air-tight. The press isn't allowed to report on specific cases; the patients have confidentiality from the press," Felix reminded him. "Just go home and come back tomorrow for the next scheduled operation. We must carry on as normal."

Henry had no idea how Felix could be so calm and

collected throughout this. Henry had some reports and research to carry out but he couldn't concentrate, so he followed Felix's advice and went home.

Annie too, couldn't concentrate on her work.

"Let's go to the police. Tell them what we know. Tell them how Felix forged all the paperwork and how James made you both go through with it all. He threatened us, Henry, we were scared. The police will understand. But we must get to them before they get to us."

"We won't make it as far as the police station. Look outside," Henry nodded towards the window.

Annie walked over to the window. A man in a car was parked directly outside their house.

"Is he watching us?" she asked.

"Yes, I noticed him following me home today. James knows I'm panicked. He's making sure we don't do anything silly."

"But how can I get out of the DNA test? I'm not hanging around waiting to get caught and then get accused of knowing the donor wasn't who they said she was. I'm not being an accomplice to this crap that you got me into!" Annie shouted.

Henry had never seen Annie this on edge before, even when she was dying.

"I promise you, if anything happens, I'll take full responsibility. I'll deny that you ever knew anything. Listen to me Annie, you don't know anything. I need you to remain calm. If anything happens to me, I need you to take care of the kids. Okay?" he demanded.

She shook her head, unconvinced.

"But Felix and James know."

"They're hardly going to talk. Please, let me see what James has in mind. And then we'll decide once and for all tomorrow."

"That might be too late," sobbed Annie.

Henry took Annie into his arms. He didn't know what to say; maybe tomorrow would be too late?

CHAPTER 36

After a restless night of tossing and turning and Annie constantly checking the window to see if the car was still outside, Henry got up as normal and went to work. He kissed his wife before he left and tried his best to reassure her. There were no kids around that morning to say goodbye to as Annie asked them to stay over at their friend's house. They were only too happy to agree to that on a school night, but Annie didn't want them anywhere near the house if they were being watched.

Henry drove to work and looked out for Andy Stewart on the way; there was no sign of him. That was a relief but once he found out that Annie didn't show up that day for the DNA test, who knew who would be waiting outside tomorrow.

Henry spotted James' car in the underground car park. Not in any rush to see what James had in mind, he remained in his car in the dark for a few moments, bracing himself for what lay ahead. Slowly, he lingered to the lift. Feeling slightly nauseous he called the lift and pressed for the ground floor. He caught his reflection in the glass of the elevator.

Did he always have those bags under his eyes? The doors to the lift opened and he walked past security. The receptionist informed him that James requested Henry to go straight to see him. He nodded. His throat felt dry so he drank some water from the cooler. This meeting couldn't be delayed any longer. Henry took a deep breath, straightened his shoulders and headed towards James' office. Without knocking, he walked straight in. Felix was also there; this came as no surprise. Henry wondered how much more Felix actually knew.

"I take it that Felix has filled you in on everything?" He directed the question towards James. "So where the hell have all these donors come from?"

"Before we get to that Henry, I thought we had an agreement; not to go to the police?" said James.

"Yes, I've upheld that end of the bargain, against my better judgement," said Henry, not sure where this was going.

"You should have made sure your wife was clear on that too. We caught her on her way to the police station this morning. We got to her just before she walked in. Here, speak to her," James passed Henry the phone.

Henry snatched the phone.

"Annie, are you there?"

"Henry," she cried. "I'm so sorry, I had to do something. I couldn't just hang around waiting for you."

"Never mind that. Are you okay? Have they hurt you?"

"Not yet but they've dragged me somewhere and

267

have a gun pointed at me. Please help me, " Annie pleaded.

"Don't worry, Annie. Try to keep calm and do what they say. Nothing will happen to you; I'll make sure of it..."

James snatched the phone back and told his men he would be in touch with them.

"You goddamn son of a bitch. She has nothing to do with this!" Henry shouted as he forced his way towards James. Felix got in-between and pushed Henry back. Felix was stronger than Henry as he tried to force his way past him.

"It's over James, you know it. Andy Stewart will be back tomorrow with the press and the police. They'll trace Annie's DNA back to his missing wife. We're finished. You did this!"

"Don't overreact. It's just one man; the police won't listen to him. We can always fake the DNA results if it comes to that. He's grieving for his long-lost wife and has gone mad," James told him calmly.

Henry pushed Felix off him and straightened his suit.

"That won't be the end of it. You can't pay everyone off. The government agency will have us under investigation if there's even a sniff of scandal. Where did the donors really come from?"

"I don't know. They're just losers. My scouts look for anyone who fits the description to order. Usually in the red light districts or the drug dealing neighbourhoods. Places where people who disappeared wouldn't be missed," James simply shrugged.

Henry spluttered; "places like Edinburgh? Where a married woman with a family wouldn't be noticed?!"

James held his hands up; "I'm not sure how she got involved. We don't pick donors from this country. She must have been in the wrong place at the wrong time. The scouts don't stop for a pleasant chat or ask for IDs."

Henry couldn't believe what he was hearing. He slumped down into the nearest chair.

"You mean, you just murder them? None of them volunteered?"

"Don't be so naïve Henry. Who in their right mind would volunteer their body?" laughed James.

"But all that money we pay out through the company to the donors?"

James tapped the side of his nose; "don't worry about the money. It's all sitting in various offshore accounts or being reinvested in other things. I'm happy to share with both of you as long as you keep your mouth shut and go along with me."

Felix sat there, looking pale.

"Felix, you're in with me aren't you?" asked James.

Felix stared at Henry, unable to say anything.

"Did you know about any of this Felix?" asked Henry.

He just shook his head; "no...nothing. I thought they were volunteers too."

James rolled his eyes to the ceiling.

"My god, for such a streetwise boy and a Harvard & Cambridge educated man, you're both so stupid. Right boys, this is what's happening. Henry, you're going to continue with your operation as normal..."

"To hell, I will. I'm not working while you have Annie..."

"Let me finish, Henry. You will carry on as normal; it's your pro bono patient today. I thought that's what you lived for? You go and operate on your poor loser. I'll sort out this Andy Stewart mess. I'll also make sure that Annie sees our point of view. And Felix, you go and do whatever it is you do," James gave a dismissive flick of the hand towards Felix.

"Henry, if you don't carry on as normal, I'll make sure that Annie does go missing. And if she can't keep her mouth shut either, then I'll make sure something happens to your children. Someone is outside their school as we speak. Now get out of here both of you."

Henry stood and stared at this man in disbelief. Felix pulled him by the arm and led him out of the office.

"Don't confront him, Henry. We can't win. Remember what he did to my mother? He has Annie and he's threatened your kids. You must put them first."

"Felix, he's murdering innocent people just to sell them on. You must have known about this?"

"No, Henry. I swear I didn't," Felix pleaded.

Henry had never visited the 'volunteer' donors

before. He didn't want anything to do with that side of the business.

"You must have? You visit all the patients to clear up the paperwork! They would have been brought here alive. How did they get dragged in here against their will from abroad without anyone noticing? Without you noticing?" demanded Henry.

"I don't go through the paperwork with them. It's all forged remember? With fake prisoner records. The donors all came on the company's private jets. It would have been easy enough to get them past security. The ones I did see were already anaesthetised by the time I saw them," Felix pleaded.

"My god, he must have had them drugged by the time they were captured until their arrival here. Those poor people..."

"I know, I know but I don't see a way out of this," said Felix. "If we tell anyone, he will kill everyone we love. He will probably kill us. If he doesn't kill us then we will be imprisoned, it's our signatures on all of the documents. My god Henry, I've signed off on everything; so have you!"

The full realisation of how involved Felix was, suddenly dawned on him.

"But we can't let him carry on with this. He can't keep threatening us and there's no way I can continue with the operations. We can't work here knowing behind the door of the prisoner's suite there's an innocent person. Some terrified person who's been kidnapped. That's unforgivable."

"I agree," said Felix. "But what can we do?"

"Leave it to me," said Henry.

Henry saw a way out. It was a long shot and might not work but he had to do something. Something extreme.

CHAPTER 37

Today was Henry's pro bono patient and the donor was actually legitimate.

"Felix, tell the prisoner and his guard that the operation is cancelled. Say the patient died unexpectedly. We'll offer suitable compensation."

"But why?"

"Trust me, just do it," ordered Henry.

When Felix left, Henry went to the operating theatre to prepare some items. Afterwards, he messaged James and Felix to meet him urgently in his office with the pretence that he needed some reassurances before he could continue. Not long after he had messaged them, they both walked into Henry's office. He sent his receptionist away on an errand and shut the door.

"What do you want, Henry? I thought I'd made myself clear. You carry on as normal, yes?" demanded James.

"I can't have you threatening us every time something goes wrong; we're supposed to be partners. So I have an offer for you," Henry gestured for James to sit down.

James laughed and sat down.

"I'm intrigued, Henry. What on earth could you possibly offer me?"

Henry walked over to James. He put his hand in his pocket and pulled out a needle.

"This!" as he stabbed the anaesthetic into James' neck and held him down by his shoulder.

"What the hell?" roared James as he attempted to stand up.

"Felix, help me hold him down."

Felix stood glued to the spot with his mouth wide open watching the two men struggle.

"Help me now, Felix," pleaded Henry.

Felix suddenly jumped to attention and helped Henry hold James down to the chair. After a few seconds of struggling, James was out like a light as he slumped forward in his seat.

"What have you done?" screamed Felix. "He'll kill us all!"

"Not if we get rid of him before he wakes up and please – keep your voice down," hissed Henry.

"We can't just get rid of him; what about his connections to the Russian mafia? Can you imagine what they will do to us if they find out we killed him?" Felix hissed back.

"They won't find out."

Henry raised his eyebrow at Felix and he suddenly understood what Henry's plan was.

"That's madness; we'll never get away with it."

"We've got to try something and this is the best I can think of. No one threatens my family and gets away with it. Quick, bring in a gurney and then fabricate a fake staff meeting to get everyone away from the operating theatre. I can set up on my own."

Again, Felix stood on the spot just staring in disbelief at Henry.

"Now!" he had to shout.

Felix quickly made his way out of the office and brought in the gurney. He messaged the staff to meet him in the boardroom and left Henry to deal with the mess. Before he left the office he asked Henry if he was sure he knew what he was doing. Henry just shrugged and reminded Felix they were desperate.

"He's responsible for the murders of god knows how many innocent people. Our families could be next," Henry reminded him.

Felix gave a determined nod which assured Henry that he was prepared to go along with this. Henry just hoped he was right.

Once Felix left the office and Henry was sure there was no staff around, he quickly wheeled James to the operating theatre covering his face – just in case. All the staff were ordered into the emergency meeting; Henry wondered what on earth Felix would tell them. He tried not to worry about that now as he was left uninterrupted to prepare James for the transfer. Once that was set up and James' body was completely covered, he messaged his assistant to leave the meeting immediately and prep the recipient.

The recipient today was a pro bono case chosen by Henry. He was slightly younger than James with no family ties. Freddie Hansen was a missionary and Henry chose him due to his voluntary work. The inclusion of Freddie in the project meant he could continue his work. It was a stroke of luck that he was often out of the country, based mainly in the most remote and poorer countries of Africa. Henry thought it unlikely the Russian mafia had much influence there and Freddie should be able to carry on as normal. He just had to persuade Freddie to do a few things for him when he woke up from his operation.

Eventually, his assistant wheeled in Freddie Hansen, who was already asleep. Henry usually liked to meet the recipients, particular the pro bono ones before the operation but unfortunately today there was no chance of that. He would have also liked to warn him of the change of donor but again, there was no chance.

His assistant, unaware of any changes, commented on how empty and quiet it was in the operating theatre today. Usually, there was a buzz about the place when a transfer was taking place.

"Are you okay, Dr Marlow? You're sweating?"

"I'm fine," he said as he wiped his brow with his sleeve.

If his assistant was suspicious, he didn't say anything, instead, he apologised for the delay.

"Felix dragged us into some pointless meeting to ensure we were up to date with our reports. I don't understand his timing when we had an operation due. You've had to do this all by yourself."

"I don't mind. Felix is under pressure from our investor – we both are. James came in today and demanded the utmost efficiency. He thinks we will be audited soon," explained Henry as he looked at James' body underneath the sheet.

Henry had a panicked thought; how would he explain to the staff that the patient would inherit James' body? He continued with the setup and performed the procedure as swiftly as possible. It was too late to back out now. At this point, he'd performed the operation so many times that he could do it automatically. Instead, he thought ahead of what he was to do and say. Felix came in to check if everything was going to plan so Henry asked him to keep all the staff away from the patient. Felix sighed as he knew this elaborate plan would probably backfire on them.

As expected, the operation was a success. Freddie's dead body was wheeled off to the incinerator and Felix told the staff present that Freddie had asked for complete confidentiality. He didn't want anyone to see him so Felix sent the aftercare team home early.

"They're suspicious as hell, Henry," said Felix.

"I don't care. I've got to wake up Freddie now and put the rest of my plan into action," Henry told him.

Felix pleaded with him that it was far too early to wake the patient and that he needed time to recover naturally but Henry reminded him they had no choice; he had to save Annie now.

"He can recover later," insisted Henry.

"It's too soon!" lamented Felix.

"I'll take my chance. I need Freddie up and about as soon as possible."

It was a risk, but Freddie's vital signs were strong. Henry was sure the risk was low as he forced him out of his deep slumber.

"Freddie, Freddie. Wake up. This is Dr Marlow. How are you feeling?" he asked calmly, trying to keep the urgency out of his voice.

Freddie woke up and did all the usual things that the recipient patients did. He checked his hands, touched his face, asked if the operation worked and looked underneath his sheets. Dr Marlow had no time to take any of this in. Felix stood mesmerised.

"Can you speak, Freddie?"

The patient nodded and spoke. He sounded and looked just like James.

"Did it work? Am I cured?" he asked the men standing by him.

Although he had the same voice, his tone seemed more gentle and passive. This wasn't the arrogant tone of James that Felix and Henry were used to. Freddie asked for the mirror and Henry warned him there had been a slight change of plan just before the operation, before handing him the mirror. Henry lied and told him the donor had pulled out but they had found a last-minute replacement.

"Okay," agreed a confused looking Freddie.

He glimpsed at the mirror briefly and confirmed it would take some getting used to.

Henry was becoming impatient and didn't want

to rush Freddie but he had to urge him.

"Freddie, there's something urgent I need to ask from you and I wouldn't ask unless I was desperate. As you know, the body you acquired is that of a criminal. It's a long story but he's holding my wife hostage. I just need you to make a call and tell his associates to release my wife."

"What?" Freddie spluttered. "What are you talking about? I don't understand what you want me to do."

"I need you to pretend to be James Talbot for a few minutes and then I promise to give you more money than you could ever need and put you in hiding. I will fast track your new passport with your new picture; it will still have your old name on it. No-one will ever know what happened to James. He will have simply disappeared. Please, I'm desperate. My wife and children are in danger and I need you to call off his goons immediately," pleaded Henry.

Henry handed him James' handset which displayed numerous missed calls during the time of the operation.

"Please," Henry begged again. "I'm desperate. I saved your life. I chose you. You owe me."

"But this was never part of the deal!" said Freddie.

"I know but if I wasn't desperate I wouldn't ask. I guarantee your safety."

Freddie sighed, shook his head and agreed. He was still groggy from the operation and Henry knew he was acting against his better judgement but he had to persuade him while he was in this vulnerable state.

Henry made Freddie change into a smart shirt and tie and tidy his hair. They waited for the phone to ring again as the phone number was blocked. For what seemed like an eternity, the phone finally rang. Henry's heart skipped a beat as he urged Freddie to answer the phone.

"Remember, Freddie. James is a cool man so keep calm and talk slowly."

"Boss, where have you been? I've been waiting for instructions for hours," asked the burly looking man on the other end of the video call when Freddie picked up.

"I've been tied up," Freddie said calmly. "Everything's worked out at this end, so let the woman go. I'll speak to you later."

James' accomplice agreed and Freddie hung up.

Henry breathed a huge sigh of relief.

"I've no idea what you've got me into but I just want to go. I need to see my mum. Make sure she's okay," Freddie told the two men.

"She's fine. She's at the retirement home, isn't she? You can call her anytime but you need to stay here for at least a day. You've been through a major operation and we need to get your new ID in order."

Freddie yawned and looked rather pale. He resigned himself back to bed and asked them to leave him alone. The two men left the room. Henry asked Felix to expedite Freddie's ID and to stay at the clinic for the night as they'd let most of the staff go home. Felix reluctantly agreed.

"What if his mob comes looking for him?" Felix asked.

"I'll decrypt the blocked number and then you just message them from James' device and tell them he's uncontactable for the rest of the day. They couldn't get past security anyway, so you have nothing to worry about. I have to go and make sure Annie is okay. Then we'll try to figure out this mess tomorrow."

As Henry walked off, Felix called after him; "I'm so sorry, Henry. I'm sorry for getting you into this."

"Me too, Felix. Me too," Henry agreed as he walked off.

CHAPTER 38

Henry called Annie from his car, relieved when she picked up straight away. She was sobbing at the other end but she hadn't been harmed and the kids came home from after-school club as normal. Nobody had approached them at school. He promised to get home as quickly as possible and tell her everything.

It was hard to believe all this had happened in a matter of hours; it felt as though a week had passed.

After an hour, he arrived home. Annie called him up to the bedroom where he found her packing. She had a glass of whisky on the side for her nerves and handed another glass to Henry.

"Please tell me we're leaving?" she demanded as she continued selecting clothes from the wardrobe.

"Yes, but we don't need to leave straight away. James has been neutralised."

"Neutralised? What the hell does that mean?"

"It means we don't have to worry about him anymore."

Henry persuaded her to sit down as he told her everything. Afterwards, Annie held her head in despair.

"That doesn't solve anything. What about the people he works for? They'll come looking for him. Andy Stewart will still want his DNA. And now that we know that people have been murdered, we can't sweep everything under the carpet."

Henry agreed that his short-term solution left a lot of unanswered problems.

"Annie, we have his device. I can get Freddie to leave a video call that he's going into hiding. If his accomplices know that he's in big trouble, they won't want to associate themselves with him."

"But you're putting Freddie in danger..." interrupted Annie.

"He'll have money and he'll continue with his missionary work in Africa. I'm sure they won't find him as long as we get him out of the country as soon as possible."

"And how do we deal with Andy Stewart?" she asked.

"We run away," offered Henry.

"That's the plan? We simply run away?" Annie stood up and looked at Henry.

Henry shrugged; admittedly, it wasn't the best plan in the world but it was all he could think of right now.

"No way, I'm not running away from this, not now I know that James is dead. I haven't done anything wrong. What would we tell the children? They love school and their exams are coming up? When Andy goes to the police, they'll dig around and find out about the murders. They'll come looking for me.

We have to come clean now," she demanded.

"We can't, there's no James to pin it on. The authorities will need a scapegoat. We're in on it over our heads. We're free to run away now; no one is watching us anymore. The kids can go to school anywhere. I can access money from the company before we dissolve it. Felix was a witness to everything; let him deal with the questions. He knows we're innocent if it comes to that."

"No, no. I've gone along with everything you've asked of me before but this is it. This is where the madness ends," she told Henry as she prodded her finger into his chest.

He took her hands and held them tenderly and looked into her eyes.

"There are too many loose ends and I don't know what would happen to us, to you. I can't take the risk. You're in possession of the body of a murdered woman. They'll make an example of us."

"I'm willing to take the chance. If no one is after us, then I'm calling the police now," she picked up the phone and dialled.

Henry admitted defeat as he sat in the armchair in his bedroom and looked out of the window. After Annie put the phone down, she came over and took his hand and crouched by the chair.

"You can still run away. I'll tell them everything I know but I'll make sure they know what a good man you are."

"If I run, I'll look as guilty as hell. Won't I? Everyone knows my face."

Annie agreed.

He knew he was too high profile. He laughed. Annie asked what he was laughing at.

"If I'd known it was going to turn out like this, I would have bloody well done the transfer on myself. At least then, no one would recognise me."

She stroked his hand and told him everything would be alright. The police were on their way over to ask some questions and then it would finally be out in the open.

"We can't go anywhere until we clear our names," insisted Annie.

Henry sighed as he shook the ice cubes in his empty glass. The whisky had gone down far too quickly. As he looked in his glass and contemplated another refill, he tried one last time to persuade Annie.

"Annie, I've knowingly been operating outside the law for years. I'll lose the company and will probably be arrested. I could end up rotting in a prison cell for years. The law is constantly changing concerning who and what crime is punishable by death. They may choose to make an example of me."

"You were only doing it under duress. I'm sure they'll understand," Annie stroked his arm.

"You're willing to take that chance on me...on us?"

Annie rested her head on Henry's lap.

"I don't know. I don't know what to do."

Henry left the room; he decided to have another whisky after all. It could be his last. As he went into the dining room to pour himself another glass, the doorbell rang. He sat down in his armchair, in the dark. Annie could deal with it; he'd had enough. He didn't want to speak to anyone. He heard some muffled voices and Annie walked into the room and turned on the light.

"It's the police; they have a warrant for my DNA and to search the clinic."

CHAPTER 39

"So that's how you ended up here, in prison on remand?" asked Joe. "And you're still working I see," Joe nodded towards Henry's laptop.

Henry shrugged; "yes, I can't seem to switch off. Even with such archaic devices as this laptop – it's better than nothing. I need something to do to take my mind off the pending court case. I promised Annie a long time ago that I would help her out on the health monitors and take them to the next level. I'm working on a way for the health monitors to measure brain activity and behaviour. Again, this may or may not prevent criminal activity. Who knows what the company will do with the information but I find it fascinating."

"Always the altruist, Dr Marlow. Faced with life imprisonment, you're still trying to improve mankind. I'm impressed. Any lesser man would have crumbled and given up by now."

"Thanks Joe, you make me sound better than I really am but as you can see, this is where my attempt at improving mankind led," Henry gestured to the small visiting room they were both sitting in.

"Anyway, that's it. That's my life story. That's how I ended up facing life imprisonment. It turned out that the police had already started investigating James and Marlow Enterprise before Andy Stewart turned up. James had always been a ladies man and he'd been accused of sexual misconduct. He never bothered with the consent forms and that led to the police investigation of James and his dealings. That's why they were only too happy to follow up on Andy Stewart's concerns so quickly. Annie agreed to the DNA test and told them everything. Obviously, they matched the DNA to Carolina Stewart and arrested us. I told her to co-operate and be completely honest. I've made it clear Annie had nothing to do with any of this. As far as she was concerned, her body transfer at the time of the operation was inside the law and that it went through the proper channels; which is the truth. She only found out later and wanted to go to the police and that's when we were threatened. Joe, I need you to tell my full story. All those protesters outside won't rest until I'm on death row. They all believe I'm the biggest mass murderer of modern time. I need my children to know the truth. This will all come out in the court case but I need the press on my side now.

Also, I thought about it last night when I found out who your father was. I have a great barrister but he's not the best. Your father was...still is the best. I want you to ask your father to represent me and Annie."

"But he's a human rights lawyer, an advocate for vulnerable groups. You're a wealthy scientist charged with conspiracy to murder," Joe reminded him.

"I'm definitely not wealthy and I'm feeling pretty vulnerable right now. If anyone can persuade him to consider my case, you can. You told me how close you are. You've heard my side of the story and if you think I shouldn't go to prison for the rest of my life then I need you to ask your father to represent me. I have such respect for your father; he's the only one I want. Could you do that for me? With no James around to hold accountable, the finger is pointing firmly at Felix and me. Do you think you can influence him?" asked Henry.

Just then the prison guard entered the room; "time's up. Visitors have to leave now."

Joe packed his bag and stood up to leave. Before he left, he shook hands with Henry.

"No, I don't think you should be locked up. James was responsible but he's not here to face his punishment, that leaves Felix. I'll try my utmost to persuade my father. You saved his life; I think he owes you."

Henry smiled at Joe.

"Thank you, Joe and thank you for listening to my story. It means a lot to me to be able to get my side out there. I want everyone to know that I'm not a monster. That I would have never agreed to the murders – even if my family were threatened. I need everyone to know that."

"They will. I'll make sure of it," Joe insisted as he turned and walked out of the visiting room.

Henry was left sitting alone after Joe was escorted out. He sat back in his chair and took a sip of water. His throat was parched after all the talking. He hoped it was enough. People thought he was a monster after all the news reports from his arrest. Carolina's husband sold his story and made sure of that. Edward Morton also came forward to the press and told them how Henry's company was responsible for the death of his wife.

Henry and Felix co-operated with the investigators. They told them everything they knew and Felix led them through every forged document. After a thorough investigation and going through these forged records, it appeared that in the ten years that James had illegally attained the donors, it amounted to almost a thousand murders. A thousand people who never agreed to the procedure. A thousand people whose families never knew their fate and never received payment. A thousand people who were innocent.

Henry and Annie were shocked when they found out the true extent of the murders that had taken place. James got away with it for so long as all of the victims were homeless, runaways or recluses; people who no one would notice missing. He'd been careful except for one of his first murders – Carolina. Who knew this would be the one to unravel it all, almost ten years later. Apart from this glitch, James' scouts had truly operated in stealth. These scouts were well-paid, silent and spread out around the world. There was no correlation between any of the missing people, most of whom were never reported. A couple of members of the staff, including the main anaesthesiologist, employed by Felix once they moved into the new premises, disappeared without a trace. With no great surprise, they had been employed under false names and hadn't been tracked down yet. Having inside staff meant the victims could be operated on without any suspicion.

The one thousand people who had obtained the bodies illegally were all tracked down and questioned. It was one of the biggest murder investigations in recent times. Henry suspected he might be in prison for a very long time while the barristers and solicitors went through every detail and every witness before the case could go to trial. He needed Patrick Slater as his trial lawyer. Patrick knew the ins and outs of all the procedures and since his wrongful prosecution of the death row prisoner all those years ago he was one of the biggest advocates against the death penalty. One thousand innocent people had lost their lives and Henry had a feeling that life imprisonment might not be enough for the prosecution. Someone had to pay; Henry knew that someone could be him.

The guard eventually returned to the room and escorted Henry back to his cell. The two men walked slowly down the prison corridor. Henry felt nervous as they walked past the other prisoners, he felt every stare and heard every whisper. He was possibly the most hated man in prison. Even so, Henry was in no rush to be confined to his six by eight-foot room; his new world.

"If it's any consolation, I don't think you're a monster," Tony, the prison guard told him.

"Thanks, Tony. Good night."

The door shut and Henry was left alone. Fortunately, due to who he was, he had a cell to himself. He was grateful for that as he couldn't imagine sharing a cell with a hardened criminal. His fellow prisoners mistrusted him and thought of him as a vulture, only after their dead carcasses for his unsavoury experiment. They were probably right, Henry initially saw the death row prisoners as a means to an end. Now he was on the receiving end.

He'd been asked a few times since his confinement if he would consider donating his body if he ever found himself sentenced to death. Luckily, that was something he didn't have to consider. The program had been shut down, unlikely to ever be resurrected in Henry's lifetime.

He lay on his bed and looked up at the ceiling. His lifetime's work, gone, just like that; all his equipment confiscated. The worst for Henry was that poor Annie had been arrested and charged with aiding and abetting. Fortunately, she was released on bail; she could remain at home to look after the children. Her solicitor had persuaded the courts that she was frightened for her family and had tried to go to the police on two occasions but was thwarted both times by James' thugs. Thankfully, it was unlikely there would be any charge.

As for Felix, he was as much in the mire as Henry, if not more. Although he had been threatened initially, it did look as though he had gone along with the whole illegal operation willingly. He was also the one who signed off on the forged copies of donors. He was the one who had initially embezzled government money which led to Henry's introduction to James. Felix's bank balance also did not help his cause. Even with his partiality to gambling, his balance was huge. He had benefited from the illegal activities more than anyone. His outcome did not look good, his assets had been frozen and if he wasn't sentenced to death, he was probably facing a long stretch in prison.

Unlike Felix, Henry's bank balance wasn't huge. He chose to donate most of his ill-gotten gains as well as pay for the operation for Charlie's nephew. This worked in his favour, as well as the character witness from his old friend Charlie, who was a respected GP and upstanding citizen of the community. Charlie pledged his support to Henry since his arrest as had many others, including Henry's colleagues, friends and patients. Unfortunately for Felix, he lacked this support network.

Everyone else who worked at the company were questioned. All were released without charge as the police were satisfied that only Henry, Felix and Annie knew the extent of the wrongdoings. With James dead, it meant all of his secrets had died with him. The police couldn't track down any of his accomplices as James had covered his tracks well. The police investigated Freddie Hansen, who at the time was terrified of being caught up with James' past and any of the families of the victims. Henry pleaded for him and felt terrible that he used this poor man as a means just to get Annie back safely. He'd managed to arrange safe passage out of the country for Freddie with the help of his supporters. Freddie would disappear and hopefully never be tracked down again as the whole world would know that James Talbot was definitely dead once Joe published his story.

CHAPTER 40

Two years later

Annie and the children ran straight into Henry's arms. He held them tightly for as long as possible. Never wanting to forget this moment, he breathed in the smell from their hair. He planted as many kisses on each of them before his barrister, Patrick Slater, interrupted them.

"The press wants to speak to you, Henry. Are you ready?"

"Are we ready?" he asked his family.

They agreed and walked out of the courthouse. The large doors flung open, and the noise from the public flooded in.

He was a free man. Henry breathed in the air and squeezed Esme's and Alex's hands. He never thought he'd see the world again after three years, locked inside.

'Henry, Henry!' shouted reporters, all asking questions at the same time. It was overwhelming as noise came from all directions; Henry had no idea what they were saying. His barrister and security guards ushered him to a podium where he could address the press.

"Make it quick, the police are getting nervous by the number of people here," urged Patrick.

Henry had no problem with that. He just wanted to get away from here with his family and catch up with them in private. The crowd quietened down and Henry spoke. He thanked Patrick for his advocacy; he thanked the public for getting on his side and protesting his innocence. He joked he never thought the protesters would ever be pro Henry Marlow for once. Public opinion turned once they read Joe Slater's entire account of Henry's story. Henry was a hero; he'd killed James Talbot, one of the most ruthless criminals in the twenty-first century. Lastly, he thanked his family for standing by him and never losing faith in him. Patrick stopped the questions and led the Marlows to the car. At a snail's pace through the press, they finally managed to get away.

In the car, Esme sat clinging to her father, telling him how much she missed him.

"I missed you too, my darling."

He looked around at his family and apologised to them again for getting them so involved.

"Have you had a hard time at school?" he asked the kids.

"Nothing we couldn't handle," said Alex.

"We just threatened to transfer their brains into hairy Zelda the meanest dinner lady," said Esme.

"Nice," agreed Henry.

It was mature of them to put on brave faces but

Henry knew from Annie they'd had a hard time at school from friends, especially at the time of his arrest. That's why they were eager to move away too and make a fresh start.

"Seriously dad, it wasn't that bad, especially since the news article came out. What were you supposed to do? Let mum die. No way. Then when you found out the donors weren't volunteers, you acted on it immediately. You got rid of that scum bag. We're all really proud of you," said Alex.

"I just wish the court case didn't take so long. I missed you so much Dad," said Esme.

Tears came to Henry's eyes; "I missed you all too."

Three years was too long away from his family.

CHAPTER 41

Before they could get away, Henry allowed Charlie to arrange a final farewell. The next night, champagne corks popped, Henry drank and toasted to all gathered around him.

"To all my friends and family who have supported me over the past three years. To my wonderful wife for standing by me and my beautiful children for not giving up on their old man. To everyone in this room, who stood up for me in that courtroom and stood up for me to the press; I just want to say, I love you all and I am forever in your debt."

Henry wiped a tear from his eye; this was the moment he'd been waiting for. The thought of the love and support he had received from these people touched him so much.

"Before we go on, I just want us all to take a moment to think about those poor people who were taken away without permission. Who were murdered for no other reason than having their lives go so wrong somehow that James and his accomplices thought so little of them, that they wouldn't be noticed. Well, we notice you all now. Each runaway, each loner, each sad individual who would never get a chance to improve their life. And not forgetting Carolina Stewart, her husband and two loving sons she left behind. A toast to all the forgotten people out there."

Henry held up his glass as did everyone else in the room. There was silence for a moment until Charlie broke the sombre moment.

"Here's to Henry and the forgotten victims. Here's to not forgetting what you achieved and what you can still achieve. Toast to Henry everyone."

"To Henry," the small gathering chinked their glasses together.

Charlie hired a house in the country, away from London, away from everyone who was unsatisfied with the trial outcome. Armed security stood out-side. There was always the risk, now the world knew Henry had killed James, some of his mafia friends might come after Henry. Who knew how deep his ties went and how much money he owed his criminal associates. This didn't worry Henry. The depth of James' guilt would surely mean no one would want to claim any association with him.

Henry was, at last, a free man and wanted to share his last few days in England with his friends and family. Annie felt she could no longer live here. She and the children received so much attention during the trial that they would no longer be able to live a normal life. Some families of the victims had also made death threats. They weren't safe and Henry agreed to get away with new IDs and make a fresh start elsewhere.

He went over to thank Joe, who had written Henry's side of the story in such an emotive, impassioned way that it won Henry a lot of support. Never before had the public heard in such detail of what actually went on behind the scenes at Marlow Enterprise. Joe attempted to keep his report unbiased but it was evident he was a huge supporter of Henry Marlow and firmly believed in his innocence. This won a lot of public support for Henry and had the public baying for the incarceration of Felix instead.

Joe also pleaded with his father Patrick to defend Henry. Without Patrick's defence, Henry was sure he would still be in prison. As well as being a brilliant barrister, Patrick spoke from personal experience of what a difference Henry made. He also spoke of Henry's determination to push through the pro bono cases and detailed every one of them. He emphasised how Henry didn't make any money from Marlow Enterprise, unlike Felix and James. Henry took Patrick's hand and shook it.

"What can I say?" he asked.

"You don't have to say anything, just keep doing what you do. Find cures, find innovations. Make this world a better place; just as you promised. Remember, if it wasn't for you, I wouldn't be here today; nor would some of the other people in this room today," said Patrick, clutching Henry's hand.

Patrick remembered Henry's impassioned plea in the court about having a lot more to do in the world. To undo the wrong that happened in the name of his experiments. Henry was determined to find a suitable alternative to dead bodies. Maybe through clones, stem cells, even robots. He wasn't sure yet, but in his self-imposed exile, he could still try to come up with a breakthrough. Patrick argued it would be a shame to imprison such a mind. A mind which still had so much more to contribute and so much knowledge to impart.

Henry promised on his release to document everything and share it with the scientific community; imparting his wisdom which so far in his life he had kept to himself. He wanted to share his passion for trying to find a cure for cancer and other diseases. There were so many theories and ideas left in him. Now unburdened from the pressure from James, he felt like that enthusiastic young scientist he was many years ago, looking for a new breakthrough. This worked in Henry's favour as the judge agreed it would be a shame to deprive the world of future cures and innovations. The judge also took into account Henry's pro bono work over the years as many of those patients came forward to make a statement on Henry's behalf, including Charlie's nephew, Monty.

"Thank you so much, Dr Marlow," Monty approached Henry.

"It's Henry to you," he said as he touched Monty affectionately on the face. "How are you, Monty?"

"Good, all thanks to you. Thanks for everything you did. Mum wouldn't have recovered had I stayed the way I was."

"And thank you for speaking up for me in court. I really appreciate it," said Henry as he patted Monty on the back.

"It was nothing, especially when I found out you used up all your savings in helping me out. If there's anything else I can do for you, please just ask. I'm forever indebted to you."

Next to thank Henry was Amelia Jarvis, who over the years he'd stayed in touch with. Amelia was one of the many character witnesses for Henry. Bravely, she admitted in court that her body transfer was dishonest as she went for the operation knowing she didn't have a terminal illness. She spoke of Henry's disgust at the time of finding out and how he had absolutely no idea what was going on. She spoke of how he was such a good man, who helped her overcome her mental issues. How he offered her support and advised her on her body dysmorphic disorder and made sure she was seen by the best psychiatrist in the world. This led her to accept herself for who she was and made her marriage stronger. Amelia spoke passionately in court that without Henry Marlow, she probably wouldn't be here.

"That was quite a speech in court, Amelia. I had myself believing I was some sort of saint," he joked with her.

"As far as I'm concerned you are a saint and you should have won that Nobel Peace Prize," replied Amelia.

Henry shuddered at that thought. At the time of

his arrest, he found out he was up for nomination for the Nobel Peace Prize for his contribution to science. Due to the controversy around his experiment, this nomination was withdrawn.

"It doesn't matter. I never cared about accolades and prizes. I just wanted to do something good. And Amelia, it was so brave of you to come forward and admit your part in the exploitation of my project. You could have faced prison yourself or worse."

"Oh, Dr Marlow. I was in such shock to find out that we weren't using volunteers. I genuinely thought it was a prisoner who was going to die anyway. When I was telling James my wish list for how I'd like to look, I never realised I was in actual fact placing an order for a hit."

With James' death, the details of how he actually went about getting the bodies died with him. Neither Felix nor Henry could divulge this information either. By hacking into some of James' messages, the police simply found descriptions and ages to various outlets. They assumed once he got a buyer, he sent out an order and one of his scouts scattered across the world would look out for someone that fitted the description.

The police managed to track down most of the victims using fingerprints and DNA. Most of the victims were vagrants, runaways, drug dealers, prostitutes, drug users and petty thieves. The police failed to track down any of the scouts and James' business accomplices. Unsurprisingly, not one of them had come forward since his death.

The court offered a plea bargain in the end to all of the recipients of illegal donors. There were too many of them to go through individual court cases. They were all extremely wealthy and could afford the best defence. The procedure could have taken years. The court system would be clogged up; it would have cost the taxpayers billions of pounds. In the end, the recipients agreed to pay substantial damages and commit themselves to hundreds of hours of community service.

Annie too, was let off with the same agreement when it became apparent that none of the recipients were actually aware the donors were taken against their will. Annie's substantial fine was paid off by Henry's wealthy supporters and Annie was only too happy to commit to the hefty community service. She felt she needed to atone for Carolina Stewart and wanted to help the less fortunate, the forgotten people. She pledged her support to a charity in Brazil that helped the homeless and the desperately poor, get back on their feet and vowed to continue even after she'd completed her mandatory community service.

Henry thanked each of his guests individually. Hannah Ford came forward as another character witness and told the court how Henry helped her overcome the issues she initially had and spoke fondly of her family. Without Henry, she wouldn't be here and nor would her young children.

Jacob Smith spoke of the gift of new life and sight. Anna Jones spoke eloquently of her life as a paraplegic or lack of life before developing a terminal illness. She spoke of all the wonders she now experienced due to Henry and how her parents were also given a new lease of life now that they finally got to enjoy having a daughter.

The Whites weren't at the party, but they attended the court case in support of Henry. Jenna White spoke of the genuine shock she encountered from Annie and Henry at the restaurant, when they accused her of making a higher bid in order to acquire the body of Lucinda Willis. And how the Marlows had no idea they had been deceived. Many other witnesses backed up Henry's account of the events; as did the phone calls and video calls the police accessed. These showed James threatening Henry and the court saw the video from when Annie was held hostage.

Feeling overwhelmed by all the support he'd received, he caught Annie's attention and motioned for her to go outside with him. They huddled together in the cool autumn evening air and looked up at the stars in the clear sky.

"For a minute there, I thought I would never get to enjoy these moments again."

"I never doubted you. You're a good man, the court could see that and just look at how people came forward and offered you their support. I feel sorry for Felix though," said Annie.

"Poor Felix," Henry agreed.

Felix fully supported Henry's version of events. He was witness to most of the meetings between

Henry and James and confirmed Henry's anguish when they discovered what James was really up to. He also confirmed the kidnapping of Annie and the immense pressure Henry was up against when Annie was dying and how he felt he had no choice in accepting the voluntary donor at the time.

Unfortunately for Felix, he didn't have the support network or contacts that Henry did. Henry wrote Felix a character statement for the court, which confirmed his belief that Felix had no knowledge of the murders. However, with Felix's embezzlement of government funds, his lavish lifestyle funded by the murders and the fact his signature was on all of the illegal documents, Felix was sentenced to twenty years, alongside the fact the court felt as though he went along with James all too easily. The court accepted Felix was not involved in any murders, otherwise he would have faced the death penalty.

"Come on, Annie, let's go to sleep. It's been a long day and I can't help but feel guilty celebrating my release knowing about all those deaths," Henry said, as he led her back inside.

Annie agreed with him so they said goodnight to everyone and made the kids promise not to stay up too late as they went to bed. Henry fell asleep as soon as his head hit the pillow.

After a few days of rest and recuperation in the country house, it was time for the Marlows to start their new lives. Alex and Esme were relieved to leave. They had received a hard time over the past few years with their father on remand awaiting trial. So Annie enrolled them in an international school in Brazil, under her maiden name. The Marlows needed a fresh start and Annie was looking forward to her challenge of helping the charity in Brazil that had reached out to her. Henry had persuaded her to accept the Brazilian charity's request for help. There were countless cases of runaways and missing people in Rio de Janeiro. It was a good start for them to make amends. Henry didn't mind where they moved to; he would be able to work from anywhere. It also helped that Brazil had beautiful beaches and great weather. It was far away from home so hopefully, they could maintain a low profile and not be constantly reminded of what happened.

Charlie drove them to the airport where they had an emotional goodbye. He promised to come out and see them as soon as they were settled.

"Goodbye, my old friend. You look after that wife and two kids of yours and try not to get involved with any Brazilian drug lords – I know what you're like," joked Charlie.

"I promise not to get involved with the local mafia or drug lords. I've learnt my lesson," Henry laughed as he hugged his best friend goodbye.

"Ready for our new lives, Mrs Marlow?" he asked.

"Ready, Henry."

CHAPTER 42

Rio de Janeiro

The Marlows had been living in Rio de Janeiro for a few weeks now. Henry had been fairly busy documenting his terminated project. Although the project was closed, maybe one day it might be considered again – although probably not in Henry's lifetime. So as promised, Henry took great care in the details so future scientists might take it on again and make it more workable.

Henry worked from home in a beautiful apartment in his new country. The estate agent helped them find a perfect apartment in a privileged area near the international school. It was luxurious with fabulous views from their large terrace and fantastic facilities with pools, a gym and not too far from the beach. Alex and Esme embraced their new lifestyle with fervent enthusiasm. So too had Henry and Annie.

Annie encouraged Henry to accept monetary offers from his supporters. Henry told her it made him feel uncomfortable but it was necessary. Although Annie was still working with her health monitor company, they weren't earning anywhere near enough money to pay for the school and their new lifestyle. Annie also wanted to cut back on her hours as she was eager to continue her community service with volunteering with the charity and spend time in Rio's favelas, the many slums in and around the city.

"Felix would have loved this apartment," remarked Henry. "Do you think we needed something so ostentatious, shouldn't we have gone for something a little more modest?"

"It's for the kids really, we've asked a lot from them to uproot themselves from their friends, school and grandparents. We've never spoilt them and why not spoil ourselves for a change? We've both worked so hard, we deserve a treat. The money you've received will easily cover the rent on this place forever. People are so generous. Besides, I deserve it. The kids and I have been through hell for the past three years, waiting for you in limbo. I know it feels slightly wrong to enjoy such luxury when everything went so wrong but whether we live in a slum or in a luxury apartment, it won't make much difference."

"People are certainly generous," Henry agreed, as he thought of all the offers he received, while in prison.

Henry was about to continue speaking but stopped.

"What were you about to say?" she asked.

Henry hesitated, but Annie urged him to speak up.

"I did have an ulterior motive for encouraging you to work with this charity in this particular city," admitted Henry.

Annie raised her eye-brow at Henry.

"One of my biggest regrets is using Freddie Hansen as a pawn. I used him to rescue you. I didn't think about the long-term effect on him and what it could do to him. Who knows how deep James' criminal activities go and what else he was involved in. That poor man, faced with a terminal disease, coming to me for help only to be used as a means to get rid of James. Now because of me, he had to change his name and go into hiding. He had to leave his poor old mum behind and he probably lives in fear of being recognised by one of James' associates on a day to day basis. Or even someone with a grudge against James. He embezzled a lot of money from the company, money that was meant for the Russian mafia and all his assets were frozen once we got caught. Someone out there might not know what actually happened and not realise that even though Freddie Hansen looks like him, it's not actually him."

"Yes, I agree. The poor man must be on edge all the time. But what's that got to do with us moving here?" asked Annie.

"Well, I know his new name so I managed to track him down. He lives here in Rio. And I wanted to come and apologise, offer sanctuary if he ever needed it and back up if he ever had to explain his situation. And to help with his missionary work."

"I thought his missionary work was in Africa?" questioned Annie.

"Usually, but for some reason, he chose to go into hiding in Rio. Look Annie, I hope it's okay but I've made contact and he's agreed to see us tonight."

Before Annie could agree to anything, the buzzer rang.

"That will be him," announced Henry as he sprung up to answer the door.

Annie followed Henry to the door. Standing there was Freddie, now known as Luca Santos. Annie gasped as she saw him. To her, it was still James, not the recipient. Henry invited him in as he handed flowers to Annie.

"Pleased to meet you," he said nervously.

She eyed him up and down as she accepted the flowers and hesitantly invited him in.

As the evening wore on, Annie relaxed. This was not the same James she knew. The old James would have waltzed in, not waiting to be invited, with an even bigger bouquet of flowers and insisted on a drink straight away. This person was more timid as she had to encourage him to come in and follow them out to the terrace for a drink. They talked on the terrace as Henry proffered his apologies once again and told Luca to never hesitate and ask them for help if he ever needed it.

Luca filled them in on what he had been up to in the past few years. He told them how he didn't feel safe in Africa any longer. There were too many civil wars and mindless murders. He described the beautiful parts of Africa that he had visited and his favourite countries and told some amusing stories about various characters there.

However, he also felt the need for a change as he'd spent so many years there. As his Portuguese was pretty good from spending so much time in Angola, he felt he would be able to integrate himself into Brazilian culture. There was so much poverty in Brazil; he decided to continue his missionary work here instead. He apologised for boring them by talking about his work so much.

"Not at all. Work is all we've ever talked about, so it's refreshing to meet someone else so passionate about helping people. I think you and Henry will get on," said Annie.

After a few more drinks, Luca extended an invitation to Henry to come and see some of the work he was involved in. Before he left that evening, he assured them both that Henry was forgiven and was now thankful for the second chance he was given. It didn't matter what happened to him from now as he would have died three years ago in his old body.

"What a lovely man," Annie said after Luca had left.

Henry agreed.

"That's why I chose him as part of my pro bono work."

Annie then punched him in the arm; "that's for not telling me the real reason you wanted to move here."

"Ouch," Henry laughed as he rubbed his arm.

"Have you got any more secrets you want to tell me?" she demanded.

"No, from now on, my life is an open book," he promised her.

"Good, I've had enough surprises to last me a lifetime."

CHAPTER 43

The Truth

The next day, as promised, Henry met Luca leaving Annie to stay at home and catch up on some work. The address Luca gave Henry was at the harbour. He told them the previous evening he lived a simple life on a houseboat. As Henry approached the harbour with its glamorous yachts, Henry spotted Luca's boat straight away, The Elixir. Just as Henry thought, it was the biggest, most ostentatious of all the yachts moored in the harbour.

"Greetings, old friend!" Luca yelled out when he saw Henry approach.

This was followed by the pop of a champagne bottle as Luca filled two champagne flutes and handed one to Henry as he boarded the yacht. Henry happily took it and clinked Luca's glass.

"The Elixir? How apt, I like it," said Henry. "But I thought you were keeping a low profile?"

"I couldn't help myself, isn't she a beauty? And we almost found the elixir of life, didn't we?" he asked as he led Henry around for a tour.

"Don't let Annie ever see this boat; it doesn't quite match your persona of a selfless missionary," Henry warned Luca.

Luca roared with laughter at the thought of himself as a missionary.

"Don't worry, I thought of that. See that small, sad looking boat over there?" Luca asked as he pointed to a boat at the other end of the harbour. "That one is actually in my name, so if Annie does come snooping, I can just entertain her on that."

After the grand tour, Luca proposed a toast.

"Finally, we did it, Henry. You and me, living in Rio de Janeiro with no one breathing down our necks. To us and our grand plans."

Henry clinked his glass again.

"Well Luca, or should I say James, it didn't quite go to plan. I wasn't expecting to spend three years in prison awaiting trial, while you got off pretty easily. I thought I'd get bail at the most, especially with the finger pointing firmly at you and Felix."

Luca looked around as there were some staff on his yacht; "shush, don't call me James again. I'm Luca now, remember?"

The two men laughed.

"Come, let's sit down and catch up. The staff don't speak English, so we're free to talk."

"Thank goodness. I've been desperate to talk it through properly with you for years. Unfortunately, the record of my life will be slightly inaccurate; I'll go down in history as some weak idiot."

"Maybe you could write your memoirs on your

deathbed?" suggested Luca.

"Maybe but I don't want to tarnish my kids name or leave them to deal with any fallout. It's okay, I can learn to live with the history books believing you were behind it all."

Luca shrugged, unconcerned with such details; the Talbot name would never be carried on. He had no interest in family.

"Anyway, since when can you speak Portuguese?" Henry asked.

"I've been here for nearly three years. I've picked it up here and there. You should definitely do the same. And while you're at it, make sure you apply to become a citizen as soon as possible. Extradition laws don't apply here. I'm untouchable from the British police. Make sure you do the same."

Henry nodded in agreement. He had every intention of becoming a citizen. The extradition law in Brazil was one of the main attractions for both men moving to this country – in case anything went wrong.

Luca motioned for Henry to sit down on a settee overlooking the ocean as the yacht left the harbour. Henry smiled as he breathed in the sea air and took in the view.

"My god, James, you can't imagine how good this feels. We got away with it, didn't we?" asked Henry.

"It certainly looks that way but please remember to call me Luca," he smiled.

"To poor old Felix," Henry toasted.

"To poor Felix, the schmuck," Luca toasted back.

"And here's to twenty-five years of friendship."

Twenty-five years the two men had known each other. During that time, they became firm friends, sharing secrets and making plans. Henry remembered the first time the two men met in that dingy, country pub all those years ago…

After years of seething over his father's death and his mother's suicide, Henry finally decided to take control. He had so much anger and contempt towards the man who had ruined his life. The scumbag, junkie, car-stealing criminal who had knocked down his father and left him for dead, would now pay for what he did. It was a pity he committed his crime fifteen years ago when the criminal courts were so liberal. If he had committed the crime now, he would have certainly faced death row. As it happened, he'd only served a measly three-year sentence, let out early for good behaviour and a promise to become clean and lead a virtuous, law-abiding life. No, Carl Roberts, Henry thought, you don't get your life back when you've ruined three other lives.

On the outside, Henry hid his contempt well. As far as everyone was concerned, even Charlie, then yes, he'd grieved for his parents but had adjusted well in adult life and concentrated on his project. Although Henry was passionate about his project, this was always over-shadowed by thoughts of revenge on Carl Roberts. After years of hoping the man would simply die in a slow painful way, it became apparent this was just wishful thinking on Henry's part. Until one day, Henry decided he'd had enough of fantasising about Carl's death and to take matters into his own hands.

Via the dark web, he made contact with someone who might be able to help him out. He'd arranged to meet the man at a bar in a quiet countryside pub, many miles from his home. This man was called James Talbot. The two men hit it off straight away. James was cool and composed; this inspired great confidence in Henry. James assured Henry he could get rid of Carl Roberts with efficiency and ease. No one would suspect foul play, especially with Carl Roberts' track record. He would simply make it look like a drug overdose. Not many people would delve too deeply into his death.

As Henry had already made a name for himself due to his findings in his project, James – who liked to keep abreast of current affairs – recognised him straight away. Henry didn't mind when James asked him questions and appeared fascinated by his work. He'd always been happy to talk about himself and his work, knowing he was far superior to most people he met. His mother noticed his ego from an early age and always reminded him he would do better in the world and get along better with people if he appeared more modest.

In her suicide note, she spoke of her despair without her husband. She apologised to Henry, told him how much she loved him and how proud his father would have been of him, but he didn't need her anymore and she just didn't have the energy or the fight within herself to carry on. In the same note, which he never showed anyone, she reminded him to be humble and kind to people. That note hit Henry hard in his heart as he remembered all the cruelty he'd shown towards his mother. Since his father's death, she became depressed and sometimes he wanted to shake her and tell her to snap out of it. He was cold and said cruel things to her as a teenager, but she never retaliated. Feelings of resentment grew towards this weak woman who was emotionally detached from him.

He applied for University abroad so he wouldn't have to face her and when he finally graduated at the top of his class with flying colours, she obviously thought that was a good point to check out of his life. Emotions of guilt flooded through him when he read that note. She loved him and he knew it deep down, but he never told her he loved her. He wished he told her before she died. After her death, he realised that selfishly, he didn't accept her method of mourning or try to understand or help her. He chose anger and she chose despair. He regretted the way their relationship turned since his father's death and vowed to take heed of her final words; to be humble and nice. He hadn't managed it with her but would strive to appear to be humble, even if it was just an illusion. He vowed to get revenge for his mother too.

So during this first meeting with James Talbot, a new friendship was born. James stuck to his word and had Carl Roberts terminated with complete efficiency. Made to look like an accidental death, no fingers or question marks ever pointed in Henry's way.

CHAPTER 44

The two men had a similar outlook on life. Both were fiercely ambitious and would not let anyone stand in their way of what they wanted. Both were prepared to do whatever it took to succeed. Henry wanted his project to be so successful that he became rich and famous. He wanted his name to live forever and for his grandchildren and great-grandchildren to read about him and to be proud.

The two men kept in touch and met regularly over the years. While Annie assumed Henry was at the office, he was spending time with his new best friend. They were of similar age and had a similar sense of humour. One difference was James was a serial womaniser, whereas Henry was a strictly one-woman guy but Henry enjoyed hearing about James' conquests.

It was due to James that Henry kept a low profile. Henry desired to be on the cover of every newspaper; to head the debates on TV in order to educate the uneducated. But after his initial public appearances, James knew Henry would find it impossible to contain his true nature. He noticed the look of contempt in the early interviews. No one else noticed this but James did, the friend who knew Henry better than even Annie and Charlie. He advised his friend that he didn't think he would be capable of maintaining this friendly demeanour in the long run. Henry agreed; he found it tiresome having to hold back his true opinions all the time. So he became the elusive but still famous Dr Marlow.

Over the years, it became apparent once his experiments were successful that his biggest barrier to success was the operation would only work with a living donor. Once he got permission to use it on death row prisoners, he came around to thinking that the barrier was actually a huge bonus. He was delighted to know criminals were the ones donating their bodies. Why not? These people were hardened criminals, who had ruined lives. They should have to make amends. Henry did not agree with the Government policy of compensating their families nor did he agree with the criminals receiving special treatment once they became donors. Henry thought they needed to be punished until the end. Once the protests started and it became clear that death row prisoners would always have to volunteer due to pathetic human right laws, this is when Henry began to think more about the future.

He couldn't rely on the success of his project on the few measly volunteers they were getting. He also knew there was the possibility the government funding would eventually be pulled and he discussed his concerns with James. Together, they came up with a long-term plan. James saw the huge potential that Marlow Enterprise presented him. Not only would he eventually be able to invest legitimately but he would also be able to use the company to clean his other, not so legitimate funds. Henry found he had no problem with that as James promised him he would be able to provide him with enough donors to keep Marlow Enterprise growing. James promised the donors would always be criminals that hadn't been captured yet, people who would never be missed and most importantly for Henry, the world would be a better place without them.

To cover their tracks, it was necessary to make sure the two men were never connected in any way. Although James was seen as a legitimate businessman, if anyone nosey enough delved too deep, they might find out more about his unscrupulous dealings. James suggested to Henry that he might need a right-hand man in the company. Someone who could easily be manipulated and to take the blame if anything ever did go wrong. So when Henry did hold interviews for an office manager, he made sure he ran all the background checks through James. Luckily for Henry, there were hundreds of candidates for the job. Any candidate with a completely clean CV and reference was ignored.

Finally, they came across a CV from Felix Carter. James quickly ascertained that this man had a serious gambling problem and Felix went straight to the front of the line for the job.

As soon as Felix entered Henry's office for an interview, Henry knew he would despise him. It was evident from the way he dressed and the way he spoke, that he was shallow and thought highly of himself. Henry suppressed a snigger when Felix name-dropped famous people he met recently on holiday and what type of car he was shopping for. Luckily for Henry, Felix turned out to be a competent office manager – apart from the stealing.

At first, it appeared Felix wouldn't take the bait; although he was responsible for millions of pounds worth of Government funding, he appeared to be genuinely interested in doing a good job. There was the question of firing him and finding someone less responsible but before Henry had to resort to that, he laid some bait. He signed Felix up for many gambling websites with his work email and telephone number. Soon enough, Felix was inundated with gambling adverts whenever he came into work. The temptation finally became too much and Henry eventually spotted irregularities in the accounts. Henry always feigned ignorance when it came to the accounts so Felix assumed Henry would never notice. Once he'd stolen a substantial amount of money; Henry sent a fake memo around the office informing the staff they were due for an audit. That's when Henry decided to get James to introduce himself to Felix and the rest of the plan fell into place.

A beautiful working relationship commenced. Henry continued to be the star of the show. James brought in numerous rich clients and had his growing workforce of scouts killing the skins and Felix signed off on everything and was kept in the loop just enough so he would always be complicit.

Since hiring Felix, James and Henry planned everything to almost perfection. James hinted to Felix he had connections to the Russian Mafia. Felix took the bait and believed him. Felix had no problem taking the money and was easy to manipulate and most importantly, he had no idea the James and Henry already knew each other.

Felix was always to be the scapegoat and when Marlow Enterprise was privatised, this became the perfect opportunity to start thinking about the other donors. The timing was always off and the dilemma was how to get it to look as if Dr Marlow was always working in duress.

Then a stroke of tragedy became a stroke of fortune – Annie was dying.

As Henry and James perused the limited stock of available female prisoner donors, both men saw their opportunity.

"How about this one?" laughed James, pointing to the mugshot of an Ukrainian prisoner.

Henry rolled his eyes. "Would you want to spend the rest of your life waking up next to that beast?"

"I don't know, Henry, she looks like she'd be good in a fight and could do some serious heavy lifting around the house."

"It's not a laughing matter. My Annie deserves an attractive skin. Someone worthy of her. Someone petite and pretty, not some hideous skin that looks like she's been competing for the shot put contest on steroids for years."

"Well then, I think it's time to put plan B into action. I have some trusted scouts out there, waiting for the call. It's just time to think about how to make Felix go along with it and how to make you look like you had no other choice and I have the perfect plan."

The perfect plan was to make Felix and Annie believe there were a suitable list of donors and that Annie had made a choice only for the this choice to be ripped away at the last minute.

This was when, James confided to Felix they could use an alternative donor. When Felix hesitated, Henry was the one who suggested that James send a goon around to scare Felix's mum. They couldn't believe their luck when Felix's mum had a stroke due to natural causes. Encouraged by Henry, James led Felix to believe the stroke was due to him and to fall in line otherwise worse things would happen. That's when Felix told Henry he had no other choice.

After the successful operation with the new dodgy process in full swing, the two men met up and congratulated themselves.

"I can't believe Felix fell for that one. I couldn't believe it when I sent that guy round to have a chat with his mum and the poor old dear had a stroke. Pardon the pun but that was a stroke of luck. Genius on your part for getting me to pretend I had somehow orchestrated the whole stroke thing," James laughed out loud.

Henry laughed too; "why thank you, James. I've been told on more than one occasion of my genius."

"Yes, evil genius though. I can't believe you made Annie go through the whole ordeal of choosing a prisoner skin that you knew was already selected by our clients?"

"I agree, that was harsh but I always knew Annie wouldn't die. It's all part of the backup; incase we ever get caught. Annie can testify how desperate we were. We had no choice. I would never knowingly harm Annie." Henry tapped his finger on his nose.

From now on they had to be extra careful and think about their cover incase things when wrong. And so far a lot had gone wrong. So many unforeseeable events occurred which meant Henry had to adapt his story, his cover and worse, involve his family.

CHAPTER 45

The first crisis occurred in Boston when Annie saw the skin she was supposed to have. He recalled how angry she was and tried to keep her from talking to the Whites. But as ever Annie was persistent and wouldn't let it lie. She was the one digging around and threatening to go to the authorities.

As soon as Henry returned from Boston, he contacted James and the two men devised a plan to keep Annie quiet.

"I don't like it, James. She knows Lucinda Willis was never going to be her skin. And she's digging around, asking questions, threatening to get the police involved unless she gets some answers."

"Annie's not stupid; I have no doubt that she'll find out. It's the perfect time to take advantage of the situation. I've got so many customers lined up. You can't possibly keep up the defence of ignorance. Let's come clean, tell Annie that the skins are volunteers but from poor countries and not criminals. Talk to Felix. I'll pay a visit to Annie at the same time. Let him witness that you had no choice."

Henry sighed. "That will work on Felix but Annie

won't give up."

"How would you feel if I send one of my men around to threaten you and your family if she insists on taking it further?"

Henry hoped it wouldn't come to that but when he returned home and told her about the 'volunteers,' she was the one who insisted on packing up and running to the police with the kids.

Henry went along with it, knowing they wouldn't get far. He'd already spotted one of James' henchmen outside. The 'henchman' was convincingly menacing. Annie fell for it as they all traipsed back into the house in the belief that they were being watched from that point forward.

Henry remembered with relish the first threat to the Marlows, when James visited Annie at the same time Henry was standing in the street with Felix. He enjoyed punching Felix and smashing his phone. Felix thought this as a genuine reaction to Henry finding out what he and James had been up to, but Henry orchestrated the whole scenario.

Although he felt nothing towards Felix, he did feel guilty about involving Annie, especially when Lucinda Willis came into the clinic; that reminded him how upset Annie was. In his mind he protected Annie as much as he could, but needed witnesses to see how desperate he was; Felix and Annie could testify to this in court. There was no way he could plead ignorance to the whole volunteer donor scheme for ten years. It would have looked as suspicious as hell. What excuse could he give for never talking to any of the donors or not noticing they were knocked out before they even met him? It was more realistic to be aware of the donors. Being forced to act under duress gave him the perfect excuse to refuse to meet them.

It was bad luck too when he and Annie bumped into Jenna White in the restaurant in Boston. The original objective was that only James and Felix knew about the illegal transfers but Annie insisted on talking to Jenna. At the time Henry tried to stop her but once Annie has her mind set on something, it was difficult to stop her.

Back on the yacht, Henry justified his decisions.

"In hindsight, I wish I hadn't told Annie about the illegal donors. I should have made something up to protect her, however, it worked to my advantage as Annie was a credible witness. Every move I made was as a backup. I wanted Felix and Annie to feel my desperation and not question my motives.

It would have looked bad in court if I had just accepted illegal donors. The jury were stupid; I told them how much I loved Annie and how I knew it was wrong but I couldn't let her die. Felix backed me up and in his trial, he even told them how he practically forced me to accept the illegal donor. The jurors' eyes filled up as I spoke about losing the love of my life to a horrible, wicked disease. Obviously, I would never have let Annie die no matter what, but the whole farce I created made the event look more believable."

"Well played," remarked Luca.

Luca read through the article again. "Good article, I can feel your panic. Poor Henry had no choice. Perfect. But it says you were the one packing up and running away?"

"Yes, I took a risk in telling a blatant lie. Annie never picked up on it or at least she never said anything. It kept her quiet – believing that we were being watched. Until the Carolina Stewart fiasco."

CHAPTER 46

The Caroline Stewart fiasco. Luca was sick of hearing about it.

"How many times do I have to apologise for Carolina Stewart? It was the first time and there's always a learning curve with everything, even murder. And you did have a rather exacting order. Remember, Henry? She had to look like Annie, no addictions, perfect health, pretty, great body, etc. Annie's skin order was tricky. And yes, I agree that was a major fuck up, but I'd been telling you we should have got out a couple of years before we did. But no, you always wanted to push it, you wanted more and more money and more attention. You got greedy Henry and that's down to you. If you had taken my advice, we would have shut the company earlier; you and Annie would be living abroad and Carolina's husband would have never bumped into Annie in the street in the first place," Luca reminded Henry.

Henry held his hands up.

"Yes, I admit it. It was like an addiction. The money was just too good to refuse. With so many rich, ill people, it was easy to exploit them. They happily paid millions for the operation. I could see why Felix was so addicted to gambling. And I liked playing the role of God. I got to choose who lived and died."

Henry recalled the conversation with Annie just a few years ago. They'd been found out. The husband of her skin had seen Annie. He knew then the Marlow Project was finished. With rumours of James under investigation due to unsigned consent forms, Henry knew it was time to enact plan z. The plan he and James hoped never to have to enforce. Henry cancelled the scheduled pro-bono. He was too popular, had too many friends and family and connections. He would never do as a body replacement for James. They needed someone unconnected, a recluse. Someone without a family. So James wouldn't have to keep up the pretence with them. That's when Freddie Hansen got his place on the project. Henry had known for months that Freddie was the likely replacement and made James study every aspect of this man's life.

However, Freddie might not get his operation today – it depended on Annie's actions. Once they got the call that Annie was en route to the police station, Henry knew they had to enforce the most extreme part of their far-fetched plan. The plan they never thought they'd have to rely on. Kidnap Annie and pretend to swap James' body out.

"It's happening today," Henry warned James.

James looked unsure. "Are you sure you can fake

the records and tests to make it look as though the operation is a success?"

Henry never doubted it for one second as he re-assured his friend.

"You'll be fine. Just pretend to be nice for once."

They laughed. It would be easy – after all, that's what Henry had been doing all these years. He even felt bad about poor Freddie Hansen; who was so excited to get called in. Get his second chance. A second chance only for James though.

The two split up. No more talk for now. They'd get together eventually once the heat died down.

"Make sure they don't hurt a hair on Annie's head," Henry reminded James.

"They won't," confirmed James. James' 'kidnappers' were under strict orders to keep Annie detained long enough for the transfer to happen. And it all went to plan.

"It was an extreme plan. I can't believe we got away with it," said Luca.

Henry never doubted it for one second. He was meticulous in everything he did, down to the nth degree.

"So James...sorry, Luca, I had no idea you were such a good actor? I was worried when they got Freddie Hansen's mum in to speak to you. Very impressive," complimented Henry.

"Why, thank you. Maybe I should consider a career in film? Ha, I didn't have to do much. I studied every aspect of Freddie's old life for weeks. We had great intel on him; I knew all about his boring life and managed to get my hands on the phone conversations with his mum. They had the same old conversations all the time. It was easy to fool her, especially since she was a bit batty anyway. I practised the way he acted, all shy and awkward. It wasn't that hard really, although I'm not sure I could be that quiet all the time. But well done to you, for picking him. He was a great candidate, a virtual loner who spent no time in the country, no family or friends. It was too easy to take on his identity. And your records were superb, I don't know how you managed to fake all the medical tests but no one picked up on them. As far as the doctors were concerned, I completely matched the other records of all the other transfers. I was worried when they went through all the tests but Henry, you truly are a genius."

Henry had been called a genius a number of times in his life. He knew he was but always faked his modesty. He didn't have to fake anything in front of his old friend.

"I certainly am," he agreed as they toasted again.

"But Henry, you're ruthless. I can't believe you got one of my thugs to threaten and kidnap your wife."

Henry sighed; "I know, I know. But I needed it to look like I was doing all your bidding under duress. That was the main part of my defence; my family would be killed if I didn't go along with you. Honestly, I felt bad for Annie; I really didn't want to scare her but I needed a credible witness to back up the threats. I knew she would never be in any real harm when I had her kidnapped, I would never do anything to hurt Annie, you know that. But it wouldn't have worked if I simply said we'd been threatened. I needed the threat to be real and I needed witnesses to confirm these threats. Also, it exonerated Annie from any blame because she was a victim. And if you remember rightly, we knew she would go straight to the police that morning. We needed time to make the transfer before the police arrested you. By having Annie kidnapped, this gave us enough time to see our plan through."

"Still, it was pretty harsh," said James.

Henry's conscience was clear, he did what he had to do.

CHAPTER 47

The two men continued discussing the article.

"The pro bonos – what a great idea. I wouldn't be here if it wasn't for them. But again, you make me look like a greedy bastard and make yourself sound like a saint in this article," said Luca.

"That was always the deal and you know it. So, what did you really think of the article?" asked Henry.

"A very interesting work of fiction," said Luca as he looked over it again to remind himself of what is said.

"Hey," Henry protested. "It was all true just with a slightly different slant on reality."

"Slant? That's an understatement. You had that reporter eating out of your hand and believing everything you said."

"Yes, well Joe was rather naive. I saved his dad's life so I think he was ready to believe everything I said."

"The pro bonos worked extremely well for you. Look at the glowing statements they all gave you in this article. Even though it meant us being a few million quid out-of-pocket," said Luca.

"Exactly, it played alongside my image of Saint Henry Marlow, charitable and good. I resented every moment of it but I chose some clients wisely, mostly Freddie Hansen but some of the others made a great defence in court."

"Like Patrick Slater?"

"Especially Patrick Slater. The best defender for any criminal."

Years ago, James was sceptical about the introduction of the free operations. Why should they give away an expensive procedure, depriving them of millions? But Henry insisted on it; it would make him look good.

"See, I was right to choose Patrick Slater. He was a do-gooder who gave up a promising monetary career to help poor losers. However, he was one of the best. I needed someone great to fight my corner; it had to be him. It also helped that his son had a promising career as a journalist. As if it was a coincidence that I chose Joe to interview me. He fell for my whole story, hook, line and sinker. I must say that was the highlight in an otherwise boring spell in prison. And then there were the blind and handicapped people, I knew the jury would love me for curing them."

Henry laughed again as he remembered the character statements in the courtroom from his patients.

"I was sitting there listening to them and playing

an imaginary violin in my head. The jury sucked it all up, every sad, tragic tale. And who was the hero of all their tales? Me!"

Luca held his hands up. "You proved me wrong."

Luca continued to swipe through the article.

"What's all that nonsense about killing a cat? Did you really find it dead?" asked Luca.

"No, the old bat, Mrs Palmer was right. I did kill the cat. The pesky thing kept coming into our garden. So I strangled it and opened up its brain. I was a fourteen-year-old boy desperate for information. What was I supposed to do, continue looking at images of brains on the internet? No, I needed to get up close and personal to find out how it really worked. When my mother made me bring the cat to Mrs Palmer, I had to run away before I burst out laughing. I couldn't believe her over-reaction. It was just a cat for goodness' sake. I dissected all sorts after that. Any living thing that came into my garden was fair game. I just made sure I kept the operations secret in the shed so my mother didn't find out again."

Luca scrunched his face in disgust.

"Sorry, Henry but that's definitely a bit weird, even by my standards. Let's change the subject. I didn't know you were expelled? I thought you were always a model student. Why mention the creepy cat thing and the expulsion in your interview? I thought it was about making you look good, not bad?"

"I had no intention of mentioning those things but that damn reporter had been snooping so I had to cover my tracks. I'd pissed a few people off when I was a kid so some were bound to come out of the woodwork. I'm surprised there weren't more. But I realised when I started university, that to get on in society, you have to conform. So I became a model student and then a model work colleague even though it was against my natural instincts."

"Yes, we all have to conform sometimes," agreed Luca, "but here in Rio, we can be ourselves a bit more."

Luca scrolled down the article and came to the passage about the fire.

"Remember the fire. Such a long time ago now," said Luca.

Of course, Henry remembered the fire. It was all his idea...

CHAPTER 48

The fire was another incident orchestrated by the two men.

"James, we've got to do something about those damn protestors. They're making me look bad. I'm sick of seeing them outside the clinic every day," Henry moaned.

The two men were sitting in the exclusive gentlemen's club in the pretence of doing some serious lobbying. James had arranged the meeting but in reality, neither men cared anymore. They'd long discussed the eventuality of bringing their own donors in. They wouldn't need authorised prisoners for much longer. But still, no one else knew this so they had to keep up the pretence that was Marlow Enterprise's aim. It was also a good chance for James and Henry to catch up. It was rare for them to meet in public outside of work.

The protestors didn't bother James; he found them quite amusing.

"I know why you hate them so much. One of them egged you years ago," teased James.

Henry remembered only too well. He'd was so

angry. James was the one who called him, calmed him down and reminded him that those protestors were insignificant. James was more concerned about the amount of money the clinic was sucking up. And here they were, meeting a lobbyist and about to bribe him with a huge amount of money. A bribe the both knew was pointless. It was that night, Henry thought of the scheme.

"It's simple, kill two birds with one stone. Get rid of the protestors and get rid of that money pit of a clinic. I'll hack into the insurance company, backdate their records to show a much higher insurance premium. We burn the clinic down, make it look like an accident and then set up outside of London. Cheaper premises, away from the protestors, state of the art equipment and money left over from the excess insurance payout."

James was in complete agreement. He trusted Henry's skills as a hacker and he knew a talented bomb maker who could orchestrate the entire scenario.

"I'm surprised no one ever found out about the explosion in the first building. Luca, that was your stroke of genius. We made a lot of money from that and we would have never been able to smuggle victims into the centre of London."

"Yes, I too have a bit of genius about me. Although I couldn't have done it without you. Without your exceptional hacking skills, the police might have noticed that we'd increased our insurance by a huge amount just a couple of weeks before. Your records were perfect, it looked like we always paid huge insurance premiums. And that silly protester, I told her to come back that night so she could have an exclusive look around the building and report it in her blog. I left her waiting for me in the office while I went back outside and waited for the explosion. What a beautiful night sky it must have been. Shame I couldn't hang around to view it, I had to go home and change. I couldn't risk turning up with any residue on my clothes."

"Of course, the stylish James Talbot can't have any dirt on his clothes. I had sick on mine! I had to force-feed myself a prawn while I was in the car. They always make me sick."

"Well, I was impressed with your commitment to method acting. Speaking of prawns, can I get you one now?"

"Stop it!" demanded Henry as the two men laughed.

"Well, in all seriousness, I do think we should have made sure the building was empty when we set off the bomb," said James.

"We've talked about this before," reminded Henry. "We needed the public on our side. People were paying too much attention to those protestors and making us look bad. This way, the public thought they were just a group of terrorists and didn't take much notice of what they had to say in future."

"Let's just agree to disagree about that one," said

James, who wanted to change the subject.

CHAPTER 49

The subject reverted back to Annie.

"Well, you definitely fooled Annie last night. She thinks Luca is so much nicer than smarmy James," said Henry.

They both laughed.

"I can't believe Annie would prefer Luca to James. I'm much more interesting company. I suppose I'll have to remember to play a bumbling idiot for Annie. Maybe keep our meetings with her to a minimum just to be on the safe side?" asked Luca.

"I agree. Annie will be busy with her community service and I'll just pretend I'm working while I hang out with you here. Just like old times."

Henry was always a hard worker, but many of the long evenings Annie believed he spent at the lab were actually spent at James' London home. Just having a drink, catching up and discussing strategy. The two men were always cautious not to be spotted out together in public. This would have compromised Henry's alibi.

"Are you really giving up? I never thought I'd hear the day you would walk away from it all," asked Luca.

"Yes, I've had enough. You try to do something good for the world. You think they'd be grateful. But instead, you get stopped at every juncture by red-tape after red-tape and constant rules and regulations. Human rights for criminals! That's a joke. 'The Marlow Project' would have worked just fine if they gave me what I wanted in the first place – all prisoners on death row. If they had, I wouldn't have resorted to murdering all those scum bags and low-lives off the streets."

"Yes, thanks for putting the blame on me for that one, Henry," reprimanded Luca.

"Very sorry about that but you understood the plan. We knew if there was any heat, there would be a dying patient lined up for you for a fake transfer. I just couldn't have any dirt thrown in my direction. My defence was how holier than thou I am. While you were just some dodgy character with links to the Russian mafia," said Henry.

Luca doubled up with laughter and had to cover his mouth as the champagne spurted out of his nose.

"And the rest of your defence, making me and Felix look like greedy bastards with all the money we made. Saintly Dr Marlow was only doing it for the good of humanity."

"Ha, yes. The money. It's always been about the money of course. And I wanted that damn Nobel Peace Prize. The timing was awful. That idiot scout of yours who killed Caroline Stewart. I thought your scouts were supposed to be professionals who did the proper due diligence on all our donors? If it wasn't for that idiot, we'd still be raking in the cash and I'd have my Nobel Peace Prize. Hell, I would have probably been knighted by now. Sir Henry Marlow, I always thought that had a nice ring to it."

"Oh yes, the money. The altruistic Dr Marlow. Where did all the money go?" asked Luca.

"To my fondest charity of all, me. It's all hidden safely in offshore accounts. Untraceable, much like yours I expect but easily accessible. I'm still profiting from Amelia Jarvis and her husband."

Luca raised a glass to that.

"She was one of your character witnesses? I organised that one for you, remember?"

"Yes, thank you. That was pretty good acting too on my part. You should have seen my performance, Luca. You would have been impressed. I made her feel pretty bad for taking advantage of my project. So much so, that she gave an eloquent speech on my behalf in court. Her husband is very generous. He's one of my main sources of income since the trial. I'm not sure what to do with all my money."

"Nice problem to have, eh? You'll have to be careful. Won't Annie become suspicious if you start becoming flash Harry?" asked Luca.

"You've known me for over twenty years Luca; you know I can always think of ways to get around Annie, don't worry about that," remarked Henry.

"I don't doubt you for a second."

Henry felt the champagne relax him and they continued their reminiscing.

What about helping out Charlie's nephew? Was there an ulterior motive to that operation?" asked Luca.

"Well, I did pay for the operation and it made me look good which didn't harm my case in court. But I would have helped Charlie out for no ulterior motive. He's my oldest friend and I'll always have a soft spot for him so I'd do anything for him. He's a good man but would never share my outlook on life. Not like you, Luca. Although you're my second oldest friend, you are the best friend I could have ever hoped for," Henry toasted again.

"Steady on there Henry, I think you're getting a bit drunk but I share the same sentiments," agreed Luca.

"One more thing," said Luca. "If you're serious about giving it all up, I won't mention it but..."

"Tell me," Henry was intrigued.

"I have a potential backer. He has billions. He'd be willing to invest in the old Marlow technology. Make it portable."

Portable? That was one of Henry's goal. Confined in the clinic near London, the operation was limiting. With portable technology, they could transfer anyone, sick or healthy. Young or old. For the right price of course.

"Interesting," agreed Henry.

"Very interesting," seconded Luca. "Forget Sir Henry Marlow. You'd be more of a deity. Playing with people's lives, choosing life for some and death for others."

Henry dismissed him. It was too soon to talk of such things.

"Never say never," Henry promised. They agreed to talk about it another time.

There was a momentary silence until Luca asked Henry if he was up for a bit of fun tonight.

"What have you got in mind?" he asked.

"We moor the yacht, go to a club and pick up a couple of girls. Are you in?" suggested Luca.

Henry laughed at Luca.

"Always the same old James. You'll never change. Leave me out of it, but go for it, have your fun. I'd rather stay in with Annie tonight."

"Always the same old faithful Henry. I thought a spell in the 'can' might have changed you, but obviously not. Such a shame, but I'll be thinking of you when I'm with two or maybe three hot Brazilian babes tonight. Plus, they don't do the pointless consent forms here. I love this country!"

"Me too," laughed Henry as the yacht moored back in the harbour.

"Don't stay out too late," joked Henry. "You've got your missionary work to think about."

"I've officially retired," yelled Luca as he left the yacht excited about his night out, leaving Henry to make his way home.

Henry strolled along the harbour breathing in the sea air. He vowed to himself to make the most of it after such a near miss in prison and try and stay out of trouble from now on.

CHAPTER 50

Henry returned home in a great mood. It had been three long years since he talked to his friend. It was wonderful to finally get everything off his chest and talk about what really happened. Over the last thirty years, he spent most of his life bottling up what he felt and James was the only person he ever met who he could be open with. He loved Annie with all his heart but he lacked respect for her sometimes, due to her eagerness and willingness to do good and see the best in people all the time. She had a loving upbringing and had never experienced what it was like to feel all alone in the world. Yet she always stood by him, no matter what and he felt so grateful for that. He was determined to make sure she felt safe from now on and he wouldn't do anything ever again that would put her or the children in danger.

He'd had a lucky escape and although he tried something monumental in the world, unfortunately, it had failed. His experiment suffered a few casualties along the way but with any great undertaking, nothing is ever easy.

For the next few weeks, Henry kept a low profile.

He messaged Luca often but knew they shouldn't be seen together too often. The plan was to introduce Luca gradually into his life otherwise Annie might become suspicious of their burgeoning friendship. So in the meantime, Henry continued with his documentation and Annie continued with her programming and volunteer work.

She was excited about the health monitor progress especially since the London based staff started implementing the work Henry had done during his three years in prison. It was just at the experimental stage but Annie's company were confident that within a few years the health monitor would not only successfully monitor physical health but it would also monitor mental health.

One evening, there was no sign of Annie. There was no answer on her phone and Henry had no idea where she was. He told Alex and Esme not to worry; their mum was probably having dinner with some of her new friends and lost track of time. He felt slightly worried as this was unlike Annie. She always let him know if she was going to be out late. Some crisis must have arisen in the favelas and Annie would have felt compelled to hang around until the crisis was averted. After midnight and still no sign of Annie, Henry decided to go to bed and try to sleep. After a couple of hours, sleep was of no avail. Henry tried not to worry but he couldn't help it. He got up to check his phone but there were no messages and Annie still wasn't answering her phone. Just then the front door opened. Much to

Henry's relief, it was Annie. He rushed over to hug her and told her how worried he was but she pushed him away.

"What's the matter? Where have you been?" he asked her.

"Just out," she replied.

"Out where? Are you angry with me? Have I done something?"

"You could say that."

"Tell me?" he asked calmly as he racked his brain trying to think of something he had done wrong.

"I need a drink," she said as she barged past him and poured herself a large glass of wine and sat down in the dark.

Henry knew it must be something bad as Annie rarely drank anything. He turned the side table lamp on and sat down beside her. She just stared at her glass.

"Please Annie, tell me. I'm really worried. Are you okay? Are you sick again?"

"No, but you are," she replied, glaring at him with a stare that made him feel uneasy. A stare he wasn't used to.

Henry didn't understand and pleaded for her to explain.

"You're sick in the head," she told him as she jabbed a finger to his temple.

"I don't follow. I'm fine. What do you mean?" asked Henry.

He had no idea where this conversation was going. Annie stood up and walked out to the balcony. She leaned over, staring down. Henry followed her.

"Annie, please tell me what's going on. I'm not a mind reader."

"You know my company is testing our brain patterns and behaviours with the health monitors?"

Henry nodded. Henry was only too happy to be part of the test group; he was always supportive of Annie and her work. The company needed various test groups, such as people with high IQ's - who was Annie. People with extraordinarily high IQ's; Henry liked to think he was in this group. Other groups included subjects with low IQ's, average IQ's, mental illnesses and criminal behaviour.

"You assumed you'd be in the genius test group?" Annie asked him.

"I suppose so," hesitated Henry, trying not to be big-headed.

For one awful moment, he thought Annie was about to tell him that his brain pattern fitted that of a person with extremely low intelligence.

"Yes, your brain pattern fit that of a genius."

Henry breathed a sigh of relief.

"But, your brain behaviour also matches that of a psychopath."

"What?" Henry laughed. "It's obviously a mistake. I'm not a psychopath!"

Henry burst out laughing and thought Annie would realise how silly she was acting.

"Come on, Annie, don't take it so seriously. The experiment is in the early stages and they've obviously got something dreadfully wrong. After all, there is a fine line between genius and madness, or so I've been told on many occasions."

"No, no. I got the results a few days ago. That's what I thought initially, but I've been sitting on it, thinking about it. Thinking about your behaviour. Your behaviour now and in the past. In Joe Slater's article about you – there were a few minor inaccuracies, just small ones. I let it go at the time. Most of the article was based on incidents that happened years ago. I assumed you got muddled. It wasn't important."

"Such as?" asked Henry.

Annie spoke of the incident when they ran into Jenna White, in Boston. In the report, it stated Henry insisted on getting answers from Jenna. As Annie remembered it, it was she who insisted on talking to the Whites and not Henry. Henry didn't want to make a scene and begged Annie to sit down and ignore them.

Another small inaccuracy was when they were first threatened. Henry said he felt paranoid and ordered the devices to detect for listening bugs. As Annie remembered it, Henry didn't seem that concerned and she was the one who ordered the listening devices. And the time right before the arrest, Henry was the one packing their suitcases and insisting they run away. Annie was the one trying to remain level-headed and hang around. In the newspaper article, it stated that Annie wanted to run away.

"And Henry, the newspaper article made you sound like a saint. You were a good man and a great doctor, but I never saw this hugely compassionate side of you. You bitched about all the criminal donors and you complained about some of the ungrateful recipients. When we first met James at that fancy restaurant, you said you felt inadequate? That you didn't understand the business side of things? That wasn't true. You were able to keep up with James and Felix that evening. I was actually impressed by how much you knew about balance sheets. And it was you and James who made me and Felix feel as though we shouldn't be there. I remember rolling my eyes as a joke with Felix because you were ignoring us.

What about the part of the article where it said women always became bored with you and you gave up on internet dating? That wasn't true. You told me you always became bored with them; that they didn't hold your interest. Charlie told me you were a 'love them and leave them' type of guy at university.

No, you're not a saint. I re-read that article again yesterday but in a different light. Everything pointed to you as the wronged party, the innocent Dr Marlow who was so naive and modest, that's not the Henry I know. And then I thought about why you insisted on moving here, to Rio. How you wanted to make amends with Luca and how all of a sudden you want to be best friends with him..."

"Look Annie, of course I told Joe Slater a side of

the story that made me look good. I was begging for my life. As for James, I couldn't admit to getting on with him initially; I couldn't align myself with him otherwise people might have got the impression that we were in it together. Look at what happened to Felix when he worked closely with James? And yes, I did bitch about some of the patients. All doctors do; Charlie's told us many amusing stories about some of the ingrates he has to treat. As for past girlfriends, their eyes did glaze over when I talked about my theories and my experiment. They were all stupid bimbos until I met you. You were the first woman I met outside of science that understood what I was doing, who could hold their own when talking with me. You challenged me. You're the only woman I've ever met who's held my interest. As for Luca, he's a nice guy. I like his company and I feel bad about duping him."

"Shut up," Annie interrupted. "I went down to the harbour tonight, to look for Luca. I found his houseboat, but there was no one on it. I hung around for hours waiting for him to show up as I didn't want to come home. But interestingly, I saw Luca return just after midnight. He didn't head for his boat; he boarded some luxury yacht called 'The Elixir.' Does that mean anything to you?"

Henry stood in silence.

"Luca was with a group of people, mostly young women. He was loud and arrogant. Just like James. Then it struck me; it was James."

Henry shook his head, "no Annie, I'm sure he was

just drunk. He must have made friends with the owner of the luxury yacht."

"Don't deny it. I asked around. It was Luca's yacht. I showed someone your picture. They confirmed they've seen you a couple of times on this yacht. You and James have been in on it all along, haven't you? You've lied to me?"

Tears streamed down Annie's face as she gritted her teeth. Henry held her hands to stop her from throwing her glass off the balcony.

"Everything I did, I did for us. I wanted the best life for us. I wanted money. I wanted you and the kids to be proud of me."

"We were proud of you. I don't understand why you've lied. Did James make you do this?" she trembled once she realised Henry wasn't denying any of this.

"No, it was always me," Henry sighed.

He couldn't see the point in lying anymore.

"I met James and used his contacts to arrange all the abductions. I wanted my experiment to be the greatest discovery of all time. I wanted my name to live on for thousands of years; to be included in history books. Most of all, I wanted all scumbags off the street. You see Annie; I was helping mankind. Not only was I saving the terminally ill but I was also getting the future criminals off the streets. They got to be part of my experiment before they messed up someone else's life. Before they killed some kid's father. Before they made an innocent person kill themselves."

"My god, it's always been about your parents?"

"Yes, Annie. I wanted revenge on all the lowlifes out there. I was trying to make the world a safer, better place."

"You killed almost a thousand people!"

"Yes, not nearly enough. Come on Annie, do you want our kids growing up in a world where they could be mugged, raped or murdered? I was ridding the world of scum."

"I can't believe what I'm hearing. You had no idea what these people did or were going to do. They could have turned their lives around. Who the hell are you to play god? I always joked about your god complex but you really do have one, don't you?"

Henry smiled at Annie; "what can I say? Maybe I do."

"But James kidnapped me. His henchmen threatened our family?"

Henry sighed. He knew Annie would fail to see the bigger picture.

"You and the kids were never in danger."

"I was terrified!" she shrieked at him.

"I would never hurt you. I love you."

"You love me? I lived in fear for years, in fear for our family. I was a nervous wreck. That's not love. You're a madman. You're a psycho!" she shouted as her eyes filled with terror.

Henry knew at that moment he'd lost his Annie, he could never get her onboard; not like James. She would never understand why he did what he did.

"Do you still love me, Annie?" he asked, although

he already knew the answer.

She cried and shook her head. She backed away from him and tried to go into the apartment but Henry, who was stronger than her, grabbed her; she dropped her glass on the floor. He couldn't let her go back inside. Henry kissed her goodbye; she tried to push him away. He wrapped his arms around her so she couldn't fight him and pushed her towards the balcony. She struggled but couldn't get out of Henry's grasp.

"No, don't!" she cried out.

Before she could say anything else, he hoisted her over the balcony and threw her off. There was a loud scream and Henry heard a distant thud as her body hit the ground.

He wept. Annie was wrong; he knew he wasn't a psychopath; he wouldn't have felt such sorrow if he was.

He went inside and called the police. Next, he hacked his way into Annie's company records and made sure to change his brain pattern behaviour on his report. If she'd told anyone about her theory, there would now be no record to back it up. He also made sure she hadn't made contact with anyone else about her little theory. Once he checked through her phone and all her files and was satisfied that she hadn't told anyone, he began practising what he would say to the police. Over the years he'd become an accomplished liar; he was sure he could convince the Brazilian police of his wife's guilt over Carolina Stewart and her mental anguish of living in her body. He picked Annie's glass up from the balcony and threw it in his face.

"Yes, Officer. I tried to stop her from jumping but she screamed at me, threw the glass in my face and jumped," is what he heard himself telling the police twenty minutes later when they arrived at the scene.

EPILOGUE

Felix sat in his cell, staring at the walls. Asking himself the same question over and over again. Why had he been so stupid? Henry trusted him. He'd given him a position of responsibility that many others refused him in the past because of his stupid gambling and this was how he repaid him. Because of him, James Talbot was introduced into their lives. Because of him, Henry's project shut down. Many others wouldn't get life-changing surgery. Because of him, hundreds of innocent people died. He had seventeen years in front of him, in the same cell, with the same prisoners heckling him day after day, reminding him what he had done. He was pleased to be given the chance to defend Henry in court. Felix knew he had taken most of the blame himself but it was the least he deserved. Even so, that wasn't enough; he couldn't live with his conscience any longer. Underneath his pillow, he took out a belt he managed to get his hands on. He knew what he had to do; he couldn't bear to live for one moment longer.

Joe Slater was shocked to hear of the suicide of

both Annie and Felix within days of each other. He wanted to contact Henry to offer his condolences and reassure himself that Henry wouldn't follow suit as he too would be carrying around an enormous amount of guilt. As expected, he couldn't get hold of Dr Marlow. Annie died in Brazil but Joe didn't have any contact details for the Marlows and it was proving difficult to get hold of him. He knew Henry wanted to keep a low profile but in times like these, he felt he needed to do something. He left a message with Charlie; Henry's best friend would probably have a contact number.

When he returned home one evening after work, he was surprised to see a postcard lying on the floor. He didn't often receive mail, especially postcards. On the front was a picture of Christ the Redeemer, the famous statue in Rio. He turned it over and read;

To Joe,

I really need to speak to you about your article. I don't think Henry's been completely honest with us. I'll be in touch soon.

Annie.

The end.

ABOUT THE AUTHOR

The Marlow Project is LM Barrett's second novel.

Lorraine lives and writes from Jávea, a small seaside town on the beautiful Costa Blanca in Spain. A Reflection of Sophie Beaumont was her debut novel written shortly after Lorraine, her husband and two young children moved to Spain after spending ten years living and working in Bristol, having never previously written anything - so perhaps the climate and beautiful surroundings are conducive to the writing process, it certainly helped Lorraine!

Her third novel will follow soon. Please check out her website for more details.

http://www.lmbarrett-author.com

Thanks for reading. If you enjoyed this book, please consider leaving an honest review on Amazon or Goodreads.

A Reflection of Sophie Beaumont: An Addictive Read with a Twist Ending.

LM Barrett's debut novel

Read all about Sophie - manipulator, gold-digger or victim?

An easy reading, guilty pleasure book with a dark side and a twist ending. A highly entertaining, racy, fast-paced book that you won't be able to put down. Can you really ever trust someone so close to you? A Reflection of Sophie Beaumont is a page-turning and gripping insight into the lengths a person will go, to pretend they're someone they're not. Perfect for fans of Gone Girl, The Woman in the Window and The Wife Between Us.

When a devastated Richard Beaumont returns home one evening to find out that his beautiful, happy wife Sophie has committed suicide it sends him on a journey to unravel the mystery of why someone with a seemingly perfect life would do such a thing.

He discovers deep and dark secrets from her past and present that he would have rather left un-covered. Does what he find out eventually lead him to agree with her suicide note, that the love of his life deserved it?

Follow the twists and turns in Sophie's life and look at both sides of the story as we learn the real reason for her demise.

Printed in Great Britain
by Amazon